Toolbox Talk

Tall Tales and Legends of Pipefitters, Welders, and Other Dudes With Trucks

Ryan Hanson and Tim Ebl

Disclaimer

Read this or don't pass go. Don't you dare skip this page!

By going past this point, you accept all blame for anything that happens for all time. You agree that Ryan Hanson and Tim Ebl are blameless (and you are full of blame) for any and all damages caused by reading this book.

The authors do not support illegal or harmful behavior.

These stories were crafted based on others' experiences, flawed memories, and hearsay. Many are second-hand in nature; a lot is just flat-out made-up nonsense.

If you think a story is about you or someone you know, it isn't.

All names have been changed, and locations have been altered or left out.

This book may contain curse words and adult subject matter of a lewd nature. If you don't know what "lewd" means, you should look it up before you decide whether or not to proceed.

Avoid prolonged exposure to sunlight.

Breaking this seal voids your warranty.

Harmful or fatal if swallowed.

If attacked by a pack of clowns while reading this, go for the juggler.

Welcome to Toolbox Talk

Who are Tim and Ryan, and why did they write this book?

Blue-collar workers get placed in a lot of crazy situations, and many of them are funny. It's a side of life that the majority of the world doesn't even know exists. The stories we've collected explore the challenges that tradies go through.

We promise that you will get some good laughs from what we wrote.

We dove into the lives of tradesmen and laborers and looked at the messed up, politically incorrect ways they acted. That was our inspiration.

We worked in construction for years. We did our time in the trenches. Our home province is full of industrial sites and tradespeople. Instead of going to college or university, many of us started an apprenticeship and got our ticket to make the big oilfield money.

We want to show you what we and other blue-collar workers have gone through.

If you've been there yourself, you will feel a connection to the characters in our book. You'll understand how messed up it is to take a whiz quiz just to be allowed to go to the job, and how hard it is to travel hours away from home and stay there for weeks at a time.

If you don't know anything about the life of construction and industrial workers, you'll get a glimpse of that way of living. It's a whole separate society, filled with a lot of fantastic people trying to make ends meet. It can be a rough journey, although it has a lot of hilarious moments and off-color jokes too.

But there is also a dark side to working in the trades.

Most of the stories are about men who worked long, hard days. They lived away from their families and were isolated in work camps or staying in hotel rooms.

These workers might have felt like they were missing out on normal life, but they couldn't just quit and get "regular" jobs. They needed an income and didn't know how to do anything else. The jobs they took let them support their wives, girlfriends, children, or even parents.

Many of them felt trapped or exploited by an uncaring system of corporate bullshit.

Industrial workers can fall prey to depression or substance abuse. Until recent years, it was considered a weakness if they discussed their feelings. So men sucked it up and tried to be tough. This just made things worse for them.

These are some of the reasons that we feel it's important to get these stories out there. Some of the tales are unbelievable, many of them have been greatly embellished, and a few walk the fine line between good and bad taste. But all of them contain fragments of reality. We hope you enjoy them.

Who We Are:

Tim Ebl is a father of three children and is happily married. He was a pipeliner, then a welder. He moved on to become a pipefitter, and that led to supervisory and quality control positions. After working with his hands and lifting heavy tools for years, Tim uses yoga to keep his body from seizing up. In his spare time, he wrote and published three books. Tim is a certified meditation coach. He worked on one book with a co-author about how meditation saved him from a devastating mid-life crisis, and how anyone could use mindfulness to improve their life.

Ryan Hanson is a father to two great kids, and has been with the love of his life since 1999. He started working in the trades as a Welder's Helper in 1998 to keep out of trouble until he decided what he really wanted to do with his life. He's still figuring that out, but he's happy where he's landed. It's been quite a ride. His rotator cuffs are so messed up from working that he needs a week to recover if he throws a baseball. This is his second book - both of which were written with Tim Ebl. He hopes to write another very soon.

The Creative Process

How did the two of us manage to write a book?

Collaboration is a challenging but rewarding experience. It took a lot of discussions, and we were both forced to give up some of our pet ideas to get the project finished.

After we each finished our rough drafts of the stories, we gave them to the other guy to read. Then we made some changes.

At the eleventh hour, we decided we had better get an editor involved. Rosalind Warren agreed to take us on, and her expert advice helped us get to the finish line. We thank her greatly for convincing us to see our stories in a different light and helping us polish them to be more accessible to anyone and everyone. We are also happy that she rediscovered the magic power of the semicolon while going through our stories.

Special Thanks:

Ryan would like to thank:

Rob for his enthusiasm and support of Cautionary Tales, Gisele for her title suggestions. Jesse for a fountain of absurd stories - keep on doing the right things. Beth and the CCMF for helping so many guys like us see that their hard times don't have to be navigated alone, without help. My coworkers, for tolerating my kookiness. Morty and Stella for being wonderful cuddle puppies on the Fridays I spend writing these stories. Terry for always giving me a heroic dose of honesty - I know there's a few in here you won't appreciate, and I can't wait to talk to you about them. Mom and Dad, And the best for last - my wife Liz. I love you, babes!

Tim would like to thank:

Josh Norman, Al Penton, Ed Wrobel, and the rest of the guys I've worked with over the years, for their crazy stories and ideas that ended up in this book.

Mike Hecek, Andrew Beers, and Corey McBain, for such a great work environment at my day job. A supportive team and good leadership are the glue holding that place together.

And to the love of my life, Nicole. I am so grateful to have you supporting me.

Contents

Clarifying the Lingo A.K.A: The Glossary

Tim and Ryan are from Canada. (They're real sorry aboot that, eh!) They are also writing about some topics that are very specific to their industry. Some of the words used in these stories might catch some readers off guard. They tried their best to clarify the meaning of them in the stories, but the odd one might have slipped their attention. Just in case, here are some specific words you may encounter and their definitions.

- **Bunny Hug:** What people in Saskatchewan call a hooded sweatshirt/hoodie. Seriously.

- **Canadian Tire:** A chain of franchised department stores that specializes in automotive parts, oil changes fishing and hunting gear, household appliances, hardware, deck furniture, clothing, boating, trailer and RV parts. Shit. Canadian Tire sells everything. Yes. They even sell tires.

- **Cutout:** When a welded pipe joint has to be removed

because it either isn't high enough quality or it's no longer needed. The welders work for hours to finish the weld, and then they have to cut all of that hard work out and throw it away.

- **Darts:** Smokes or cigarettes. "Let's go smoke a dart."

- **Ginch:** What Albertans refer to as tightie whities, unmentionables, undies, or underwear. Also known as gonch, gotch, or gotchies, and sometimes gitch in other parts of the country

- **Goon Spoon:** A shovel used for digging. "Grab that goon spoon and give us a hand!"

- **Highway of Death:** The dreaded Highway 63 from Edmonton to Fort McMurray. Also known as Suicide 63 and Hell's Highway due to the large number of deaths that took place over the years. This road is 450 kilometers long and winds its way through some of the most boring forest and swamp terrain on Earth.

- **Jump Hours:** Bonus hours paid to an oilfield worker that he did nothing to earn. Welders think jump hours are their God-given right. Hardly anyone else ever gets a jump hour, no matter how hard they work.

- **Lockout:** One of the most important safety precautions at an active industrial plant. Every place has a different way of doing it, but each lockout must prove that all pressure, electricity, or other hazards from the system have been eliminated. It keeps people from working on a pressurized pipe or electrical system that could kill them.

- **Loonie:** A common name for the Canadian one-dollar coin, named for the bird (a Loon) depicted on the coin. Canada eliminated the dollar bill in 1989 and replaced it with the Loonie. "Do you have a loonie for the shopping cart?"

- **Lumberjack Effect:** The effect that a man with a beard, wearing plaid and carrying an axe, often has on others. Common symptoms of the effect include uncontrollable hormone rushes, declarations of love for the plaid wearer, and attempts to grope the lumberjack

- **Lumberjill:** A female lumberjack.

- **Nanaimo Bar:** a highly sought-after dessert with a crust of chocolate and cookie crumbs, covered with vanilla buttercream filling and a chocolate glaze. It's named after Nanaimo, British Columbia.

- **Pervert's Row:** The front row at the strip club, right up at the stage. See: **Sniffer's Row**

- **Piss Test:** A pre-employment drug test, where you give a sample of urine to get tested for drugs. A worker might also get this test after a safety incident. See: **Whiz Quiz**

- **Pulling a Slip:** Trade Union members are dispatched form their local union hall. Instead of a job interview, a qualified tradesperson is given an employment slip to show to their new employer.

- **Randy** from **The Trailer Park Boys:** Randy is a character from the hit TV show **Trailer Park Boys**. He was the fat assistant trailer park supervisor, was famous for eating fifteen cheeseburgers in one sitting, and never wore a shirt.

- **Rock Truck:** A large all-terrain dump truck that could crush a pickup truck like a bug. Quite often driven at high speeds right past work crews on foot.

- **Shafts:** A milky alcoholic cocktail that includes an extra dose of strong coffee. "Hey everybody! Let's all go to Leopold's and down some shafts!"

- **Shutdown:** When an industrial facility needs to do large repairs, they shut down the entire place. A large number of temporary workers invade the place. Welders, pipefitters, laborers, electricians, millwrights, and other tradies work long shifts day and night until the plant can be turned back on. Then all of the temporary workers get laid off.

- **Sin Bin:** Also known as the **Penalty Box**. This is an area in ice hockey or rugby, off the field of play, where a player who commits a foul gets sent to sit until the penalty is up.

- **Smoke Pit:** An outdoor designated smoking area that usually contains crude seating, a fire extinguisher, and a metal pail full of cigarette buts that no one ever cleans.

- **Sniffer's Row:** The front row at the strip club, right up at the stage. See: **Pervert's Row**

- **Tailgate Meeting:**   **1.** A safety meeting before work begins. If you don't have an office handy, the field foreman opens the tailgate of his truck and puts the safety paperwork on it so the workers can sign in.   **2.** An emergency shit on the side of the road, behind the meager barricade of your truck. "Quick, pull over! I gotta have a tailgate meeting!"

- **Tradie:** A tradesman or tradesperson. These are skilled manual workers in a particular·craft or trade. Tradies are considered professionals with practical knowledge of most aspects of their trade. Examples include pipefitters, welders, electricians, plumbers, and hairdressers.

- **The Trailer Park Boys:** A popular Canadian television show, depicting several denizens of a Nova Scotia trailer park and their zany, expletive heavy, politically incorrect exploits. It's a hoot.

- **Toolbox Talk:** A short safety meeting before the start of a work shift. The supervisor reads the talk in front of a roomful of workers, who all pretend to listen. If someone falls asleep due to the utterly boring nature of the experience, his buddies smirk and wait until the speaker calls the sleeper out.

- **Toonie:** A common name for the Canadian two-dollar coin. Canada eliminated the two·dollar bill in 1996 and re-placed it with the Toonie.

- **Touque:** **1.** A stocking cap or beanie, sometimes made out of wool. Canadians use these to keep their brains from freezing.   **2.** A foreskin

- **Whiz Quiz:** A pre-employment screening, where you give a sample of urine to get tested for drugs. A worker might also get this test after a safety incident. See: **Piss Test**

Chapter 1

Russ and the Magic Bus

I'll never forget the day Russ tried to kill a busload of screaming, airborne oilfield workers.

The job was out in the sticks, as usual. When I first heard about where we were headed, I would have backed out of the job. Everyone knew about the living conditions at Camp Cruella. That was the nickname that everyone gave this shithole at the end of the earth.

But my wife and I had a baby on the way, and I needed cash. I said goodbye to my honey and made the long trek out to the location.

This wasn't a dry camp. It's a good thing because the only way to live through living in it was by drinking your face off. That made the delivery driver, Russ, one of our best friends. He was a rock truck driver by day and a hotshot driver by night.

When Russ was in that dirt-moving truck, he was an unstoppable madman who went full throttle all day long. A rock truck is a giant all-terrain dump truck that could squash you flat if you got in its way. It can crush a pickup truck as easily as a frat boy crushes empty beer cans on his forehead. We all steered clear of Russ and his daytime activities for fear of getting run over.

Russ was always doing supply runs for the guys after work. The closest town was two hours of rough logging roads away. So when we needed any essentials, like smokes or booze, Russ was our man. For a small fee, he could get you whatever you needed.

You might wonder what it was about Camp Cruella that made it worse than the others out there.

Let's start with the fact that it had been condemned, but they had decided to open it up after it had been sitting empty for three years, just for us.

Imagine what kind of vermin can get into a camp with no humans around. Beetles, mice, maybe a bear? I know the mice and beetles got in for sure because they were still there when we arrived.

I saw my first mouse in the dining hall. I was standing in line holding my tray, waiting to sample some fine work-camp cuisine. The sign said today's entrees were beef stroganoff or mac and cheese. I saw sudden movement out of the corner of my eye at floor level.

"Look, a mouse!" the guy behind me shouted.

Then the line moved forward. We loaded up our plates with food prepared by what looked like institution escapees.

That night in bed, as I lay there trying to fall asleep, I heard suspicious rustling noises coming from the end of the room. I lifted my head off of the stained pillow and looked. There was my new buddy, Mickey, checking out my duffel bag.

I jumped up, and he ran for it. Bending down to look closer, I saw the tiny hole in the wall that Mickey or one of his tiny relatives had chewed into my tiny room. I wadded up some paper towel and stuffed the hole tight, then went back to bed.

It was a few days later when I had one of the best meals Camp Cruella could offer. Instant mashed potatoes and turkey log.

If you haven't had a turkey log, what a treat you're missing out on. Here's how it works. First, one of those big meat factories scrapes all the leftover turkey parts off the floor and drops them in a big hopper. Then a machine squeezes and glues them back together in a long, log-shaped meat bundle of wonder. The turkey billionaire pats himself on the back for inventing a way to sell leftover garbage and gets busy dreaming up more evil atrocities to sell to the unsuspecting.

After languishing in deep freeze storage for a few years, this meat rollup gets shipped by truck to whatever institution you are forced to eat at. It might be the funny farm or a prison. Or maybe it's a place like Camp Cruella, which is the best of both the funny farm and the prison combined.

Next, it gets overcooked and placed on a steam table to marinate in its own bacteria for several hours.

And finally, the jolly camp server carves you off a few hunks, as many as you want. Why not serve you extra since they got this golden goodness pretty cheap? To top it off, they slap a few scoops of instant mashed on the tray, slather it with mass-produced gravy, and away you go.

Anyway, my belly was full of instant mashed potato, turkey log, and delicious instant gravy.

It was minus thirty-five Celsius with a stiff wind. The dormitory they had me in was cold. The furnace barely worked, so we were all wearing our long johns and toques to bed so that we could wake up alive instead of like a popsicle. For those of you that don't know, a toque is what Canadians call a stocking cap.

I saw Russ leaving the hallway to our dorm.

He stopped to talk to me. "Hey, John. I rigged you guys up with some auxiliary heat! Stay warm," Russ slapped me on the shoulder as I went by.

I was apprehensive yet hopeful as I opened the door of the bunkhouse. There was a muffled roaring noise. I couldn't believe it.

Russ had a steel bucket sitting on a steel chair in the middle of the hallway. Inside the bucket was a tiger torch, burning bright. The thirty-pound propane tank was nearby. This couldn't be safe!

But it was warmer in there that night.

We had a forty-five-minute ride out to the pipeline right-of-way. Forty-five minutes of blissful bumping and bouncing in a yellow school bus. The biggest struggle was that the seats were designed for students, who are typically shorter and thinner than working guys. Some of the lovely men I spent time with on that bus were overweight and over six feet tall, so they didn't fit well in those seats.

Our bus driver, Shelley, did double duty as a rock truck driver after we arrived on site. She parked the bus near our work area and left it accessible so we could warm up and have coffee inside. All day long, Shelley went back and forth in a rock truck with loads of dirt. She was an active lady. Then she drove us back to camp.

The other rock truck drivers didn't have to work nearly as much. No one wanted to do double duty, but Shelley never complained.

Her bus driving skills were impeccable. A friendly demeanor, smooth stops, appropriate turning speeds, and absolute professionalism. We didn't realize how spoiled we were.

One night, Shelley had an incident at the parking lot just as she pulled in to park the bus. She collapsed on the steering wheel and had to get an ambulance ride to the hospital. It was a blood sugar problem. We all hoped she would be able to come back to work soon.

The next morning, we arrived at the bus, wondering who would be the new driver. Russ sat behind the wheel with a big smile on his face.

"Good morning, fellas! Let's get out there and get back to work!"

We all piled in and found our cramped little seats. No one was surprised when Russ started to drive that yellow piece of shit the same way he drove his yellow rock truck.

The bus lurched out of the work yard as if it had Tourette Syndrome. Russ swore at the traffic like he had Tourette's too. He locked up the brakes at every stop sign. We were feeling like milkshakes. That didn't stop the usual suspects from falling asleep like the worn-out party animals that they were.

Halfway to work, there was a train track crossing. It was at the bottom of a huge valley, with a steep hill on the way down. Every morning when we crested the hill we could see those tracks at the bottom. It was easy to look both ways for a mile or so, so we always knew if there was a train.

On average, a train would be coming about half the time. It was a busy crossing.

There were no lights, just a stop sign. Our usual driver would calmly pull up to the stop sign, look both ways, and proceed when safe. If we had to wait, we waited. What's the rush anyway, on the way to work?

Apparently, Russ never got the message that safety is the number one priority when you're driving a crew bus with twenty-odd souls on it.

We came to the top of the hill that morning, and Russ saw a train about a mile away. He must have done the math and decided that we needed to beat that train. Russ floored the pedal, and the bus lurched down the hill.

All of us who were awake suddenly became even more awake.

"Russ! We aren't gonna make it!" One of the guys yelled.

Russ just leaned forward in his seat, steely determination in his eyes, as he willed the bus to go faster.

The train bore down on us like a big boy at an all-you-can-eat buffet. We were all going to die!

As we picked up more speed, we went faster than a yellow school bus should ever go. The back end bounced so much that every little bump had us airborne.

There was the crossing. And there was the train, speeding towards it. Its horn blared as it tried to put on the brakes, but there was no stopping that monster.

The bus started across, and I looked without blinking out the window at that train. It got bigger, faster, and closer. I could feel death approaching. It was like a scene from a movie, but not a happy flick. It was from a movie where everyone dies.

We just made it across. The hump at the rail crossing launched the entire bus what seemed like feet off the ground, and we all floated past that train in weightless freefall. Then the bus slammed back to Earth.

Those who had been sleeping were now awake, probably because of all the screams and that huge plunge that pounded us into the seats like a plane coming in for the worst landing ever.

"Ha! Ha ha ha ha!" Russ cackled with glee. He sounded like that deranged uncle you never leave alone around small children or old people. Russ grinned like a maniac all the way there. Everyone else was completely silent for the rest of the drive.

We all appreciated life more than usual that morning. The air smelled sweeter, and the laughs were louder. But we all dreaded the ride home. Were we going to live and make it back to see our loved ones? Only time would tell.

Russ moved dirt all day like a possessed man, roaring back and forth with his yellow truck. We eyed him uneasily from a distance.

Late that afternoon, Shelly got chauffeured out and got behind the wheel of the bus. We all let out a sigh of relief. As we piled back on board to journey home, we thanked her from the bottom of our hearts for showing up. She smiled and proceeded to drive uneventfully and peacefully to town. Russ wasn't with us.

Back at Camp Cruella, I headed straight for the smoke pit before supper. I was in no rush to go back inside that dilapidated pile of mold and mouse-infested junk we were living in.

Russ was there by himself. I lit up a smoke and headed over to him.

"Russ! They didn't let you drive the bus back to camp."

"Drive it? They wouldn't even let me get on it!" He said with his madman's grin.

And then I realized that Russ never wanted to drive the bus, ever.

He just made sure that it would be the last time he would have to do it.

Chapter 2

The Wrong Way to Pass a Piss Test

L isten, I want you to know something before I get into it. I'm not some crackhead. I don't have a substance abuse problem, maybe an impulse control problem, but definitely no substance abuse issues. I like a good beer occasionally, a shot of rum in some cola if I visit my mom and dad, and sometimes even a puff of a joint or a couple of edibles on a Saturday night. So sue me.

With that out of the way, we can mosey on to the meat and potatoes of my story.

In 2016, The Federal Government took the final steps to legalize weed here in Canada, and by 2018 they had cemented the recreational use of pot into law. The Government of Canada placed itself into a market formerly the dominion of bikers, Asian gangs, and old hippies with secret fields of green gold in the B.C. interior. The Government decreed that they would now be the biggest drug dealer in Canada.

Many of us who were working in the oil and gas industry thought that the requirements for the pre-access drug and alcohol tests would be either waived altogether for marijuana or at least dialed back to check for impairment. In a rare reversal of fortune, the Government proved quick to change, and industry did not. This is how I found myself with this humiliating tale to pass along to you, dear reader.

For those unfamiliar with the whole process, a person like me (electrician by trade) working in the oil and gas business might have several jobs in a year, depending on their chosen career path. Some keep local, working near the cities in fabrication shops that are stable, reliable, and long-lasting. Others might prefer the industry's more lucrative and less stable construction side. Another option is the shutdown and turnaround industry, which is my bag. Short bursts of intense hours, several days in a row. A good shutdown would last about three-to-four weeks with maybe only one day off in the middle to keep on the side of the labor laws, with twelve-hour shifts until it is over. I can hit two or three of those in a year, make enough to pay the bills, and have the rest of the year off. I'm bad at math, but that's, like, eight or nine months off if you do it right. The catch is, in between each job you have to do a pre-access drug and alcohol test. Every damn time.

A pre-access test usually goes like this. You arrive at a private medical facility for an appointment at your chosen time. They confirm your identity and give you a breathalyzer test. Unless you are a giant fucking moron and showed up drunk for the test, that's an easy pass. If you make it through the breathalyzer, you are handed a lidded plastic cup with a temperature monitor stuck to the side, which you must fill with piss, usually to the halfway point or better. While you are engaged in this process, a nurse monitors you closely to ensure you are not cheating the process through "adulteration," which usually means fudging the test by drinking a high-dose vitamin solution before your "whiz quiz."

Adulteration can be determined by your appointed piss sommelier focusing their eye on the color and quality of your "donation" (their word for piss) to see if there are any odd variations in color. Too yellow is no good. Too clear? Also, no good.

Neon green? You're a cheating fuck. No job for you! After they give it the scrutinous eyeball, your hot bladder beer is usually sent to a lab for analysis or a quick panel test on the spot to check for all the possibilities, including methamphetamines, opioids, cocaine, and, yes, legal marijuana. I always wondered if there was a Hunter S. Thompson Award if you simultaneously tested positive for everything. I never wanted to find out for myself.

Once inside the testing facility, you are stuck there until you pee. If you leave, no matter the reason, the test is over, and you have forfeited the job you were looking forward to starting. They also restrict the amount of water you consume while you are there. You can't have anything to drink unless you have a shy bladder and can't pee. Some places even take your phone, wallet, and keys while you're in there. I don't know what purpose that serves, but them's the rules. After you fill the cup to the halfway mark or better, you spray the rest into the bowl, but you're not allowed to flush. The collection facility staff must do all flushing of the toilets. There is tamper-proof tape on the toilet tank and handle. It's quite a process.

I had been off work for some time, five months to be exact, and the bank account was starting to get a little low. I called a guy I knew who was looking for electricians to do some instrumentation work at a big shutdown that would last for five weeks. It started right away, which was a little unexpected. I thought it would have been at least a couple of weeks out, and I would have had time to sweat out all the weed I had in my system from the past five months. The trouble was, I had been out snowboarding the weekend before, and some pretty lady had some edibles on the hill she wanted to share with me. I wish I had a higher level of self-control, but I'm a single guy in my thirties, and my willpower for weed is as weak as my ability to resist a pretty face. Combine those two in one situation, and any mental fortitude I might have been capable of gets flushed down the shitter. I suspected there was a slight chance the edibles I ate on the ski hill might have pushed me over the edge for a test, but I didn't want to say no to the job, so I risked it, and I failed. There's a first time for everything, I guess.

Failing a test is not good. It guarantees that you probably will never work for the company that booked you the test ever again. I had to admit to my contact at that company that I fucked up. My friend who lined the job up for me was pretty disappointed I wasn't coming to work for him. After chewing me out on the phone, he threw me a bit of a bone. "Listen," he told me, "there's a path through this stuff for guys like you. You need to get onto RWEP. A few guys working with me are on it, and it keeps them from losing work."

RWEP stands for "Rapid Worksite Entry Program," a voluntary program for schlubs like me with poorly timed impulse control problems. It works like this, I volunteer for the program and get a substance abuse counselor assigned to me. I cannot admit to using legal government marijuana edibles outside of the recent instance on the ski hill to the counselor, or I get placed into a one-month rehab program – no shit. After they decide that I am not a chronic substance abuser, I will undergo a series of urine tests - six in total - over four weeks, where I must piss clean each time. Once I beat the six tests, they will issue me a card, and I can skip the pre-access testing requirements and go straight to work at any future jobs. There is a small catch. I would now be subject to random testing at unknown intervals while I was employed. These random tests are less stringent than urine tests and use an oral swab to check for impairment. I have no problem avoiding the 'Devil's Lettuce' when I have a job, so this seemed like it should be a no-brainer.

The first five tests went perfectly fine. I showed up, "donated," and left without incident each time. I should have known when I got up in the morning for the final test that things were going to go sideways.

I live with my older brother, who is between jobs and looking to return to work like me. The morning of my final test, he had to be at a training course. His truck was in the shop, and he needed a ride from me before I went to my appointment. It put me at my whiz quiz about an hour earlier than I needed to be there, but I'm a good brother, so I agreed to give him a ride, and being a good bro himself, he offered to take me to breakfast. With the prospect of a greasy diner breakfast in my guts, I got up earlier than usual that morning to make sure we both had time to eat.

As soon as we stepped out of the apartment into the unseasonably cold Calgary air, I sensed things wouldn't go well that day. I had been inside our apartment playing video games for the last week. I had gotten into my third playthrough of "Far Cry 5" and hadn't left the house the whole time. I had no idea how cold it had gotten, and goddamn, it was minus thirty-five, at least. The wind pushed hard from the side, almost knocking me to the ground when I got out into the unprotected expanse of the parking lot. We fired up my little old car, a sweet nineties BMW that I call "Gerty," cleaned the thin, dry snow off her and scraped the windows. We both jumped in, shivering and blowing on our waxy white bare fingers to try and warm them up. I decided to drive off. Gerty always warms up faster when you get her on the road. After driving a few blocks, I knew Gerty wasn't feeling her spry European self. She wasn't warming up. We got to the diner for breakfast, and I left her locked and running in the parking lot while we ate, hoping that the car would warm up in that time.

I don't usually eat until noon, so breakfast is a treat for me, and I was enjoying packing everything I could into my face that morning. Sausage, bacon, toast, and hash browns, and I even got an extra basted egg with two cups of coffee. By the time we left, I felt stuffed and satisfied.

Gerty hadn't gotten any warmer that whole time. As we got out of the diner, I immediately saw that there was still an opaque layer of thin frost on the window. We got into the car, and I wiped enough of the icy glaze off the inside of the windshield that I could drive it safely. The building where my brother was taking his course was close by. He tucked his hands in his pockets and his chin in his jacket, enjoying the cold five-minute ride to his class. I dropped him at the front of the building and after a quick goodbye consisting of, "You're welcome for breakfast, fuckface. Get your car fixed," He ran into the building, leaving a trail of cold breath behind him. I drove away in Gerty without seeing him enter the building. I wanted to get to my piss test as fast as I could. I cruised another five minutes to the testing facility, alternating hands between the steering wheel, the gear shifter, and coat pockets, cursing my stupidity for buying a stick shift. I cursed every red light I hit with the lowest words in my vocabulary and tried to invent some new words.

At the piss test clinic, I ran to the door and pulled on the handle. It was locked. The place didn't open for another five minutes, and I was the only car in the parking lot. I ran back to Gerty, the cold causing me to make pathetic noises under my breath with every step as I ran across the crunchy snow. I slipped on a spot of smooth ice and went down hard. I got up and dusted myself off, the snow in my ear already melting and starting to freeze as the wind continued to punish me. I got back into Gerty, started her up, and looked around for something - anything - to keep me warm.

I took my jacket off and used it as a blanket, tucking my head under it. I stayed that way for five minutes until I finally heard another car pull into the parking lot. I popped my head out from behind the comfort of my jacket. I watched a pair of small ladies that looked like they might be the nurses who worked in the clinic. They were all bundled in full-length parkas, the kinds that cost a thousand bucks but are like wearing a warm cup of hot chocolate. The nurses shuffled from a toasty cream-colored minivan to the front door. They removed their mittens to unlock the front door. I jumped out of Gerty and made my way to the door. The clinic ladies hadn't even entered the building when I grabbed the door handle and let myself in behind them. They shot me a concerned look as I barged into the ecstasy of the heated space, and I had to assure them that I had an appointment, but I was a little early.

The clinic nurses got the lights turned on and the computers going, letting me shiver alone in the waiting room before beckoning me over to check me in. I gave them my name, confirmed the paperwork, and locked the contents of my pockets in a small locker in the waiting room before one of the nurses, a quiet, pretty lady about my age with big, kind eyes, led me into a private room for the breathalyzer.

I blew a 0.000 - because I'm a winner!

The nurse handed me the familiar empty cup, marked a line about halfway up with a sharpie, and led me to the toilet. This particular facility operated on a heightened level of professional suspicion. The nurse was in the bathroom with me, on the other side of the stall door. She gave me the same parameters before I shivered into the stall, alone, while she stood outside, listening for any shenanigans I might get up to. "No flushing, no washing until after I check the test. Place the cup on the back of the toilet when you are finished."

I had done several whiz quizzes at this stage of my career, and not since the first test had I experienced "stage fright" until now. The cold had shrunk my unit down to a retreated turtlehead. My once modest penis was now a shriveled and timid nub. I pulled at it with cold hands and stretched it into the cup. I tried to clear my mind, working every mental faculty to envision a flowing mountain stream, a waterfall, a hot shower - any imagery that might start the flow. Instead, I thought of icicles, snowmen, an angry Yeti, and the first twenty minutes of 'The Empire Strikes Back.' All cold thoughts, negative thoughts that kept my pee hose unable to function. I held my sad, cold unit for a minute or two before giving in to the fact that nothing was coming out yet.

Admitting defeat, I zipped up, leaving the still-empty cup on the back of the toilet before I left the stall. The nurse returned me to the waiting room, giving me a half-cup of water to sip. I paced the room, ears and fingers tingling as my blood started to find those previously cold vessels, alternating my hands between my pockets and the room-temperature cup of water. I fidgeted and sipped until the water was gone. I finally was starting to feel warm.

I looked around the sterile waiting room and wanted to be anywhere else. I started flexing my abdominal muscles to see if I could force the feeling to pee. I felt a twinge, just a little flutter above my pecker, but it was enough. I flagged the nurse down, and she escorted me back to the tiny bathroom stall for another attempt. I got into the stall, closed the door behind me, and saw the nurse moving around through the crack of the door. As I held my junk over the bowl, I could feel the need to pee evacuate my nether regions with every move she made out there. I had psyched myself out. Outside the stall door, the impatient nurse shuffled around again.

"You okay in there?" she asked. As soon as her words came out, any remaining urge to piss hopped on a rocket, strapped itself in, and left the fucking planet.

I took a deep breath, feeling disappointed anger at myself. I wanted to tell the nurse off for interrupting me, but I was afraid that it might result in her throwing me out, which would also mean failing the test. I dropped the cup on the back of the toilet and left the stall.

"Still nothing?" the nurse asked.

I shook my head and returned to the waiting room. There were two more people in the room now, a man a little older than me and a woman younger than myself, and dammit, she was good-looking. I could feel their judgmental gazes on my back as the nurse handed me another cup of water. They knew I was a failure - a low-down, dirty, no-pissing failure of a man. I thanked her for the water, going out of my way to be over-the-top polite. Looking for a silver lining to my situation, I remembered that I was no longer cold and shivering, took another deep breath, and paced the room while I sipped the water until it was gone. I tossed the paper cup into the trash can and flexed my abdominal muscles, trying to force myself to pee. I leaned against a wall to give myself something to push against—some more leverage. I wanted to give it my all.

I pushed my upper back against the wall, pushing on my guts with my abs, using my clenched legs to give the whole process a little extra 'oomph.' I was starting to feel a little fullness in my lower abdomen. It was working! I unclenched my legs and abs for a minute and relaxed everything before repeating the whole process. The man and woman sitting comfortably in the waiting room looked at me like I was an alien, but I didn't care how I looked.

A nurse called the woman donor from the waiting room and asked her if she was ready.

"I think so," the woman said before the other nurse escorted her out of the room.

I returned to my exercise of trying to piss. I clenched everything again and held my breath this time, working my neck muscles into the process. It probably looked like I was giving birth, but I didn't care. I just wanted this to be over. An unmistakable heaviness filled my abdomen. This was it! I unclenched my muscles. Dread hit me as I relaxed. A heaviness had formed in my guts, but not that familiar front feeling of a full bladder. It was the uncomfortable feeling in the back, like an internal puppeteer trying to push his hand out of my ass. I had worked my guts into needing to poop. I clenched my butt cheeks to keep the sensation at bay.

I sat in one of the chairs and fought the growing urge to poop, hoping that having my legs in the sitting position would somehow stop the urge. It didn't. I began to squirm in the uncomfortable plastic chair and had to stand back up. *Come on,* I thought. *Hold it together. All you have to do is pee.*

After another minute of pacing the waiting room, the sensation became unbearable. It took every ounce of my concentration to keep from farting. My stomach and intestines were making groaning and gurgling sounds that brought with them sharp, stabbing sensations. The more I tried, the harder it was to maintain composure. Things were getting dire. I had to shit badly, but I couldn't leave the clinic. I flagged the nurse down with my right hand, my left arm clutching my stomach tightly in a futile attempt to keep the pain at bay. She came to the counter ever so slowly, as my intestines quaked with every step she took.

"Are you ready *now*?" she asked me, picking up the sample cup. She turned to leave before I stopped her with a tap on the shoulder.

"No," I told her quietly, "I have to go to the bathroom."

"So, you're ready then?

"No. I have to use your bathroom, though."

Confusion crept across her face. She wasn't putting it together. *Fuck. She was going to make me say it.*

"Number two," I whispered.

"Excuse me?" She asked.

"Number two," I reiterated, a little louder this time, "You know? Number two."

"Number two?" the nurse asked. Still not putting it together. I could see the moment in her eyes when it clicked. "Oh! Number two?"

Finally, I thought.

"Yeah," I said. Another stabbing pain jabbed me below my navel. "Is there a bathroom I could use?"

The nurse looked over her shoulder at her colleague.

"He has to use the bathroom," she said to the other nurse. "Number two."

"Are you kidding me?" The other nurse shot back at her, not realizing how close they were to a brown deluge in their waiting room. "He can't do that here."

"Can I leave and come back?" I asked, my voice rife with desperation.

"You can't leave before you provide a sample." my nurse said, "If you leave for any reason, we have to report it as a refusal to donate, which they consider to be the same as a fail."

"I don't want that," I said. "But isn't there something you can do? It's an emergency."

"This has never happened before," she said.

The more seasoned colleague said, "He could use one of the collection rooms, but all the other rules apply. You'll have to be in there with him."

Horror filled the nurse's face. She looked at all five foot-eleven of wincing, shit-pained, stupid me, and I saw the horror on her face round the bases. At first base was a look that said: *Screw this guy. This is not my job.* That quickly faded as her thoughts rounded second base to: *But this poor guy will lose his job!* Third base came with a big inhale. This Saint of a lady was going to help me out. Home base was a steely look.

"Okay," she said. "Let's go." She straightened her back and went to the side door to let me into the collection area.

She didn't have to tell me twice. I accompanied her, half doubled over from the gut-wrenching pain. She talked as we walked, telling me the rules still applied. I could wipe, but no flushing. All flushing had to be done by the collection staff. She would have to work the toilet handle on my behalf. Good Christ, had my life come to this? She let me into the stall, and I hurriedly fumbled with the door and then did the same with my belt. The pain in my stomach was so bad that I had trouble with the most basic tasks. I managed to get my belt off, my pants undone, and my pasty ass sitting on the bowl. I saw the nurse through the too-large space in the stall door. Bless her heart, at least she had turned her back to give me a little privacy. I hung my head in shame but also to clear my head. I am not one for praying or meditation, but I would say that I was doing both at that moment.

A low hiss left my asshole as I began my silent prayer. *Please don't be loud, please don't be loud, please don't be loud,* I repeated in my head. I tried to think of quiet things. Mouse footsteps. Ninja boots, Charlie Chaplin. Anything quiet. Push out the noisy thoughts. Push out the noisy thoughts. No tubas. No foghorns. No fucking loud exhaust pipes on custom-tuned foreign cars.

God was not hearing me that day. My prayers went unanswered. Though I had been trying to clench my stomach to slow-release the contents of my guts, the symphony began to play. First came a drum-roll of rapid-fire farts like a distant machine gun followed by a sad, dry 'plop!' Next came two notes. The first was a higher pitch than the second.

My ass was trying to play the theme to 'Jaws.'

I caught a glimpse of the nurse through the crack in the door as the thunder fell outta me. Surprised by the sound, she quickly turned her head, then returned her gaze to the wall opposite where she stood, her hand shot up to cover her mouth and nose.

"I'm so sorry," I moaned to her pathetically.

She said nothing.

The hits just kept on coming. With a sharp stabbing pain, everything began to leave my bowels, causing a disgusting melody to echo through the collection room.

"Ahhhh!" I cried in pain as my stomach cramped up. More turds fell out of me. Poops and musical toots, no doubt prompted by the greasy breakfast I had eaten earlier that morning. I should have known better. Diner food always gets me.

"Are you okay?" the nurse asked. Despite the circumstances, I could tell she was genuinely concerned.

"I'm so sorry!" I pleaded, not even answering her question.

I kept pooping soft serve. The weird bum noises eventually tapered off, and in my final moment of relief, I started to pee. Fuck, fuck, fuck!!!! I tried to hold it in, but the floodgates had opened up. There was no stopping it now. I hung my head for a few seconds to pretend

I was somewhere other than where I was. I heard the nurse shuffle her feet in a subtle, non-verbal reminder that she was waiting.

"I'm so sorry." It was all I could muster.

The nurse cleared her throat and said, "It's okay."

I reached out for the toilet paper, batting at the wall where it should have been, blindly trying to unroll a hearty wad. Instead of touching the standard roll of paper that should have been there, my hand hit an unfamiliar metal object instead. I looked over at the peculiar dispenser before registering what it was.

Single squares of toilet paper from a box instead of a roll. God-damned poop tickets.

Perfect. I grabbed as many as possible, like an angry old man waiting his turn in the line at a deli, and wiped up as best as I could with those useless, tiny squares of non-stick paper, careful not to get any on my hands. I stood up, buttoned my pants, and buckled my belt.

I looked at the bowl. A giant 'turdberg,' with only ten percent of its mass above the water line was left behind. A giant, disgusting hulk. I looked to the ceiling, to the sky, to the great beyond, but I found no relief.

"I'm done," I said.

"Okay," she replied.

She got herself ready.

I opened the stall door and let the nurse in. This poor lady had to give my monstrosity its final send-off. She shuffled into the tiny stall. With my eyes on the floor like an embarrassed puppy, I scooted out of her way as she entered. Her hand was held over her mouth and nose. She avoided looking at my shameful remains. She didn't look at me. She pressed the toilet handle down hurriedly.

The toilet sighed and gulped, but my payload was not delivered. The entirety of the ticket-topped mountain just sat there like a slug as the water accumulated around it. Her hand reluctantly darted to the handle again, holding it down longer. The water ran until the bowl was dangerously full.

But the turd remained.

"I think it's plugged," she said, pushing past me and out the door. She was trying to look like she wasn't in a hurry, but I could tell she was. I followed her to the waiting room, which had begun filling up. Three more people were waiting now. As the nurse and I entered, the lady who had gone in later than me was already leaving, having made her 'donation.'

Color me green with envy.

The nurse went back behind the counter and quietly informed her colleague of what had gone down – and what had failed to go down - in the collection room. She bent low to her colleague's ear, whispering to her. The nurse returned her attention to me, bringing the empty urine sample cup to the counter.

"Do you think you're ready?" she asked.

"No," I solemnly replied. "I went already."

The nurse grimaced, exposing her bottom teeth in a display that made me think she was partly embarrassed for me and partly trying not to laugh.

"Oh boy," she said. "I guess I'll get you some more water?"

"Yes, please."

I watched as her colleague turned away from me, the phone receiver to her ear. I knew she was calling a plumber. The nurse brought me a full cup this time, another sign she wanted me out of there. I sipped it down in a few gulps and looked at the time. I had only been there forty-five minutes. The test has a maximum time of three hours, after which you fail and are kicked out. I had another ninety minutes to pee.

I sat down on one of the molded plastic chairs, sipped water, and watched the room fill up with other whiz donors. I got another cup of water and another after that. I watched as other nurses came into the office. They spoke to each other quietly behind the counter, telling my story, spreading the virus from one ear to the next. They had a hard time containing their gasps and laughter. One was bold enough to point at me and say, "That guy?" before she was shushed. That prompted the other 'donors' to begin wondering what I had done.

Seventy minutes had gone by since I first noted the time. I had been there almost two hours, and my bladder finally started feeling a little full. I hopped out of my chair, bounded to the reception desk, and announced that I was ready. The nurse snapped up the cup, and I accompanied her to a different collection room. I noted that the whole back room was filling up with my smell. They had designed the collection areas for urine only and had not installed fans in any of the rooms. My smell tainted the air throughout the facility, turning the place into a haunted house full of the ghosts of every egg salad sandwich ever eaten. I handily filled the cup this time, left it on the back of the bowl, and left the stall. The nurse checked the temperature and color, poured my pee into two separate containers, labeled them, and gave me the paperwork before she flushed the toilet and let me wash my hands.

"Your results should be ready in two-to-five days." She told me. "There is a number on your sheet to call for the results."

"Thank you," I said flatly. I took the paper from her hand and made my way back out to the waiting room. The plumber had already shown up and was being pointed in the direction of my shameful mess. He had come prepared for war. The plumber had the one-hundred-foot toilet snake that comes on a two-wheeled dolly cart. I collected my possessions from the locker and made my way out, ashamed but triumphant. I would not have to do this ever again!

The weather had warmed up a little, and the warm winds of a Chinook had begun to blow in, seemingly bringing my better fortune with it. Gerty had no frost on the windshield. I hopped in and fired her up, spinning the tires in the slush as I fishtailed out of the parking lot and entered late morning traffic. I laughed as I drove myself home. The ladies in that clinic would have a story to tell for years to come. It had been quite the ordeal for me, but I realized that I was going to be a piss clinic legend. I was the guy who came in to donate a urine sample and clogged the toilet with a massive shit.

Chapter 3

The Night a Guy Named Nipples Saved Me From Getting Bootfucked With Flip Flops

Have you ever met someone, and within fifteen minutes, you knew you were gonna be best buds? That was how I felt when I met Nipples.

Nipples was tall, skinny, and had a scruffy beard. He kinda looked like Shaggy from Scoobie Doo, and he even had Shaggy's love of 'Scoobie Snacks' and weed.

We had some great conversations while we worked. It didn't matter if we were putting up snow fences, moving around pumps and hoses, or chucking skids. Nipples and I had a blast.

Everyone still called him by his "real" name back then, which was Connor. But one day we accidentally discovered his true name. It had to do with one of our epic conversations about Batman.

I had never met such a big Batman fan. Nipples knew every comic storyline, every movie, and every villain in the Batman universe. That's how we got onto the topic of Batman's suit, and why did it need to have nipples.

Nipples was all fired up about the masked superhero's costume. "George Clooney's 1997 Batman Suit was the start of something great. Do you know why? Because it had nipples. And now, a Batman suit has to have nipples, or it's a waste of my time."

I wasn't sure it mattered. "Why would Batman build a suit with nipples on it? Isn't the whole point of an armored breastplate to protect your nipples, not showcase them?" I asked.

"Look, you want your Batsuit to confuse your enemies and strike fear into them. Don't you find the idea of a dude dressed like a bat, coming at you with his nipples erect, kinda scary? Like a witch's tits on a minus 30 morning, only she has a mask and a cape, and she punches the shit out of you!"

"I don't think that if I'm in a fight situation I'm gonna notice a dude's nipples. He's punching me in the head with his bat gloves and kicking me in the nuts, and that's distracting."

"But that's when you look down and see the nipples, and you realize that anyone who builds nipples into their armor is crazy, and you get really scared. That guy obviously isn't worried about rules or social conventions, or due process. He's gonna kill you! I'm telling you, it strikes fear in the hearts of criminals."

"Shit, no. No nipples. It's like some sorta latex sex suit with those on it."

"Listen to me. I gotta insist on Nipples on my bat suit. Nipples on everything! I freaking love nipples!"

"Okay, Nipples, you've convinced me. He's the freakiest Batman."

And that's how Nipples got his nickname.

At the end of the pipeline job, we had some cash in the bank and wanted to head somewhere overseas. But the two of us were travel noobs, so we asked where some of the other guys had gone. One of the welders we were working with told us we needed to head to Thailand.

"It's a great place. The food is fantastic, the people are friendly, and it's so warm there. Forget this minus twenty Celcius shit. And everything is cheap! Just watch out for that second type of woman, or you'll be sorry."

That really got Nipples' attention. "Second type of woman? Well, what are we waiting for?" It turns out we should have asked more questions.

The Thailand trip was happening. We bought a couple of plane tickets and went on an adventure.

We didn't plan it that way. We were just lucky enough to hit Thailand at full moon party time. If you are into that giant beach bashes, that's when you should go. It's the biggest party event in Asia. Guests from all over the world celebrate on the beach every month when the moon is full. We found ourselves at Koh Phangan, full of booze and other substances, having a great time.

Nipples was off schmoozing with a couple of girls, and I was dancing my butt off right there on the beach. I got partnered up with this Thai girl who was slightly taller than me. That could have been a warning flag.

I'm not a tall guy, but a lot of Thai people are shorter than me. That includes most of the Thai guys.

Picture it: a gorgeous, tall Thai girl dancing on a beach with an inebriated white guy. Where was my Spidey sense? It was buried under alcohol.

Things were moving along pretty fast. She was touching me in all the right places. I was starting to think it was time to make my move.

That's when my buddy Nipples showed up, and he seemed a little distraught. "Josh!" he yell-whispered at me. He pointed at his throat.

I had no idea what he meant, so I kept dancing. "Nipples, what's wrong? You choking?"

The girl laughed. "Your friend is called Nipples? That's funny."

"Yeah, it's a long story," I smiled at her as we ground on. "Nipples, I'm busy."

He grimaced and pointed at the center of his throat again.

I turned away and kept dancing with the girl, who had a hand on my arm.

Nipples didn't give up, though. He leaned in close and drunk-whispered, "Adam's apple!"

I was totally confused. Bible talk on the beach? What the hell was Nipples up to? But I saw him looking at the girl I was dancing with knowingly, and suddenly the pieces fell in place. I clued in.

This lady used to be a guy!

I pushed clear of her and tried to get a little space, but she just came right back in and started rubbing against me. In sudden shock, I pushed her back, just a little too hard. She fell on her butt in the sand and let out a little squee.

Now she was angry. She jumped up and ran straight at me. She started hitting me, not that hard, really, but it was annoying.

I hadn't noticed how many Thai girls there were in the area, but there were plenty. When they saw what was going on, all of her friends mobilized. Before I knew it, a circle of girls was shoving me and hitting me.

This magic circle started to cause some damage. Their fists had a lot of power per square inch, and this wasn't the vacation I signed up for. I was getting beat up by a bunch of girls, or guys, or maybe both.

It was too much for my alcohol-soaked brain. With a lurch, I went down face first in the sand.

As I lay there, confused and annoyed, these colored plastic blobs kept coming in and hitting me right in the face.

Pink, blue, green. What was going on? It took me a few seconds to realize what was smacking me in the head.

It was their flip-flops. These girls were bootfucking the shit out of my face with their flip-flops, and it hurt.

I staggered back up, and at least five of these hot-looking girls or boys kept hitting me and yelling words in Thai. I didn't have any choice. I was going to have to start fighting back.

Nipples pulled one off of me and tossed her onto the sand. I started swinging. I had to defend myself, right? I laid a few haymakers right into the middles of a few of these girls. They screamed and ran for it, leaving Nipples and me standing there.

We were right beside a beach bar with plenty of onlookers. Four bodybuilders covered in tattoos had seen the whole thing go down, and they were pissed at us.

"You two losers can't hit the ladies. We're gonna fuck you up!" one of them yelled. They all stood and started moving in our direction. We ran, and they chased us, determined to teach us a lesson.

We ran away from the beach, down a busy little street, the four white dudes hot on our tail. But as soon as we hit the crowd, they gave up and went back to their bar.

I bet that in their version of the story, we were the bad guys. They were the heroes who saved the girls.

I can see one of the meatheads telling the story while showing off his massive tribal tattoo.

"So there we were, sitting at the bar," the bodybuilder would say while taking big swallows of his energy drink. "And those two fuck-wads started punching these girls right in the face! There was blood everywhere. But we taught them a lesson. They woke up in the hospital with their jaws wired shut, covered in bandages."

The way Nipples tells the story is like watching a spy movie.

I was getting beat up by a bunch of girls, so he pulled me to safety. Then he made sure I escaped all of those tough gym rats, and we jumped on a scooter. That was when we outran the Thai Mafia in a city-wide scooter chase while being shot at, only to escape by jumping off the dock onto a barge loaded with fish.

Nipples always did have a vivid imagination.

But looking back, I really second-guess myself. Was Nipples right about the ladyboys? Were they actually guys? If so, they were still pretty good-looking. I kinda wish he had left me alone to find out.

Chapter 4

Smokepit Confessions

I quit smoking six years ago. You know all the reasons. It's expensive. It makes you stink. And it eventually kills you. All those reasons informed my decision to finally get some nicotine gum and quit that filthy habit once and for all. And quit, I did. Cigarettes are now a thing of the past, a puff of smoke in the rearview mirror, and let me tell you – I don't miss it. I don't wake up coughing anymore. I can climb a flight of stairs without losing my breath. I don't have one weird yellow finger. I have money for other things, for fun hobbies that add enjoyment to my life instead of melting minutes off it.

I had been a secret smoker. Because I worked in the dirty environment of a piping fabrication shop, it was hard for my wife and kids to tell the smell of welding fumes from the scent that a half-pack of darts would pollute my clothes with every day, and I would shower and brush my teeth as soon as I got home. It had been a secret shame that I am happy to have conquered.

Chances are you know someone who has quit smoking. Maybe they replaced their smoking habit with the ever-fashionable white clouds and glycol-sweet smell of a battery-operated vape – aka "The Douche Flute." Smoking is way out of fashion, and rightfully so. It's the worst. Now that it's been six years since I've paid to put that shit into my lungs, I cringe whenever I have to walk through a cloud of it and shiver whenever I have to follow a stranger into the warm space of a building in our frigid winter, only to be slapped with the pungent funk of Canadian tobacco on their winter jacket. I have noted that this experience has become scarcer as time passes, and more people have stopped smoking altogether. I think we're all better off for it.

I'm glad I don't smoke, but I must admit that I enjoy other aspects of smoking. Break time in the smoke pit was one of them. Job-site lunchrooms were usually quiet places where folks read books or quietly scrolled their phones. In contrast, the grey haze of a job site smoke pit was full of raucous laughter, dirty jokes, self-promotion and congratulation, and moments of brutal honesty that could only come from people who have embraced such a subtle death wish. What is it that Kurt Vonnegut Jr. said about cigarettes? "A classy way to commit suicide."

Besides a specific type of camaraderie, I made a lot of good connections. It was a conduit to networking that you didn't get if you sat in the lunchroom, and it led to some great opportunities. Rubbing elbows with the older, disagreeable fuckers who ran the jobs went a long way. It resulted in more than one unexpected promotion and several bucks per hour in a raise – events that would have never happened had I spent my breaks in the lunchroom reading Vonnegut.

It was in the smoke pit that I found an unlikely kindred spirit one day. In exchanging self-deprecating stories about our odd personality traits over some lunchtime coffin nails, I confessed my darkest secret to my colleagues:

I am deeply disgusted by stickers.

It borders on paranoia and phobia. Fruit stickers are the worst, I told them. I would have to remove them from the edges of the lunchroom tables I would sit at on each job I went to. That was always the first thing I had to do at a new job, and it grossed me out. I would handle the filthy stickers with a sizeable prophylactic wad of paper towel to remove them from my sight before I could sit down and relax. I'd silently curse the Neanderthal who put them there.

I told them how I would recoil in horror as my young daughter would greet me at the door when I came home from work with tiny cartoon character stickers on her fingernails. Eventually, those little stickers would come off her fingernails, and I would find a filthy Sponge Bob on the bottom of my favorite pair of socks. There was no saving the socks at that point. I would throw them right in the trash, making sure the stickers didn't touch me.

They laughed smoky laughs as I told them how bile would rise in my throat if I went through a drive-through and had to confront the reality of the faded stickers that the weather had half-washed off under the window. The more they laughed, the more I told, cutting the punchlines of my self-ridicule with drags of my cigarette. After my laughing coworkers had taken turns grinding their spent smokes out on one chosen post at the entry to the smoke pit, I noticed that one guy remained, my foreman Sean.

"I thought I was the only one," said Sean, looking around to see if anyone else was listening, lighting up another cigarette, even though the break was over, which gave me license to do the same.

"What?" I asked.

"Stickers. I fucking hate them." He pointed to his hard hat, "See any there?"

"No."

"That's because they're goddamned disgusting, and there's a special place in hell for the fuckers who insist on sticking them on everything. I could never mention it to anyone because I know it's weird. You're the only other person I've ever heard of who feels the same way I do. I thought I was alone," he confessed.

You might think we're both fucked up, but it was the kind of weird honest moment that could only have taken place in a smoke pit. Laugh away, but now that I've quit, I miss those bizarre, honest moments. They were where someone could find intimate trust from guys who typically didn't open themselves up.

Smoke pits were a comforting place to be when you were out on a remote job, away from family and friends. They were a quick way to break the ice with new coworkers, have a laugh, and find people who could understand your frustrations. At fifty cents a smoke (in those days), it was cheap therapy for people who didn't know they needed therapy, and while I was a smoker, I lapped it up.

There was a flip side to smoke pit conversations. Sometimes the level of honesty was too much. You would hear something out of left field that made you wonder about some people. I've heard of people's uncomfortable perversions, brutal assaults they've committed, and other criminal activities. Occasionally I even heard the odd gruesome war story.

Eventually, I was hired on to a night shift at a five-week plant shut-down north of Fort McMurray. I naturally couldn't resist the pull of the closest smoke pit and found myself in its orbit immediately. After the required two-day orientation, I got my bearings and met my fore-man –a grizzled smoker – who gathered a few other lost-looking souls and me from the orientation shack. He walked us all over to where our lunchrooms were and proceeded to light himself up a smoke with a beat-up old zippo.

We did a lot of smoking at that job. It was one of those 'hurry up and wait' jobs where you didn't get out into the plant unless there was an immediate need for your skills. They wanted to keep the number of workers in the facility to a minimum.

Out of the ten or so of us in the crew, the smokers got to know each other well over trips to 'The Pit.'

Five of us regularly attended story time in the smoke pit on that job.

There were two welders on the crew, Ben and Andy- both smokers. Ben was not a cigarette smoker, but he would enjoy smoke breaks with the rest of us as he puffed away on a big old Bilbo Baggins pipe and pleasant-smelling tobacco. He was a funny guy with fantastic stories.

Andy was a quiet guy who would enjoy the conversations in the smoke pit in silence. He was what I would describe as an 'intense listener.' Andy had an accent that I couldn't place. His English was good but still developing. I knew he was listening to the bullshit the rest of us barfed out every night, putting the words into his vocabulary for later use.

For fitters, we had two Daves - Young Dave and Old Dave. I had worked with Old Dave before at a construction job. He was a gruff, funny, good-natured dude who told his tall tales with a booming voice you could hear for miles. Young Dave was a bodybuilder type and a hard worker.

We all quickly got along, primarily working, playing cards, smoking, and repeating the process over five weeks of darkness and welding light.

A couple of weeks into the job, all of us smokers were killing time in the pit, and Young Dave was complaining about the showers in the camp. While he was getting cleaned up at the end of his last shift, someone walked into his bathroom stall while he was buck-naked and soapy in the shower. Young Dave's chosen stall had a malfunctioning lock, and another dude strolled right in. Old Dave had worked there when everyone in the camp had to get clean in gang-style showers. There was no such thing as privacy back then, and he couldn't resist letting all of us young bucks know how good we all had it.

"Back in the day when Christ was a cowboy," Old Dave boomed, "When the gang showers were there, you'd either wake up early for a shower or make sure you got in there late. You sure as hell didn't want to be showering when the shift changed. The showers would be half-full of dudes that were hungover and angry from the drinks they had the night before, and the other half would be dudes from the other shift who tried to have a couple of beers at the lounge, trying to miss the crowd in the showers. I'd be minding my own business, and a brawl would start in the middle of the shower room. Fist flying and dicks swinging. Things got interesting back then."

"You ever get into it with anybody, Dave?" Ben asked through puffs of his pipe.

"No, but my buddy did one time. I thought about breaking it up because he was getting his ass kicked. With all of us being naked, that was the kind of fight my buddy would have to get out of on his own."

"Yeah, right," said Young Dave. "You probably dropped the soap, hoping someone would notice."

"Not this cowboy!" Old Dave said. "Besides, I liked it when the fights broke out in the showers. At least no one was jerking off."

We had a good laugh at that. All except Andy, who had been looking at us all with curious regard through his thick round glasses that gave his eyes a distorted magnification. He was working his way through a cigarette that he held near his mouth the whole time he smoked. He went for a significant drag before finally asking in his peculiar accent, "What does this mean, to 'drop the soap'? I don't understand."

Ben explained to him what it meant to drop the soap in prison. Andy thought about it for a few seconds, still not laughing. After another nearly motionless drag, he ashed his cigarette into a bucket and said, "I dropped the soap many times in the prison shower. Never did that happen to me."

An odd hush fell over the group. What did we just hear? This polite, quiet, and kindly man had done time. It was a lot to process. We all sat around, eyes wide for seconds before I finally spoke up.

"YOU have been to prison, Andy?"

"I was in a military prison in my home country."

"Holy shit Andy! You were a prisoner in a military prison? How long were you in for?" I asked.

Andy shrugged his shoulders. "Six months."

"What did they send you up for?" asked Old Dave.

"It is a long story," Andy replied. "And I am not a good storyteller."

"You're going to have to try," Ben said, "I have a feeling this is too good not to hear!"

Andy looked around and saw that we were all waiting on his story. His cigarette had gone out.

"You need a smoke?" Young Dave asked.

"Yes, thank you," Andy said, ever polite.

Young Dave handed Andy a cigarette and lit it up for him. Andy took a drag and came to life. This is the story he told us:

In the military, I was a soldier on the ground. The unit that I was in was tasked with border patrol. My government knew that there were lots and lots of drugs coming through the borders, and we were supposed to find the smugglers who were doing it.

The border there at that time was a very complicated place. Many people would move through the hills on their way to other places. There were limited places to cross the border, and the section we patrolled was five hundred kilometers. Many people would walk or drive across wherever they wanted. Refugees. Farmers were moving animals from country to country. Heavy equipment. Families with small kids who have relatives in both countries. Mixed with all these were terrible people who brought weapons and drugs into my country. The government wanted to stop all illegal crossings.

There were insufficient resources and people to keep everyone from unlawfully crossing, so they told the military to let people cross unless someone thought they were smuggling drugs. We left people to cross until the government could find a better solution. We didn't take prisoners for illegally crossing. We only took prisoners if they were smugglers. These were our instructions.

For three years, we looked for heroin, hashish, and opium. We searched vehicles and found nothing. We searched people and found nothing. When we reported back to the people at the top, we told them we found nothing, and they lost their minds!

"How the fuck can you say you found nothing when drugs are all over this country?" they would say.

The government put significant pressure on the men at the top, and then they took it out on us.

The morale in my platoon was terrible. We thought we were failures. We increased the searches. We looked at women. We looked at the kids. We searched more people. We searched more vehicles. We searched more bags. We took cars apart and cut car seats open. We always found nothing. We started to turn on each other. Someone would blame *me for not looking where they thought I should have looked. I blamed someone else for not looking where I thought they should have. Sometimes these arguments would lead us to scuffle and fight with each other.*

Soon, none of us were talking to each other. The next patrol we went on was silent. I didn't care anymore. I wouldn't search for anything. I watched people move towards the border to another country with their families. I was furious, and I cursed everyone else in my head. I cursed the government, the high ranks, and my fellow soldiers. I cursed myself. I was feeling very sorry for myself. I wanted to help my country out. I was a patriot and knew that the drugs moving across our borders funded worse activities in the neighboring countries. I wanted to catch these bastards. Not just because it was my job but because I wanted to keep my country a good place.

One day, I noticed the animals. There were a lot of sheep and goats. Some cows and donkeys. It occurred to me that we never checked the animals before.

I walked over to a herd of sheep and grabbed one. The farmer with them looked at me nervously as I checked the animal. I felt the sheep's skin, like the sheep was under arrest. I frisked the sheep. There is nothing. I grabbed another sheep and did the same. Nothing. Another soldier called me over the radio.

"What the hell are you doing?"

"Checking the animals," I told him.

"You're fucking crazy," he says.

"I know. It's a crazy world. What have we got to lose?"

"You're a moron."

"You sound like my father."

"What would your father think of you groping sheep and cows?"

"He would think it was better than walking around with my thumb up my ass, doing nothing," I said. "He might even help me out."

He agreed. He started to look at the sheep, donkeys, and cows too. Soon none of us were looking through cars and bags. Now, all of us soldiers were checking animals.

The sheep farmers started to get nervous. They watched us molest their animals, but they said nothing. I began to suspect that they might be guilty of something, but we still had to get proof.

I grabbed another sheep. I took a look at the animal. As I examined the sheep, I noticed a big bulge, a big square hard thing under its skin. I laid the sheep on its side and started looking under the hair. There were stitches there. I opened stitches with my knife, and a bag of drugs fell out of the infected wound.

Holy shit, I found the drugs!

I radioed the other soldiers and let them know.

The farmer saw me with the bag of drugs. He panicked and made the animals move faster, waving his arms and shouting at the livestock. Another smuggler started whipping the animals with a stick to get them going. The smugglers were five minutes away from crossing into another country, and we couldn't stop them after they crossed. I called over the radio to the others and told them what I had found. I was the closest one to the smugglers. They asked me to radio in for orders, and I did.

I switched the radio over and called the command center.

"We have visual on the smugglers," I told him.

"You're sure?" the Commander asked, "You confirmed this?"

"Affirmative," I said. "We have visual confirmation of the drugs and the smugglers. Permission to engage?"

"Do not engage," the Commander says. "Wait for air support. A helicopter is on the way."

I thought to myself that a helicopter was twenty minutes from getting to where we were, and the smugglers were five minutes from crossing the border. They would be gone with the drugs and would change how they smuggled next time.

We would have to repeat this terrible process all over again. Command would surely reprimand us, and the drugs would continue to flow.

"There's no time!" I told the Commander. "They will be across the border in five minutes. How long until we can get air support?"

"The helicopter is fueling now. Twenty minutes out."

"I am opening fire," I said.

He yelled at me over the radio, "Do not open fire! Air support is on the way! Do not open fire!"

Fuck that, I thought. If I let them go, surely someone higher than my commander would hear about it, and Command would no doubt take it out on us to deflect from their incompetence. I had had enough of their bullshit. They couldn't see what was going on. They didn't have boots on the ground. They didn't have to shit in a hole for weeks. The Commander was in his office, sipping expensive coffee. He got to see his family every night. What reason did he have to put an end to this situation?

None.

But I did.

I turned the radio off and grabbed my RPG-7. I threw the tube over my shoulder, flipped the safety off, and sighted-in a crowded area where I would hit the most smugglers with an explosion.

I launched the grenade.

Sheep and people parts flew everywhere when the grenade exploded. The air in front of me became a fountain of dirt and guts.

My comrades came running. They saw other smugglers running for the border and finished them up with machine guns. When no more *smugglers were left, we walked through piles of guts and body parts until air support showed up - thirty minutes later.*

They were useless.

We returned to the base, happy that we finally stopped the fuckers, but the commander was not pleased. He was furious that we disobeyed his orders. I got a court martial when he found out that I shot first. I took the fall for the other guys in my platoon too. Nobody else went to jail, only me.

Six months I spent in there. I read. I wrote letters.

Higher-ups got medals for what I did while I sat in prison.

Six months! It was long enough for me to start thinking, 'fuck this,' you understand? I got out of prison and was dishonorably discharged from the military.

Well, fuck them,

I learned to weld. I came to Canada.

We looked around at each other as Andy nonchalantly continued to smoke.

This guy, I thought, has *seen some shit!* I had never heard anything like that before.

"Oh-my-fucking God!" said Ben. "How many guys did you blow up, Andy?'

"Seven men. Fifteen sheep." Andy replied. "I feel bad for the sheep. They did nothing wrong." He took another drag of his smoke.

My dark sense of humor caused me to think that he was trying to be funny, and I chuckled a little. He snapped his head in my direction when he heard me chuckle. The look on his face was indescribably placid. It was like what he had described was just another day at the office. I looked down at the ground, suddenly intimidated by Andy's eye contact. What I thought was a look of misunderstanding and confusion had revealed itself for what it was; a thousand-yard stare of someone who had seen and lived some horrors that most of us should never have to imagine. The silence got awkward.

"Well, it sounds like you were a good shot!" Young Dave said, allowing us to laugh again, and we did – nervously.

"Hard to miss with RPG-7," replied Andy.

After Andy left the Smoke pit, Ben looked up at me between puffs of his Hobbit pipe and said, "Remind me not to fuck with Andy."

After that job ended, I never saw Andy again.

It's been a few years since I quit smoking. It was a struggle to get here. I had to keep myself from going into smoke pits for the longest time. I knew I would immediately start up again if I went into one.

I have the willpower now to drop in on a smoke pit without feeling the need to have a cigarette. The smell of cigarettes bothers me now. But I sometimes can't help visiting a smoke pit when I find one. I can absorb some weird magic and hear the tall tales and dirty confessions I love. Sometimes I still throw one of my goofy stories out there to get a laugh or make people's eyes widen in disbelief. Nothing has ever come close to Andy's confession of the time he annihilated seven drug smugglers and a herd of sheep with a rocket-propelled grenade, but maybe one day I'll hear something that will top it.

Until that day, I'll keep wandering through them. Maybe I'll see you there?

Chapter 5

This is Why I Will Never Cook Bacon Buck Naked Again

Mama always said, "Never cook bacon naked." Okay, she never said that. But she should have.

What she did tell me was to always wear shoes in the kitchen.

"What if you spill boiling water or grease on your feet? How are you going to wear shoes with big grease-burn blisters on your feet? You won't! And it's going to hurt so bad you won't be able to sleep. So put on some shoes or at least socks!"

It was good advice. If I had taken it, I would have avoided getting into one embarrassing predicament that I don't think I will ever live down.

But then, I never did what I was told. I guess that's why I ended up as a pipeline welder in the first place.

I was working away from home, eight hours of travel from my apartment. The company had given me a living allowance to find a place to live near the job, so my girlfriend and I found a good deal on a furnished basement suite. The furniture wasn't the best, but the rent was cheap.

Leanne bought a few decorations and cheap curtains. She brought some bedding from home and put a waterproof mattress pad on the bed.

"You never know what happened on that mattress," she explained. "Maybe someone was murdered on it."

Other problems in this apartment needed attention. There was a rip on the couch cushion that Leanne was going to sew up, a drip from the bathroom sink that I could fix easily, and the plastic shelving in the fridge door had a big crack in it with a piece busted off. We picked up the necessary supplies so I could tackle the repairs on my day off.

That Saturday, we went out with the boys and cut loose. It was a real bender. We got kicked out of the pub well after the last call and stopped at Mark's place for a few more drinks before we called it a night.

Leanne and I passed out minutes before the sun came up. The new mattress pad worked like a charm.

I woke up six hours later with the sun shining straight in my face. No blinds on the window yet. As I rolled off the bed, Leanne moaned. I could tell she felt as hungover as I did. She grabbed her earbuds, put on some music, and went back to sleep.

Craving a big, greasy breakfast, I stumbled out into the kitchen nook. I was only wearing my underwear, but I thought nothing of it.

Sunday was no-pants day. I opened the fridge, found the bacon, and put some in the pan.

As I shoved the package back into the fridge, I saw that broken shelf on the fridge door. What the hell, I thought. I might as well fix that now and get it out of the way.

I flipped the bacon, then got the tube of superglue we had picked up.

The package said, "fast-bonding, high-strength, instant adhesive engineered to bond almost any material." I figured it would work on plastic fridge shelves.

I got the glue open and squeezed some onto the surface inside the fridge door. Then I left the project for a moment, took a couple of steps to the stove, and used my trusty spatula to keep the bacon from burning.

Back to the gluing.

The surfaces were tacky now. I carefully fit the pieces together, held them for a moment, then let go. They stayed in place. Success! I reached over, grabbed the spatula from the counter nearby, and tried to head back over to the frying pan.

"What the fuck!" I yelled as my foot refused to lift off the tile. And it hurt like hell.

In my hungover state, I had applied way more glue than needed, and it had dripped onto the floor. I had glued the skin on the bottom of my foot to the tile of the kitchen.

I carefully tried to lift my foot, but it was no use. I was stuck. If I pulled too hard, it would tear my skin right off. Swearing, I went to put the spatula down. That was when I realized that it was glued to my right hand.

I tried to get it unstuck. No go. "Shit!" I cursed.

Realizing the bacon was about to start burning, I reached out with the spatula and managed just barely to turn the dial off.

"Leanne! Honey! Need some help out here!" I yelled uselessly. She couldn't hear me. She was a sound sleeper to start with, and she had her earbuds in and her music blaring away. I yelled until I was hoarse.

As luck would have it, my phone was on the far end of the counter, out of reach, so I couldn't text or call for help that way.

The fridge door was still open, and my body was blocking it, so I couldn't even shut the fridge. I sighed and tried to think. I tried to use the spatula to pry my foot off the floor.

That didn't work.

What else did I have? I could reach mustard, ketchup, pickles, salad dressing, eggs, bacon, and beer. We didn't have much else in the fridge. I cracked a beer and poured it around my foot. It had no effect.

I grabbed the squeeze bottle of mustard and jammed the tip under the edge of my foot. All that accomplished was that I got mustard all over my foot.

With a sigh, I chugged the remaining beer and tried to wipe the mustard from my hand onto my leg.

I reached into the fridge and got myself another beer. Then I leaned against the fridge door and tried to wait patiently. It was starting to get chilly standing here, practically naked, in an open fridge door. After about an hour, Leanne woke up and came out of the bedroom.

"Good morning!" I said brightly.

"What are you doing?" Leanne asked me. "Having a few beers for breakfast?"

She took in the scene. Me in my underwear, shivering, holding my third beer of the day in my left hand and a spatula in my right. The fridge door was still wide open. There was mustard on my leg, my foot, and the floor. "Why is there mustard on your foot?" she asked with deep suspicion. "You know you don't even have the stove turned on, right? That bacon will never cook."

"Yeah, honey, I realize that," I said. I took the last swig of beer. "I started cooking the bacon, but I ran into a little complication."

"What, you were too thirsty and had to stop for a beer and mustard break?" she asked.

"Not exactly."

"Well, what then?"

"You remember that broken shelf? I tried to fix it," I said. "I might have gotten a little sloppy with the glue. My foot is stuck to the floor."

Leanne was looking at me like she had just won the Stupidest Boyfriend On Earth contest. "So what, you smeared mustard on it to fix the problem?"

She went over and turned the bacon on, then tried to take the spatula from me. "What, you glued this too?" She was grinning now. She pulled her phone out of her sweatpants pocket and took a step back.

"No! No pictures!"

"I'm not taking pictures," she chuckled as she held up her phone. "I'm making a video, dummy. Now tell me again how you glued your foot to the floor and why your hand is stuck to that spatula?" She turned the phone down a little bit to make sure my mustard-covered foot was captured for posterity.

"This isn't funny," I said.

"Trust me, it is," she said with a grin

"Stop recording. I'm serious," I said.

"How serious can a guy be when he has glued his foot to the floor and glued a spatula to his hand?" she asked.

She had a point.

Eventually, she got some nail polish remover to unstick me from the floor. She finished cooking breakfast —but not before she sent the video to everyone we knew.

As the video went viral among our friends and family, I thought back to my mother's advice. If only I had slipped into my Crocs and a teeshirt before I started cooking. I would have saved myself from quite the ordeal.

But then, I never did what I was told.

Chapter 6

You Can't Read at a Strip Club, Even if it's Called "The Library"

I'm not your normal pipeliner. I like to read. It's a hobby that gets me through living on the road, far from my family.

These days we've got it pretty easy, with ebooks, smartphones, and tablets. But twenty years ago, it was a lot harder to find something to read if you weren't in a big city.

I found myself trapped in a remote northern town. There wasn't a lot to do but work, eat, drink, try to pick up the small-town girls, and sleep. I was married and trying to be a good boy. Every couple of days I went to the pay phone and made a collect call back home to talk to the wife. I avoided the local ladies, on the theory that what I wasn't shopping for I wouldn't buy.

The town was practically deserted. The only library was in the school, so that was off-limits. You could get a newspaper at the gas station, but otherwise, there was no reading material in this place. No magazines, no paperbacks, no comic books. Unless free Gideon Bibles from hotel nightstands were your thing, you were out of luck.

There was another library, but it wasn't for reading. It was for looking. The bar's name was The Library.

The crew went to the local strip club, which was entertaining at first. I went down there too, but it wasn't really my thing. I'm the kinda guy that doesn't like window shopping. If I'm at the store, I want to take something home. I decided I had better stop staring at naked chicks if I was going to be a good boy and go home an honest guy.

Back then, it was a lot easier for unfaithful bastards to screw around and get away with it. We didn't have social media, so no one was posting pictures of extra-curricular activities. Who would know unless one of us told on his buddies? We were a long way from home, and lacking in female companionship. It was a recipe for disaster.

Unfortunately, it was the only bar in town. If you wanted to go play pool or drink a beer with your friends, you didn't have a lot of options. You ended up at The Library.

The guy who named that tavern was a genius. The local joke was that you could tell the wife you were going down to the library because that was the name of the local saloon. Of course, the town didn't actually have a real library. There were only about 50 people living there, and I had my doubts about how many of them could even read.

I can imagine how this "dad" joke went over every night.

"Well honey, it was a tough day at work. I'm gonna go down to The Library and catch up on my reading."

The wife rolls her eyes. "Yeah. Right. Ok, what books are you taking out now? *The Idiot's Guide to Pole Dancing*? Or how about *Watching Strippers Demean Themselves For Dummies*?"

When I left home, I knew what kind of place I was headed to, so I prepared. I had three actual library books with me.

This was before cell phones, the internet, and such. If you wanted to read, you had to buy a book or borrow it. So before I left the city, I swung past the big brick book building and checked out a few books. I'd been studying hunting and survivalism, my new passion. I had the book *The Old Pro Turkey Hunter* and another about wild game cooking.

We were staying in this cheap motel on the edge of town called The Satellite Inn. It had a color TV and one of those giant satellite dishes on the roof. I had a roommate, of course. We were all trying to save money.

Ken was religious. He liked to tell me how we were going to go to hell for things like drinking and carousing. He wasn't much fun to talk to, so I read while he was watching TV.

One night I didn't want to sit in the motel room and read while Ken bombarded me with his church propaganda. I wanted a beer, I wanted non-religious company, and I wanted to read my book. So, I took it with me to The Library. It seemed only natural for someone to actually read something in a place named after a house of books.

The place was fairly busy. The special was a steak sandwich and fries, and this was the only place open after 6:00 PM. Everyone else from the crew was there, other than Ken. What else would they be doing on a Wednesday night?

When I walked through the door, it was between shows. The only sounds were from the crowd that filled the place up.

They had a little raised dance floor and stage, complete with Sniffer's Row. There were a few tables a little farther back, which had pretty good lighting. I picked a seat and sat down facing away from the stage.

Slim Jim, one of the guys from work, came over. "Brainy! What are you doing in here?" He always called me Brainy after he found out I actually LIKED reading.

"I got sick of listening to Ken's Bible thumping and came down for a beer."

"Well, get over here where the action is!" He pointed at the tables up by the stage where the rest of the guys sat with jugs of draft and big glasses in front of them. "You can't see the tits from back here, Brainy. For a smart guy, you're slow on the uptake."

"Nah, I'm gonna relax back here with this." I pointed at my hard-cover copy of *The Old Pro Turkey Hunter.*

"A book, in The Library? What a nut!" Slim Jim laughed and slapped me on the shoulder, then walked toward the john shaking his head.

The waitress brought me a mug of draft beer. I took a big swallow. Not bad.

The speakers crackled to life as the music started and the next show began.

"All right, guys, give it up for Brandi!" The first lady came out of the back with a cigarette in her hand. She took one final drag and sucked that smoke right down to the filter before putting it out on the ashtray at the closest table. Brandi released a big cloud of smoke as she climbed the steps and started her show.

I turned to watch her for a minute, but it was nothing I hadn't seen before.

She was somewhere between 40 and 50, and past the time most women in that trade find something else to do with their evenings. But she didn't let her age slow her down as she pranced back and forth. She slipped off some lingerie and flopped out a couple of large assets.

Her top half didn't defy gravity. As she shimmied and bounced, her boobs swung around like a couple of overfilled lunch bags.

There was no air of mystery. The only mystery was why so many guys were cheering her on.

She bumped and ground through her show with the precision of someone who has done the same thing thousands of times, and I was totally uninterested. I pulled my book out, turned away from her, and started reading.

She finished that set, and the music stopped. Another song started, but I hardly noticed. I was enjoying my beer. I knew that Ken was probably back in the hotel room praying for my soul. I was in no rush to go back there.

Suddenly, in mid-swing and mid-pole twirl, she must have gotten the DJ's attention to get him to cut the music. I turned to see what was going on.

Brandi left the pole and pointed at me. From the edge of the stage, she yelled, "I'm not going to dance until this asshole stops reading!"

The whole bar burst out laughing.

"Now you're in trouble, Brainy!" Slim Jim yelled. "Reading in The Library isn't allowed!"

That started the crowd off again. A couple of guys were laughing so hard they couldn't breathe. I didn't think it was funny at all, and neither did the dancer.

"I'm serious!" Brandi screamed. "How you can you READ when the goods are up on stage?" she shook the goods to make her point, and they bobbed around like a couple of overstuffed balloons that needed more helium and less sag. "Get this guy out of here or I'm gone!" Now the whole place was chuckling.

I don't know if anyone would have been heartbroken or not if Brandi had stopped dancing. But at least one guy wanted her to keep going, because he yelled "Asshole, out! Asshole out!"

Someone else yelled, "Yeah! Asshole, get out!"

Then everyone else started in too.

"Asshole out! Asshole out! Asshole out! Asshole out!" They all chanted in unison, holding their drinks up and pointing at me. Even the bartender was in on it.

Brandi was back at the pole, yelling, "Asshole out! Asshole out!"

A bouncer came over. He was laughing so hard that there were tears in his eyes. "Buddy, you wanna put the book away or leave," he said with a big grin. "Brandi will get the stuffing beat outa you if you don't watch out."

I stood up, chugged my beer, and left. I knew when I wasn't wanted. As I carried my book out of The Library, the music started up again, and the crowd got even more serious about worshipping Brandi.

The next few days at work were painful. No one would let me forget about the time that I dared to read a book at The Library. The nickname Brainy was definitely stuck now.

Age Discrimination Epilogue

A few years later, I came across a newspaper article about that little northern town and my favorite pole-dancing friend. Brandi was standing up for her workplace rights. It sounded like The Library wanted her to retire.

Brandi took The Library to court for wrongful dismissal. They wouldn't let her dance anymore because her assets were no longer in their prime.

I can't imagine why they didn't want nude dancers to keep going well into their 60s. What's the world coming to?

I never found out if she won the right to keep showing her naughty bits into her golden years.

But if she is still there, whatever you do, don't turn your back on her and start reading your phone screen. She'll probably lose her cool.

Chapter 7

The One Where I Cheat on My Girlfriend With My Wife

I am a pipefitter. When I signed my apprenticeship, my father – also a pipefitter – cautioned me, "Welcome to the trade, son. There's no life like it, and no wife likes it."

He was right. It didn't take long before I found myself out on the job, and one of the things that I noticed was that a staggering amount of the guys I worked with were either divorced, in the process of getting divorced, or some variation those. I had a great relationship with my wife, Lisa, who had been with me almost from the start of my apprenticeship. I never thought I could be one of those guys. I always tried to stay close to home, and chose the less lucrative shop or maintenance jobs nearby rather than the big money makers. Working at the big-dollar mega projects meant I would be away from home, stuffed into a work camp for weeks at a time.

Eventually, my luck ran out. The job I was at had run its course after I had been there for two years, and I found myself unemployed for the first time in a long time. The layoff happened right before the weather turned bad in late October. The timing of the layoff meant that it was likely that I wasn't going to be seeing a paycheck until March or April of the next year.

A few weeks of unemployment passed. I checked the job boards at my Union Hall for work daily, sometimes driving to the Hall if there was a job. The jobs remained scarce. If there was a job, it would quickly get snapped up by other people who were higher up on the 'out-of-work' list, which organized the unemployed union members by the date they were laid off. I wasn't high on the list.

It wasn't long before Christmas came. Soon after that, we were broke. I signed up for employment insurance benefits which usually took three weeks to show up. It wasn't enough to cover the bills.

By New Year's Day, we were into overdraft in the bank account, and there were still no signs of work on the horizon. I started to look for non-union work, which was frowned upon. I started calling non-union employers. I sent resumes to shops and sites in towns two hours away. It was useless. No one had any work on the books until March when the snow started to melt. We were fucked.

February flew by, and then March. I had been out of work for five months.

I got good at making biscuits from scratch. We were living by cooking whole chickens and using the bones to make soup, and we consumed a lot of Kraft Dinner and instant noodles.

Having little money for gas, I stopped driving into the union hall to attend the daily job call-out. I was stuck waiting now.

I played video games. I gained weight. Before I knew it, I had packed on thirty pounds.

Finally, a former coworker reached out to me with an offer for a fly-in-fly-out camp job at the only game in town—a major new construction project in the boonies outside Fort McMurray. The shift was fourteen days on and seven days off—the last day off was sacrificed to a late afternoon flight back to work.

The credit cards were maxed out, and the employment insurance benefits were used for food and rent. Our cell phone bills were overdue.

When it was time to go, I happily went.

Two weeks away from my family proved harder to deal with than I thought. I flew home for the first time, and my family met me at the airport. I was so starved for real life after my first fourteen days, that my first seven days off seemed like a race to cram in as much as I could before I went back to the sensory deprivation of camp life for another two weeks.

We went shopping, out for meals, and took the kids to movies. My home life suddenly seemed busier than a shift at work. Like a glutton, I gobbled up as much life as possible in that one week off.

Most of my life was now spent in the company of manly men. The superintendent was an old rodeo cowboy, and he liked the alpha-male type. He made me a supervisor, and I drank his tough-tasting brand of Kool-Aid.

I became nasty.

I was leading a group of guys who were unhappy to be there. Most of the guys on my crew began to complain. They thought the way our superintendent ran the job made it feel like a prison. If this was Shawshank, I was Captain Hadley, and I leaned into the role.

If someone asked me what I thought was a stupid question, I was more than happy to dismiss them with a meanspirited reply. My superintendent rewarded me with positive feedback for every harsh interaction I had. I came to idolize his authoritative nature.

Remembering how I felt looking through the couch cushions for lost change to buy an extra box of macaroni and cheese just a few months before, I met and exceeded his expectations. My usually happy-go-lucky personality was overwritten with a new program – the belligerent asshole.

I became uncaring and cruel, but I got results.

"You have the stick," the Superintendent counseled me, "If your guys do what they are supposed to be doing, you don't need to take the stick out. But if they want to fuck around with you, then you whack 'em!"

For two weeks at a time, for the next five months, I wielded "the stick."

It wasn't long before there was graffiti of me in one of the bathroom stalls. One picture depicted me being screwed from behind by the superintendent. My friend was drawn too, waiting for his turn at my butthole. Captions were placed above each character so people could tell who they were. My favorite part of that piece was the arrow pointing to my friend's pecker that said, "NOT TO SCALE: INLARGED FOR DRAMATIC PERPOSES."

We laughed at that.

Another bathroom stall had a more artistic portrait of me with a swastika emblazoned on my hard hat. I took a picture of this masterwork with my new smartphone and shared it on Facebook. At the following day's toolbox talk, I showed my crew that I had posted it to my profile, and gave the artist, whoever they were, tips on correctly drawing the swastika next time.

"You have to offset the thing forty-five degrees. If you draw it with the axis straight up and down, it doesn't convey the Nazi theme you were going for!" I boomed at them, showing them the photo on my phone. I did a good job pretending I didn't care, but no one with any self-worth wants to be compared to a Nazi. Here I was, pretending I was okay with it.

When I next went home for days off, I knew something was going wrong.

On my last night at home, Lisa informed me that she would no longer be driving me to and from the airport. She didn't give a reason.

"What do you want to do next time I come home?" I asked her.

"I don't know. Whatever you think," She replied.

"Any ideas? Is there anything that you'd like to do? There's the Food Festival we could check out."

"If you want to go, sure."

"What do you want to do?" I asked her.

"I'm good with whatever. I really don't care."

The Lisa I knew would have loved the Food Festival. The more I tried, the more I was convinced that there was something seriously wrong. I decided I knew what the problem was. I was away too much. That had to be it. I didn't want things to go on like this, and I knew I would have to quit my job if I wanted to make things better at home.

On my next rotation at work, I quit.

I explained my situation at home to my superintendent. He slapped me with a ninety-day ban from working for that company after telling me he felt bad for me. Prick.

Quitting my job didn't have the effect I thought it would. Nothing changed at home. I'd never seen her like this before. We moved around the house opposite each other. She avoided looking at me or touching me. Whenever I would try and talk about anything, it wouldn't even build up to a fight. Worse, she was just wholly disinterested in me.

I prowled around for a local job and soon found a place that offered me a job supervising a fabrication shop. I was going to be home every night just like I used to be. I thought everything was going to be as right as rain. We would turn this around.

"I got the job," I told her. "The one at the fabrication shop. It pays more than what I was making at the last place too."

"Great," she said.

"Yeah!" I agreed.

I could tell she didn't care, and I was getting sick of the cold shoulder. One day we were both sitting on the couch watching a hockey game. She was as far away from me as she could be, jammed into the opposite arm of the sofa. I'd decided I had finally had enough.

"What is it with you?" I asked.

"What do you mean?"

"You know what I mean. What more can I do here? Aren't you happy that I have a better job close to home?"

"I guess I'm amazed that you didn't do it sooner if that's how easy it was."

"What the fuck," I said, fuming. "What will it take here?"

"I don't know."

"That's what I'm talking about! You just shut off. I have no idea what I'm supposed to do. Every second I spend with you feels like I'm waiting at the airport for another flight north. I fucking hate this. If this is how it's going to be, I don't think I want to be here anymore."

"You do whatever you have to do."

It bothered me that she didn't care. I should have let the situation cool down. I had spent too much time getting results I wanted by acting like a prick at work, I figured it would work just as well at home.

"You know what? Fuck you!" I shouted. "I don't need this shit from you! If you don't want me around, you could just fucking say it, but you're too much of a coward to say anything at all."

She stood up from the couch. The fight was on.

"A coward? Fuck you!" Lisa yelled back. "You think these last few months have been fun for me?"

"I don't know what these last few months have been like because you don't even fucking talk to me anymore!"

"I'll tell you that for two weeks at a time, you aren't home. I get the kids to school. I make breakfast, lunches, and suppers. I make them do their homework. And then suddenly, you come home, and everyone has to break their routine to be in party mode until you go back to work. When you are here, you're plugged into your fucking phone."

"If I'm plugged into my phone, it's because you have become an emotionless zombie."

"I wonder why that is?"

"I wonder too. I feel like I'm waiting for a flight to work every day. You don't talk to me. You don't care that I'm here."

I looked for a response from her, but there was nothing. She just watched me in silence. I've never been good at silence, so I kept on going.

"You know what? If you won't talk to me, maybe I should leave."

"Do whatever you want."

"Watch what you say here," I warned.

"I'm not saying anything."

"If you want me to leave, I'll leave," I said.

"I don't give a fuck what you do."

"I'm not staying here if you don't want me here."

"I didn't say that. I just said you should do whatever the fuck you want."

I lost it.

This hadn't gone the way I thought it would have. I stormed upstairs and grabbed suitcases out of the closet. I began stuffing all of my clothes into them. My kids came out of their bedroom. I tried not to look at them. I knew they were scared and confused. If I looked at them I thought I'd completely break.

I jammed all the clothes and belongings I could into the suitcases and hauled everything down the stairs and out the front door. She followed me outside. I don't remember what we were saying to each other, but I was yelling and swearing. I think she returned every spiteful word I hurled at her.

We'd never fought like this. Eleven years together - gone in a white-hot flash. I got in my truck and left.

Now I was homeless. I called my best friend from high school to see if he would graciously allow me to have his couch while I figured things out. He had let me stay there while I was in school or the odd time I had to come and work closer to his house than mine. Thankfully, he let me stay with him. I wouldn't have to live in my truck.

After a couple of weeks, I wanted to come home. I had made a mistake, and I knew it. I knew what I had done wrong, fixed the problem, and was willing to work things out and rebuild. After eleven years together, I thought she should have been too.

"I don't think that's a good idea," she said.

"Come on. I'm sorry. Can we just start over?"

"You told me that if you left, you weren't coming back."

"I was mad. It was a mistake," I admitted. I just want to come home."

"You can't," she said.

I started to accept that it was a lost cause.

I got sad, stressed out, and depressed. My darkest shame - I started listening to City and Colour. I was really into feeling sorry for myself. It was my new hobby. I'd started working out, but I wasn't eating well. I was losing weight fast.

I was talking through my problems with another friend who had just gone through a bad break-up himself. We traded sad stories before he told me, "Fuck her, man. You know what you should do? Put yourself up on a dating site, dude. Get yourself back in the game."

I hadn't even considered this. There were no dating websites the last time I was single. I thought that maybe if I made a profile, it would make her jealous and I could see if she still cared.

I announced my intentions to Lisa. I was going to put myself out on a dating site and would start seeing other people. She called my bluff.

"Do whatever you want. I don't care what you do."

That was it, I thought. If she didn't care about me seeing other people, it really was the end of us. I made a profile that night, posting a mysterious-looking picture.

I met one lady on a snowy day in November at a trendy pub. I was talking fast like I always do when I get nervous. She had been split up from her husband, she told me. He was a cheater - escorts. It had been a couple of years since she broke up with him, and their divorce had been finalized a couple of months ago. She had just started putting herself out into the dating world again. She asked me how long I had been split up from my wife and recoiled when I told her only a few months.

"This is too soon for you to be doing this," she told me. "You don't even know if it's over yet."

"I'm pretty sure it is," I told her.

"Maybe, but it's too soon to tell. Besides, you probably don't even know who you are without her. How long were you together?"

"Since 1999, I said. Twelve years now?"

"Oh yeah," she said, "It's too soon. You should at least take a couple of years to figure out who you are. She would need the same amount of time. Be a good dad. You shouldn't be on a dating site. You never know; you might wind up back with each other. One lady I worked with thought she and her husband had grown apart, and they both ended up almost divorcing. It wasn't until they both had affairs with other people that they realized they were meant to be together. They patched things up and are now one of the happiest couples I have ever seen!" It was good advice, and a hopeful story.

It was a shame that I didn't listen to her.

I went on one more date with someone almost as fresh to the scene as I was. Her name was Rebecca, and she was a host of a local evening radio show. After messaging each other over the dating app for a couple of weeks, we met in person. She seemed interesting and interested in me. She had been separated for a few months longer than I had been, and the end of her marriage sounded much more complicated and final than mine was. She had a great sense of humor about the whole thing and we really hit it off. We agreed to see each other again and exchanged numbers.

I told Lisa about the meeting and was surprised by her reaction. She got pissed off and lit into me.

"So what? Do you love this girl?" she demanded.

"I don't know," I said. It was the best answer I could give. Things were out of my control and happening so fast. I was confused.

"For fucks sake," she said. "You're a mess. You need to figure your shit out!"

"What the hell, Lisa? I told you I was going to do this. You've been a zombie around me for months, and now you decide to let me know what you're thinking?"

"Don't you think this is all a little too soon?"

"I don't know what I think," I told her. "Can I come home?"

"I still don't think that's a good idea," she said. "Maybe you could go talk to someone."

"What, like a psychologist?"

"Yes."

"I'm not the one with a problem here. Maybe you should fucking go speak to a psychologist."

She hung up on me.

I didn't feel any better after that phone call. I couldn't sleep. I showed up to work late most days. I was always tired from being out at night with Rebecca, who kept later hours than I did.

At lunchtimes, I would sit in my truck and field more emotionally charged phone calls from Lisa. After she'd hang up, I would have a full-on panic attacks after every conversation. Lisa was right. I should have talked to someone, but I'm a stubborn, pig-headed man, so I did nothing.

I wasn't effective at work. I would come in late. I would take excessively long lunch breaks. I would work late into the evenings to make up for it, but mostly did nothing. My lack of effort was noticed by everyone. If I did try and manage the workers, make improvements, or discipline anyone for breaking the rules. The guys would go around me to John, my manager, and I'd wind up getting a talking to from him.

I hired a worker who was still technically incarcerated. He was a great guy and a hard worker, but John caught on to the fact that something was wrong after the receptionist alerted him about the serious-looking lady who would sign in at the front desk every Wednesday to meet with me.

"That's Chad's parole officer," I told him.

"Why does Chad have a parole officer?"

"Because he was in prison," I answered.

"How long has he been out of prison?" John asked.

"Technically, he's still in prison," I told him. "He goes back to a halfway house every night after work, and they lock him up. If all goes well, he'll be on full parole in a month or so. He's a good worker. I figured you be okay with it. Besides, people who want to work here aren't exactly falling out of the sky."

John was not impressed. "You might want to clear that with us next time."

After spending Christmas apart, Lisa and I started to settle into the new reality that this was our new normal. I got my own apartment in a seedy walk-up complex a little too close to the 'hooker-y' part of town. I rarely stayed there. I was spending most of my time with Rebecca. Things with her were moving fast.

Lisa had also struck up a relationship of her own with someone, a tall guy named Frank. I pretended I was okay with that. We tried to keep things civil. I researched child support and voluntarily paid her the full amount every payday. She found a job that kept her close to the kids. Both of us kept the peace with each other, as neither of us saw any benefit to making lawyers rich.

I saw the kids as much as I wanted and took them to my apartment every other weekend.

I had practically moved in with Rebecca. Most of my clothes were at her house. I had toothbrushes at her place and mine. If she wasn't home, I hung out with her kids and was a sudden stepfather to them.

Sometimes I had no idea how I got there or who the fuck I even was.

One night, Rebecca got curious about my past relationship.

"Why did you and Lisa break up?" she asked.

"I was working way from home, and we had a fight."

I gave her the condensed version.

"Did you guys fight a lot?"

"No," I replied. "Almost never. She just stopped talking to me one day. She got pissed off that I was never home. I couldn't take her giving me the cold shoulder and blew up on her."

"Well, I think it's noble for a guy to go to work and provide for his family. If you were making good money, I wouldn't mind if you went away to work," she said.

I knew she meant well in saying that. I knew I had given her little information on which she could judge my personality, but this was when I knew I was in the wrong place and with the wrong person.

"Well," I said, "I don't have to worry about that anymore. I'm home every night now, and I'm never going back there again."

Rebecca was unfamiliar with what I did for a living and how I felt about it. I knew she didn't know how difficult I found it, spending two-thirds of my life at a remote work camp. But I knew I didn't want to be with someone who was okay with me sacrificing precious moments for money.

With Lisa, I'd had someone whose most significant issue was that there wasn't enough of me in her life, and I had blown that all to hell. The next time I spoke with Lisa on the phone, I told her about the conversation with Rebecca.

"For what it's worth, I always hated it when you had to go away," she said.

My heart sank.

One day I got a text message out of the blue from Lisa with a link to a music video for a song called 'One Foot Before the Other' by a guy named Frank Turner. I had never heard of him, but she had seen it and thought it reminded her of me. I watched it and liked the vibe immediately.

It felt nice to be decent to each other again.

Soon I was doing the bi-weekly kid exchange at Lisa's house. We chatted for a while, and exchanged stories of what was happening in our other lives.

Neither of us was happy.

She asked me if I could show her how to use Netflix on her TV so the kids could watch it. I showed her how to use it when a movie caught her eye.

"What's that one?" she asked, "The wine one."

It was a documentary I had heard of about a rock star starting a winery in Arizona. I heard that it was good. I ignored that I was supposed to meet Rebecca somewhere, and my wife and I watched the whole movie together.

I would later lie to Rebecca about where I was and what I was doing.

Lisa and I began exchanging text messages more frequently. None of them were angry. I started finding excuses to see Lisa, and she would find excuses to invite me over. Frank had started working out of town.

And just like that, I wound up cheating on my girlfriend... with my wife.

After that, I knew that I had to break things off with Rebecca. It was wrong for me to have started something with her in the first place.

While Rebecca had gone to visit her family, I picked up the kids from Lisa for the weekend and took them with me to Rebecca's house where I proceeded to remove all my belongings, I loaded everything into my truck with the help of my kids.

I felt genuinely hopeful for the first time in ages. I took my kids out for a fun day with Dad to the mall and then out for pizza. Later, at my apartment, I was in the middle of watching a movie with the kids when Rebecca called.

"Is everything okay with us?" she asked.

"Why?" I asked, not wanting to ruin her weekend with her family.

"I had a dream last night," she said. "It was so real. I dreamed that you took all of your stuff out of my house and wanted to break up with me."

Rebecca's ex had used a similar mystic trick to manipulate her when they were together. She told me about it, she might not have remembered that she did. Anyway, it wasn't going to work with me. I knew one of her neighbors had likely seen me remove all my stuff and decided to squeal on me. She was likely trying to protect who'd told her.

"We should talk about this on Monday," I said.

"I knew it," she said, bursting into tears. "My dreams are always right."

I hoped to have had the conversation after that weekend, but that plan was shot. I had to rip the Band-Aid off over the phone.

"Are you sure your neighbor across the street didn't just see me take all my shit out of your house a couple of hours ago?" I asked.

She was a wreck, and I felt bad that I had been responsible for this. A weekend meant to be relaxing for both of us became a flood of emotional text messages and upset phone calls. I probably should have waited until after the weekend to haul my shit out of her house, but I was hellbent on doing what I wanted from that point on.

Over that same weekend, Lisa broke off her relationship with Frank. Lisa and I both agreed that we needed to hit the reset button on everything and let the situation cool down. We'd see what the landscape looked like without other people involved.

By the time Monday came, I was stressed out and I needed a 'me day.' After taking the Monday off, I called John and let him know that I would be extending my leave to include Tuesday. I sat in my apartment and enjoyed the quiet.

Rebecca was scheduled to fill in for the regular hosts of the morning show at the radio station while they were on vacation Bad timing after I had called our six-month relationship off. I got to listen to the aftermath on the morning radio as I drove to work. Rebecca had no scruples about dissing me on the air, and there were plenty of callers to back her up.

"BLEEP that guy! You deserve better, honey!" One caller passionately blurted.

"He doesn't know what he had! You can do better than him."

"He did it over the phone? What a coward!"

I had never had so many people mad at me all at once before. I found the callers hilarious and kept the radio on while they lambasted me. I had every cubicle busybody in the city mad at me. I'd always wanted to be roasted, but this took all my expectations right over the top.

Rebecca briefly came on. She was still very upset. Her cohost had to do most of the talking.

"If you're just tuning in," the co-host said, "Rebecca has just had her boyfriend dump her. She's still very upset, but she's a trooper. We told her that she could have the day of, but she wanted to come on anyway. She thought you'd be disappointed if she didn't. Please keep those calls and texts coming to let her know that you all think she's fantastic. If you want to tell her what an ass her boyfriend is too, we're more than happy to hear your thoughts about that too."

I could hear Rebecca sniffling as she cried into the microphone. She'd hardly said anything. I turned the station off. It was morbid that I could listen in on her grief.

I got to work with a new purpose. I was going to be a better employee, starting right now, I had decided. I backed my truck into my parking space outside our office trailer and bounded into work with a spring in my step. I bid 'good morning' to the three planners I shared the office with as I strolled by their desks. They were usually quiet guys, and I didn't notice anything unusual about them that morning as I was laser-focused on getting to my desk and righting the ship.

When I got into my office, I saw that my computer was gone. I looked around the room, checking the windows for signs of a break-in. There was no sign of forced entry at the windows. No splintered wood on the door jam.

It must have been an inside job. A prank? I turned to the planners.

"Guys, did we have a break-in last night?" I asked them. "My computer's been stolen!"

I heard one of them mutter, "I don't know, man."

I looked around the room. It dawned on me that something was wrong. John walked through the door and waved for me to follow him. I babbled about thieves and my stolen computer as we went through the main reception area and into his office. From the hallway, I saw our Human Resources guy waiting in John's office.

"Shit," I said. "I'm getting fired."

There was an awkward pause in the room as John and the HR guy looked at each other, trying to decide what to say next.

"Ummm, yes," was the best that John could muster. "Please sit down."

I had always been a competent, hard worker. I had never been fired before, but for several months prior, I had seen this coming, but I didn't expect it today of all days. Just when I had decided I was going to do better.

"I'd rather stand," I said, getting madder with each breath. "What do you need from me? My Blackberry?"

I whipped my company-supplied phone out of my pocket and tossed it on the desk.

"Do I have to sign something?"

John stared up at me wide-eyed. This wasn't going how he had planned.

"There is a form to sign," John said. "There's a process we need to follow."

"You have to follow it," I said. "I don't. I'm fired."

"Well, yeah," John said, "But we need to have an exit interview."

"FUCK YOU! That's my exit interview!" I fumed. "Where's the goddamned form? Let's sign it and get this shit over with."

John produced the form, which had been sitting on his desk, ready to go. I saw a line with my name below it and scribbled my signature, flipping the pen on the desk for John. The HR guy signed as a witness to my signature, then turned his attention to me.

"Hey man," he said with a soothing voice, "I can't let you drive home in your emotional state. You'll have to give me your keys. We'll call you a cab. It's an Occupational Health and Safety Requirement."

He held out his hand.

"No problem," I said, seething. "My keys are in my pocket. I'm not going to give them to you, but you're welcome to try and take them. I'll warn you though, as soon as you touch me, I will break your fucking nose."

"Okay," he said, putting his hands in the air. "I won't touch you."

"Are we done here?"

"I would like just to have a conversation with you," said John. "I'm sure you would feel better knowing what this is all about."

"I know I'm a good worker," I said. "I've been through a rough time lately, and I don't need to hear what you think this is all about."

I left John and the HR guy in the office. Neither of them followed me out. I got into my truck and sprayed gravel with the tires as I accelerated out of the gate. My mind raced all the way to my apartment. I had never been fired before. I couldn't afford to be out of work again. Lisa and the kids depended on me. I looked at my watch. It was eight in the morning. I had to figure this out when I thought about The Union Hall. The pipefitter call-out was ten o'clock. I'd head over and see what they had.

I got to the Union Hall early for the call-out. I felt stupid that I was about to be back working on the tools, but it beat the alternative. I checked the job board. I was sure I'd get something. Sure enough, I walked out at eleven o'clock with a new job at a different fabrication shop. I went for the required drug and alcohol test before I drove back to the place I was just fired from. One of the planners called and told me he had gathered my personal effects for me and had them in a box, ready to go.

When I got to the shop, John was waiting for me. The sting from being canned was mostly gone, and I respectfully shook his hand. Lots of people out there who have been fired will tell you that their firing was because their boss was a douchebag or some other guy had railroaded them. Both were true in my case. John was a douchebag, and I suspected that the lead hand had been going behind my back to John since I started there, but in the end, I got fired because I didn't do my job properly, and I knew it.

My focus had been on my own personal issues and not on keeping the shop productive and safe like I was supposed to. I hadn't been doing what I was hired to do, and despite the backstabbing and John's douchebaggery - I hadn't been earning my keep. I deserved to be fired.

"No hard feelings," I told John. "I had it coming."

John was surprised.

"Well," he said, "It takes a bigger person to admit something like that. I want you to know that there are no hard feelings here too. I'm sorry we didn't get to see what you're capable of, and I hope you find a new job soon."

"I already have one," I told him. "Orientation tomorrow."

"Wow! That was quick!" John said, surprised.

"I don't fuck around!" I said. "See you guys."

I hopped back into the truck and left that place for good.

I told Lisa the whole story. She was shocked.

She let me know that she decided that she was going to take the kids to visit her family in New Brunswick for most of the summer and she drove out there with the kids as soon as school was finished.

I hunkered down by myself in the little apartment. I'd gone to work every day and did a good job - like the old me. I read books, something I loved to do, but never did when I was with Rebecca.

I worked on a pipefitting bench for the rest of that summer - building pipe at the shop. I'd go home every night and spent time with myself.

I remembered who I was again.

In mid-August, Lisa came back with our kids. I moved back into our house, and at night, after the kids went to bed, Lisa and I would sit together and talk about everything. I'd smoke cigarettes, and we'd just open up about everything until. She told me how things were for her before we had split up.

"It all started for me when I was at the airport to pick you up after your first two weeks in camp," she told me. "There were some other wives there waiting for their husbands, and I overheard them all talking with each other about how they all liked their husbands being away all the time, because it meant they got to hang out with their girlfriends and do whatever they wanted. One of them said that they preferred it when her man wasn't at home."

"Shit," I said.

"I never thought I would think about you that way, but after a while, your coming home was a disruption. You got to be the fun guy for a week, with movies and ice cream. And then you'd fly off, and I would have to be the miserable bitch with the alarm clock and rules. I resented that you were up there with none of those responsibilities."

"It's not like I was having a great time up there," I protested. "It was a fucked-up place to be for two weeks. Everyone was awful, and I was awful with them."

"I noticed," Lisa said. "So did the kids. Do you remember when I asked where you wanted the camera repaired?"

I bowed my head in shame, "Yeah." I admitted.

We had been at a mall. I had brough our camera with us in the hopes I could find a repair shop to fix it. I had gotten sand in it during a beach day the year before and it had stopped working.

"You said to me, in front of the kids, 'At a camera store, where the fuck do you think?' Do you remember that?"

I did. Fuck.

"Do you remember when we went for beers with Dan and Candace, and you openly commented on her looks right in front of me like it didn't matter?" She asked.

"Yeah," I admitted, ashamed. "I didn't mean it."

"I know," she said. "But it was rude, and you still said it. I knew it was out of character for you, but it seemed you kept getting further away from the guy I married. You were never an asshole before, and it shocked me. It was such a harsh twist from how you act when you are at home."

"That's the kind of shit that went on at work," I admitted. "I let it come home with me. I was trying to fit in with the guys up there. I didn't want to lose my job. I was scared of being unemployed for months at a time like I was before I started that job."

"I liked it when you were at home before. We didn't have money, but we spent time with each other. Then you got the phones for us. When you were home, you'd stare into your phone. Sometimes I'd say something to you, and you wouldn't even hear me. It was like I was talking to a wall."

"Two weeks of camp life had got me living in my phone." I reasoned. "It was my only connection to the world I cared about. I'd gotten so used to looking at the thing while I was at work, it just became a habit."

"I look at mine too much too," she admitted. "When you were away, it was nice to chat with other people over Facebook who didn't act like assholes. That's how I met Frank."

"I fucking knew it," I said.

"I was lonely," she admitted. "You weren't home, and if you were around it was like I had a new husband that acted like a dick."

It went like that for a while. Months. I knew I was guilty as charged, and shared some of my grievances I had about her. It felt good to air our grievances.

"You get restless," I told Lisa. "And when you do, everyone else has to uproot their lives. We've moved six times in the last five years."

"I know," Lisa admitted. "I'm working on it."

In case you haven't been paying attention, I am still the bad guy in this story.

It has been over a decade since these events all transpired. There is not yet an ending to my story, so I can't (won't) offer up any further details. 'Happily Ever After' is a fairy tale ending, and a bad guy wouldn't end his own story that way.

Chapter 8

Quoth the Raven, "Leave Your Truck Window Open Nevermore"

We called him "The Raven Whisperer."

Darcy, our overweight supervisor, was twice the man I was. You couldn't miss the big guy coming toward you with his blue coveralls and large gut.

It was against the rules to have anything to do with the wildlife on any of these oilfield sites, but that didn't matter to Darcy. He was always screwing around with the ravens.

He liked to drop some food or a wrapper on the ground and wait about five feet away until a raven landed nearby. "Hi, pretty bird. How are you today? Are you looking for a snack?" he'd say in a low voice.

Darcy was encouraging these big black birds to be more of a problem than they already were. They were always hanging around the worksite, waiting for us to screw up and leave a garbage bag out or a dumpster lid open.

If ravens were lucky enough to find a garbage bag in the back of a truck, they had a blast ripping it open and looking for food. You would come back and have a big mess to clean up. All the dumpsters had to have the lids closed whenever there was no garbage going in. Otherwise, the birds would make an unholy mess of things, spilling half of the contents out on the ground.

Darcy didn't care about all that. He just liked ravens.

Carlos and I would see him out there murmuring to one of the birds as we went to and from our various jobs on the worksite.

Carlos was one of my favorite co-workers, so I made sure to try to team up with him when I could. He was happy, good-natured, and hardworking. He sent all of his money back to his family in Mexico. Since we spent so much time together, we spent some time observing Darcy and the ravens and having a good laugh.

Ravens don't judge you for your weight, or if they do, they never let you know. The birds always seemed interested in whatever Darcy was whispering. Sometimes they got pretty close to him. Too close, in my mind. They have big, mean-looking beaks and claws that are meant to catch and rip open small animals. Of course, they never attack humans, but what if you cornered one? I didn't trust them to keep their beaks to themselves.

Getting caught messing around with wildlife could cost you your job. We were supposed to avoid interactions with deer, bears, foxes, and birds. The only thing we were supposed to do was report a sighting of wild animals inside the work zone. We weren't supposed to chase them, interfere with whatever they were up to, or feed them. We weren't even allowed to take pictures of animals (or anything else) on site. But the rules didn't say anything about talking to the animals.

We figured as long as Darcy whispered to the ravens, it was none of our business. Besides, he was our foreman, so if he was busy having a chat with a big black bird, then he wasn't in our faces barking orders. Whatever kept Darcy talking to animals instead of to us was a good thing.

One day a couple of other guys and I were installing a new valve and piping at the north end of the project. We liked it over there, away from the rest of the action. It was peaceful in this out-of-the-way area.

Carlos spoke up. "Is Darcy giving that raven a bag of Doritos?"

We looked over to see Darcy crouching down by a bag in the middle of the road. A raven was sitting on the fence nearby, turning its head this way and that as it studied the fat man beside the Doritos. It looked scruffier than the rest of the birds. Its feathers were ruffled, and it looked dingy.

Darcy stood up and backed away from the bird. Immediately, the raven made a break for the bag. It landed, pulled a chip out, and flew back to the fence.

A couple more ravens arrived. It looked like the first raven got worried that he was going to lose his lunch. With a low "caw," he swooped in and grabbed the whole bag. Unfortunately for him, he grabbed it by the bottom. As he lifted off, the bag turned upside down, and everything fell out. The poor scruffy raven landed on the fence, holding an empty bag.

I swear, the other ravens laughed at him. Their caws sounded just like they were saying, "Hahaha, Doofie, you screwed up again. You're such a dumbass! You can't even bird right."

Another one was cackling, "Yeah, loser, we're gonna leave you holding the bag!" The two laughing ravens swooped down and grabbed some of the dumped chips.

Doofie dropped the empty bag and said, "Sad caw. I am a worthless raven." I could picture his dejected expression as he shifted from foot to foot on the chainlink.

We all had a laugh at the poor raven's expense. Then we went back to our bolt-up and torqued up the studs on that valve. After we finished up and put the tools back on the truck, we went for our lunch break.

Back in the lunch trailer, all the guys filed in and took our spots. We workers took our little slices of real estate seriously. You didn't dare sit in another guy's spot, or you would get punted.

At one end, the card club fired up a game of crib. These guys always cribbed away at lunchtime.

The two crane operators sat together every day, talking about crane-guy things. They were too good for us non-crane folk.

Most of the men had to sit on cheap stacking chairs with no padding. That wasn't good enough for our fitter's table. We had rolling chairs that we had liberated from an unused office one lonely winter night shift. We put little signs with our names on the backs so no one would steal them.

Trent, a tattooed fitter who spent all his spare time at the gym getting bigger, sat down and asked, "Where are my Doritos? They were in my lunch bag." We all knew that one day a week was a cheat day for Trent, where he could eat whatever he wanted. The rest of the time, he was on a Chris-Hemsworth-style diet: Only rice, broccoli, and chicken. Because of his strict regimen, his treat day was a huge deal to him. You wouldn't take this roid monster's Doritos unless you had a death wish.

He stood up. "Which one of you fuckers took my Doritos?" Trent always wore his coveralls a size too small so that all his muscles would pop, and he had his sleeves rolled up to show off faded black tribal tattoos on both arms. He cut an intimidating figure.

He walked around the trailer and stared at each guy. The veins were popping on his forehead as his arms started to shake a tiny bit. It was scary.

Carlos and I looked at each other. We knew the ravens had them now, but we didn't say anything.

As the days went by, other things went missing. It was baffling why anyone would bother to steal food. Most of it was items we could get for free in the camp anyway, so why steal from your buddies? You could just bring your own from the camp lunch bagging area. Stealing lunch was a personal dig, a passive-aggressive way to hurt someone.

This was definitely true for the special items, like bags of chips. These weren't free. They came from the vending machine.

We saw Darcy feeding sandwiches and pastries to Doofie and his beaked pals almost every day after that. We couldn't figure out why he thought he could get away with it forever. We knew he would have to pay the piper eventually.

Not surprisingly, food only went missing from guys that Darcy didn't like. It seemed like he was doing it to see how mad he could get them. Darcy didn't like Trent. Carlos and I thought that it was probably because Trent was in fantastic shape and Darcy was not. He was jealous of Trent and his amazing physique.

Everyone started cluing in that the culprit had to be our supervisor. He was the foreman, and his office was at the end of the lunch trailer. He was in there "doing paperwork" while everyone else was out working. Darcy never brought his lunch inside until noon; he kept it out in his foreman's truck. Everyone else thought that Darcy was eating the stolen snacks himself, but Carlos and I knew the truth.

It was on the tenth day of a fourteen-day shift that Trent totally lost it.

A few of us were walking up to the lunch trailer, chatting away. We stopped talking when we heard a loud bang inside and the sound of chairs scraping on the floor. I opened the door to absolute mayhem. Jacked-up Trent was standing in the middle of the room beside a table that he had just flipped over. There was food debris everywhere.

"Which one of you fuckers took it?" He yelled as he turned around and pounded his fist into another table so hard that the plastic top cracked. Then he flipped that table too. Lunch bags, coffee mugs, and playing cards went flying. All the guys sat there open-mouthed and staring. No one knew what to do.

Trent marched the length of the trailer to Darcy's office. Everyone gave him a wide berth, they jumped out of the way as he stormed through.

"You lazy piece of shit, what are you gonna do about the stealing?" Trent yelled at Darcy. "Or did you take it?"

Darcy was turning red. "Did I take what?"

"My Nanaimo bar!"

We all cringed. The camp lunch room put out Nanaimo bars only once in a while. Those three-layered coconut, cookie dust, and chocolate desserts were hard-won commodities in these parts. Most of the time, all there was for sweets were crumbly, sad chocolate chip cookies and cardboard muffins.

Trent missing his Nanaimo bar was as bad as a momma bear missing her cub.

"Is that why you're so fat? Stealing lunches? I bet you're in here scarfing down all of our snacks while you sit around pretending to do paperwork!"

"Get out of my office right now, or you can go straight to the gate with a security guard escort," Darcy told him.

Trent threw his arms in the air and stomped out. Darcy quietly shut his office door. We all looked at each other and the trail of destruction with wide eyes and grins. This shit was getting real.

Nothing else happened for a couple of days. We cleaned up the lunch room and settled back into our routine. It seemed like it had blown over. But that was just a lull in the storm, the eye of the hurricane.

We were heading to the trailer for afternoon coffee when we saw a big crowd gathered around Darcy's foreman truck, a diesel F350 with a lift kit. I couldn't tell at first what was happening. There was movement inside the truck. What was that black shape smashing around in there?

As we got closer, we could see that a raven was trapped in the truck. It was frantically flapping back and forth, trying to get out. The window had been left open a few inches, just enough for a crafty bird to have squeezed in. But apparently, the bird couldn't figure out how to get back out. It banged back and forth in there like a moth at a lightbulb.

Darcy ran out of his office, moving faster than I had ever seen the big man move. His gut was bouncing from side to side as he came to a stop by his truck. "What the hell?" he yelled. He yanked open the door, and his raven friend escaped. Doofie flew in a straight line into the forest and vanished.

Now that the door was open, we could see that the truck was a mess. A brown paper lunch bag was ripped open, and Nanaimo bars were smeared all over the seat. There was bird shit on the dash. Scratches from the bird's claws were everywhere.

"Who put these in here?" Darcy held out a ruined Nanaimo bar in one big fist. The chocolate and the sweet yellow filling squeezed out of his shaking fist. "And which one of you arseholes opened my window? When I find out who did this…"

I saw Trent at the back of the crowd. He had his phone out, recording the whole thing. There was an evil smirk on his face as he posted the video to social media.

Darcy walked over to Trent, holding the Nanaimo bars. "This was you. Admit it." Trent smirked and walked away without saying a word.

Doofie never came back. In fact, it was like the ravens blacklisted Darcy. It was kinda sad, really. Darcy tried for a couple of weeks to get one of them to come to talk with him. They weren't having it.

They had all seen what happened to Doofie, and they weren't taking any chances.

Chapter 9

Lust's Open Window

"Dear Penthouse,
      I never thought this would happen to me...."

I've heard lots of crazy shit from people I've worked with. Most of those stories are so ridiculous that they aren't worth repeating. Every once in a while, though, I'd hear something so specific and bizarre that I couldn't help but believe every word.

It was another late night getting everything set up at the pulp mill. I had been hired on to help organize the logistics at the shutdown. In two weeks, a hundred people would be running around in this nightmare of boilers, pressure vessels, and kilns, and all of them would need tools, electrical cables, and lighting where they would be working. Our job was hauling all the shit up the network of stairs and catwalks that snaked through this hot, smelly dump. I had never worked in one of these places before, so I was following around the small crew of guys that had been hired on with me.

The supervisor on the job was a beefy mouthpiece named Sweeney. That was his last name. I don't think he ever told us his given name. He was one of those guys who hit thirty but was still mentally in High School. He had a habit of only referring to people by their last names, which became a habit that we all picked up too.

I was grouped up with two other guys, a happy-go-lucky welder named Watson, and a witty and smart-mouthed apprentice, Barrowman, who was only a few years out of high school.

The mill was far from where we all were living, and we were all staying at a cheap local motel, trying to save some of the living allowance that was part of our wage.

After a weekend off, I noticed the usually energetic Barrowman had not joined us in the lunchroom, and I figured he must be outside having a cigarette.

"Yo," Watson called after me. "Can I bum one?"

"Sure," I said before heading outside, Watson in tow.

We caught up with Barrowman in the smoke pit. He has seemed uncharacteristically withdrawn and quiet the last few days. I chalked his behavior up to his inexperience and thought he might be a little scared of speaking up. He was the youngest one in our group. Seeing him there, hunched over and staring blankly at the ground made me think that something else might be happening. I sat down beside him on the bench.

"Everything okay?" I asked.

"No," Barrowman replied.

"Well, shit. You want to blab?"

"Not really. It's kind of fucked up."

Watson heard that part of the conversation and moved closer. "How fucked up?" Watson asked.

"Super-fucked up. I don't even want to say."

"Nothing illegal, is it?" Watson replied.

"No. I don't think so." Barrowman tossed his cigarette into the bucket on the ground and dug into his pocket for another.

Here we go, I thought. *He's going to blab.*

"Okay," Barrowman said sheepishly as he lit another cigarette. "I'll tell you guys, but you can't tell anyone else."

Watson crossed himself in a display of old-world Catholicism. I could not offer the same religious gesture with any honesty, so my good word would have to do. "I won't say anything. I promise."

Barrowman looked around, ensuring no one else was in earshot, and then he told us his story.

Guys, I never thought this kind of thing would ever happen to me.

On our last days' off, I skipped going home and hanging out with my roommate. I get along with the guy and everything, but he's a little too wild for me. The guy works on a road crew, and everyone he works with, including him, smokes weed. When he's at home, the green clouds are constant. I like weed too, but I'm trying to avoid it in case I bang my thumb with a hammer at work and have to do a piss test. I figured it would be better for me to give all those guys and their constant weed smoking a break, so I called up my mom and dad, who still live in my old hometown. They were pretty happy to have a visit from their son, so I drove straight out there as soon as we went on days off last rotation.

My mom and dad have a house on a few acres near a small town between Edmonton and Hinton. I made the drive and chilled with my parents and their dogs for the first day. I enjoyed some home-cooked food and watched some football with my old man. We played some crib and just took it easy.

That Saturday, I had just finished helping mow the lawn when my sister, Jenny, pulled into the driveway. She is working in Edmonton for the summer break. She had just finished her first year of university. I knew she was probably there to freeload some leftovers and just visit like I was. She's a good kid, two years younger than me, and I always have a great time when she's around. She helped me get the lawn cleaned up and helped my mom cook supper.

After we ate, Jenny suggested that she and I go to the town bar. I knew this meant she was looking for her older brother to spring the cash for her drinks as she is a broke-ass student. Sure. I went for it. I'm a good big brother.

We got into the bar around nine o'clock and got a table. Soon the place started to fill up. A bunch of people from our high school days began to file in, and it became a makeshift reunion for everyone. Before you knew it, we had pulled a few tables together to get everyone sitting down. It was a pretty good time.

I noticed that there was one girl there I'd had a massive crush on in school. Her name was Julia. She was across the table and a few seats down from me, but occasionally I would catch her checking me out. She'd get caught looking at me and would look down at the floor nervously, doing that cute, sexy lip-bite thing every time. When I was in school, I always thought she was out of my league. I don't think I ever even spoke to her back then, but here we were — adults in a bar, flirting.

Typically, if I'm at a bar, it's with my buddies, and we are all just there to get hammered. I'm usually the guy who gets too fucked up to be effective at picking up the ladies. When I noticed that Julia was checking me out, I laid off the sauce and ordered a non-alcoholic beer in case I got to talk to her. I didn't want to blow any remote chance I might have had with her by being a stupid, drunk asshole later on. I excused myself from the table and went to the bar to get myself a non-alcoholic beer. I was waiting for it when Julia sidled up beside me at the bar.

"Hi-ya, Barrowman," she said.

"Hi-ya Julia."

"What are you getting yourself there?" Julia asked me as the bartender set the 'near-beer' down on the bar.

"Fake beer," I said.

"Trying to stay sober, huh?"

I don't know what came over me. I have never been a forward guy, but I think all the time I spent working this job with all of you guys with no filters might have had some effect on me. Without thinking, I blurted, "I just don't think a guy should be sloppy drunk when talking to a beautiful girl in a bar."

Julia lit right up.

"So, you gonna buy a beautiful girl a drink, or what?" she asked with a smile.

Julia and I spent the rest of the night talking. Eventually, we got a table of our own in a quiet corner. By that point, the table we had been sitting at was getting raucous, with several people hitting their limit. One of them, a big rugby jock named Stevey, breezed past Julia and me to retch his guts out in the bathroom. We both laughed at him. We could hear him heaving over the music with the bathroom door closed.

Julia and I hardly had anything to drink the whole night. We nursed our drinks as we sat and chatted, catching up. She was going to school in Calgary for a business degree and hoped to move into Law after that.

She was intelligent, funny, and pretty. I was shocked that she seemed interested in me, but she was laughing at all my jokes.

I told her about what I was doing for a living, about working in the trades. She told me she liked a guy who knew how to build things. It couldn't have been going any better. After a couple of hours, It seemed like Julia and I had known each other, like, *really* known each other, for years instead of minutes. She kept edging closer to me, and before long, she just grabbed me and planted one on me, leaving me a speechless mess. She laughed at me a little when she saw that she had mentally incapacitated me with a quick kiss. She was right next to me now, her left arm around the back of my neck, sipping her drink with her right hand.

"How come you never talked to me in high school?" she finally asked.

"I never thought you'd be interested in me. Besides, I knew I was a moron. It takes a guy at least twenty-two years to grow himself a sack." I thought I might've taken the conversation too far with that last remark.

"Is that so?" she asked me before sliding her right hand down my stomach as she brought it down to my crotch. She grabbed my dick and balls, not hard enough to hurt me, but hard enough to let me know she meant business. She waited until I turned my head to make eye contact.

"Yeah. There it is. Do you have any plans for using this thing?" she asked me.

"I hadn't planned on it," I replied.

"Well, I might be planning on it," Julia said.

"Really?"

"Really," she assured me, loosening her grip.

I had been exercising all my willpower to keep myself from bonering out, but I had failed miserably. A considerable steeple had grown up against the zipper in my jeans.

"I liked you in high school and always wanted you to talk to me. Besides, you're returning to work in a few days, and it's the end of summer. I'll be going back to school in a couple of weeks. We won't get the chance to see each other for a long time after this weekend. I'm saying that we might want to make the most of it."

"I'm staying at my parent's house," I told her. "My sister is there too. I'm sleeping on the couch. We can't go there."

"I'm at my parents' house too," Julia said. "But my bedroom is on the second floor, and my parents are on the main floor. You can tiptoe like a ninja, I bet!"

"You bet I can!" I said, pantomiming some slick martial arts moves with my hands. "I *am* a goddamned ninja!"

"Well, let's sneak out of here, ninja."

Julia laughed and grabbed my arm, walking me out of the dingy small-town bar into the eerie pink-blue light of the late summer night sky. The bar was a few blocks from her mom and dad's house, which was built on a large private lot.

Her dad had built the house in the eighties, and when real estate was cheap, he had bought the lots on either side of the house and amalgamated them into the property. A long asphalt driveway lined with boulders and old trees led to the house and a three-car garage. The place was well kept, as Julia's mom was a renowned green thumb who always won awards for her garden. I could make out some of her mom's handiwork in the dark as we made our way up the long driveway.

The house was dark, with only the pale front porch light on.

"Are you sure they won't wake up?" I asked.

"Positive," Julia assured me. "My mom takes a pill to help her sleep every night, and my dad could sleep through a nuclear explosion. We're safe. Trust me."

"Okay," I whispered as we walked up the front steps. Julia opened the unlocked door. I winced, half expecting the hinges to creak, but the door swung open without a sound, and we stepped inside. Julia tugged on my arm and silently pointed to a door at the end of a long hallway.

Her parents' room.

She pulled me up a stairway to the second floor. Her room was far enough from the room her parents were sleeping in that I breathed a sigh of relief, finally believing we wouldn't be caught.

The room showed signs of belonging to a girl with too many clothes and didn't know what to wear. There were scarves, shirts, shoes, bras, and jeans all over the place. Julia's bedroom window had a nice view. I had a brief chance to enjoy it before she was all over me.

Julia grabbed me, and we made out heavily before her hand shot down my pants. I was already hard, and she took a moment to uncouple her face from mine to breathe, "Take off your fucking pants," into my ear.

I obeyed.

She looked down at my hard dick and pulled on it, smiling at me the whole time. I've been with a few girls, but none made me this horny.

Julia dropped to her knees and put me in her mouth, giving me the best head I have ever had. She kept looking up at me with her otherworldly blue eyes. We kept going like that for a few minutes, and I started to feel like I was going to blast off. I didn't want to get to the end so soon, so I stopped, pulled out, and helped her onto the bed.

I realized I was standing there with my pants down and a tee shirt on and thought I probably looked like 'Winnie the Pooh,' so I took the rest of my clothes off while she unbuttoned her jeans. I helped her slide them off before I got to work on her panties. I pulled them off as she unclasped her bra, letting her gorgeous boobs out. I took a moment to realize what a lucky guy I was before I spread her legs and began kissing my way up from her left ankle.

I've never considered myself a ladies' man, and as I said before, my usual interactions with women usually ended in my getting too drunk to talk to them. But I did have a fling with a forty-something divorcee last year. I wound up hooking up with her after meeting her at a nightclub. I had sex with her. It was pretty good. She called me a couple of days later for a booty call. As soon as we got down to business, she looked at me with disappointment and sighed before saying, "You young guys are all about the dick. Not one of you knows how to eat a pussy."

Then she showed me how.

Now with Julia, I used everything she'd taught me. I slowly teased my way up before lingering around the target area with some breath and a slight brushing of the lips. Once she started to get impatient, I went in. I explored the area around her clitoris until I found her spot. Once I got it with my tongue, she seemed to slow right down, holding her breath for several seconds before taking a deep breath.

"There?" I asked her.

"Yeah. Yeah." She took a handful of my hair and pushed my mouth in deeper. I kept a steady pace, concentrating my tongue around that spot, straying away slightly, but never for too long, just as I was taught. I listened to her breathing to gauge my pace, increasing the intensity as her breath quickened and she clawed at my scalp.

A few minutes later, I felt her give way. My hands massaged her inner thighs, and I felt her leg muscles relax, her breath stopping for several seconds. She stopped moving, paralyzed by the unstoppable approaching orgasm. I kept pace as I had been taught. This was not the time to speed up, stop or slow down.

Soon, I felt the pulse of the muscles around her pussy retract and then push forward, a seismic wave before the big quake hit.

And hit her, it did. Her torso rose off the bed as she tensed up with the big moment. I pulled my mouth away from her to watch the impact of my handiwork. She fell back onto the bed, still writhing and shaking, her eyes clamped shut so hard they wrinkled at the corners. I had given my last partner — the divorcee — several genuine shiver makers, but the orgasm Julia was having was bigger than anything I had ever seen.

I kept watching, waiting for the waves to subside before I resumed.

But they didn't stop.

She let go of my hair, and her arms were now straight out, her hands locked at the wrists. Her fingers were twitching.

Something was wrong.

I stood up and called her name, "Julia? Julia? Are you okay?"

She didn't respond.

I got down near her ear and called out to her again. Still, there was no response.

She began to shake. Her arms wiggled awkwardly from side to side as her head twisted back and forth. Her legs eventually started shaking too.

Frozen with fear, I looked at her wrist as she continued to spasm, but no bracelet was there to alert me to any medical condition. I finally resorted to getting on the bed beside her and gently slapping her cheeks to see if I could snap her out of it. I tried that for what felt like two minutes of nothing happening – and then I panicked. Horrified and terrified, I jumped off the bed and gathered my clothes. Her eyes partly opened and locked onto mine as she shook on the bed. It looked like she recognized me, but she couldn't speak.

I gathered all of my clothes into a ball, opened the window, and tossed them out. I jumped out after them, rolling down the shingled roof, scratching my shoulders, knees, and back on the cheese grater surface of the shingles as I tumbled down before I fell the nine feet-or-so from the lip of the roof into one of her mom's prize-winning flower beds below, destroying a cluster of roses as I landed. I got up, staggered through two more flower beds, and picked up my clothes.

I limped down her long driveway as fast as I could, putting on my clothes as I hobbled away. I tripped a couple of times and scraped up my face. I managed to get myself mostly dressed before I got to the end of the driveway, throwing my shirt on as I made it to the main road. I walked to my Mom and Dad's house — an hour-and-a-half walk with the limp I had. The sun had started to come up by the time I got in.

Jenny had already made it home and had helped herself to the couch I had planned to sleep on for the night. From the smell of rum wafting from her, I don't think she had been in any shape to make it up the stairs to her old room and just flopped on the couch. I took her bed and laid there staring at the ceiling all night, freaked right out. And that is why I've been weird since we returned from days off.

Barrowman had reached the end of his sordid tale. Watson and I stared at him. Both of us were wide-eyed with shock at what we'd just heard.

"What?" Barrowman asked. "Why are you fuckers staring?"

"You just left her there, having what sounds like a seizure? Didn't you get help or anything? What? What the fuck, dude?" I stammered.

"I panicked," replied Barrowman. "But I know she's okay."

"How?" asked Watson.

"It's a small town. If she'd died, I'd have heard by now."

"Holy fuck!" Watson spat as he turned around and raised his arms in a wild gesture.

"What else was I supposed to do? Go wake up her mom and dad? *'Hi folks, you don't know me, but I was chowing on your daughter, and now she's in her bedroom — naked — having a seizure! Send help!'* I don't think that would have gone over so well."

"You might have called nine-one-one?" I suggested.

Barrowman thought about that for a few seconds. "Yeah," he said. "Maybe I could have. I don't know, guys. I never even got her phone number. I did get my sister to get it from one of her friends who used to play ringette with her. The thing is, I'd still love to go out with her again. I've been thinking about calling her up and explaining myself. Do you think I should?"

Watson and I shared a stunned look.

"I wouldn't if I were you," I said. "I think that ship has sailed."

"Really?" asked Barrowman. "Maybe she doesn't remember what happened?"

"Even if she doesn't," I said, "I'm sure she's smart enough to put two-and-two together. You fucked up, buddy. It's over, Casanova."

"Dude," Watson chimed in, "What you just told us is one of the most fucked-up scenes I've ever heard about, and I've seen been through some shit. The only reason you should call her is to apologize."

The conversation was broken up by Sweeney, who emerged from the main building door and crossed the road to join us in the smoke pit. Sweeney sat beside me and lit a smoke, oblivious to the story we had just heard.

I watched Barrowman shrink away and head for the door, back upstairs to sit in his dark cloud of love, lost to a freak occurrence.

'*He's young. He'll get over it.*' I thought.

"What's wrong with Barrowman?" Sweeney asked.

"He had a bad date," Watson replied.

"How bad are we talking?"

"Eleven out of ten," I replied. "It's actually impressive how bad he screwed up."

"Shit. That sounds pretty bad."

"What are we doing the rest of the night, boss?" Watson asked Sweeney.

"This is it," replied Sweeney. "We're all out of tools and material to put out. We were supposed to get another truckload of parts tonight. The guy who was supposed to deliver everything got himself shitfaced, so it looks like that plan is out the fucking window."

"What's so funny?" Sweeny asked as Watson and I both cracked up at the same time.

Chapter 10

Saved by the Welder

Nowadays, hardly anyone has to run a shovel for a living. With all of this modern equipment like hydro-vac trucks, you don't see a bunch of guys running goon spoons or Mexican backhoes for days on end. Not every small company wants to pay for a truck to come in, though. Why spend thousands on a big hydro-vac unit when you can hire some cheap laborers and give them some shovels?

After high school, I was hired on with a local construction company as a laborer with no experience. So when I started out in the world, my first job was digging ditches. Someone had to do the grunt work, and it was dummies like me who didn't have a plan for our lives.

I didn't sign up for ditch detail. No one said, "Hey, James, you wanna dig ditches all summer?" If I had known that my summer was gonna be spent on a shovel, I would probably have found something else to do with my time. ANYTHING else. But, I got tricked into digging all day by hand, me and a couple of other fools who said yes when they should have said, "No thanks, I'd rather be broke."

I was partnered up with a guy named Nick, a twenty-two-year-old headbanger who was full of tall tales about how great his hot rod was. Trout was our leader, a more experienced pipeliner who knew what we were supposed to be doing out there. I can't remember Trout's real name because no one ever used it. Trout was on our little crew to drive the truck and keep us newbies out of trouble.

The new pipeline was going to come through, and they needed to know where the existing lines were so we didn't accidentally hit them with the excavator. The only way to get the job done safely was to dig down by hand and find that pipe. The locations were marked with stakes so we would know where to look, and the markings were usually accurate.

The first few pipelines we dug up went like clockwork.

On day one, the three of us carefully dug down a few feet and found a yellow plastic gas line that ran to a farm. I was a bit too rough with the shovel and put a good scar on the plastic, but Trout said it wouldn't matter.

On day two, we exposed a phone line in a ditch beside a gravel road, again pretty close to the surface.

The rest of that first week was similar. Find the spot to dig using the stakes. Dig down to the depth they gave us while listening to Nick talk about his car. Be careful not to damage the line.

We had no idea that we were being set up for hell week.

On Monday, we followed the foreman's truck into buttfuck nowhere to uncover the next relic. We pulled over onto an approach and got a tour of the spot. As we walked away from the truck, mosquitos zoomed in to find breakfast.

"What a bug-infested shithole," Nick complained as we all slapped mosquitos. Trout smirked at him in amusement. He was too tough to whine.

"The line locator tells us that this six-inch pipe goes right through here." The foreman pointed across a weed-infested field beside the dirt road. There were wooden stakes with ribbons on top showing where we were supposed to find this pipe.

"It's going to be about five feet down," he continued. "It'll be a yellow jacket, so whatever the fuck you do, don't scar it up by smashing your shovels into it. You got that, Trout? I want to see that pipe in good shape when you guys are done so we don't have to fix it!"

"Sure, boss," Trout said around a mouthful of chew.

The foreman drove off. We grabbed our shovels and liberally applied bug spray to keep the mosquitos from sucking us dry. Trout lined us up at the location where the new line was supposed to cross this old pipe, and we started digging a trench down to find it.

That day was a hot, sweaty, mosquito-filled yack fest. Nick just wouldn't shut up. He and Trout were opposite when it came to the number of words used per day.

Trout was an Easterner with a strong accent. He always had a wad of chew on the go, or a dart (cigarette,) or both. About the only thing that came out of his mouth was spit or smoke. He never said anything negative; I'll give him that. He was there to get the job done, and he wasn't going to whine about it.

Nick made up for it by babbling nonstop about some of the wildest topics I'd ever heard. Like that whole "Flat Earth" idea.

"Listen, you think the world is round, but do you know anyone who has gone all the way around? That's because it can't be done!" Nick jumped on his shovel to force it into the sticky clay and pried a lump of earth half the size of his head out of the ditch. He hoisted it up and thumped it on a rock near the edge of the ditch to force the clay to let go of the shovel.

The dirt quality here was terrible. It was sticky, heavy clay that just would not come off the shovel after you managed to get it on there, so we had to tap the shovels on the ground or on a chunk of wood to get it off. It was frustrating to work with.

"What about those pictures of the Earth from space?" I asked.

"That's all fake! They never went to the moon, and they keep releasing this propaganda to make you think the Earth is round."

"But why would they do that? It sounds expensive." I liberated another shovelful of clay from its underground prison.

"They lie to you to keep you under control. They don't want you to know that the Earth is flat in every direction, so they stop you from going there. There are patrols up North and you can't get past them."

"Okay," I said, "Do you know anyone who's seen these patrols or even tried to get there?"

"Well, no, but anyone that does get up there goes missing. That's why we don't hear from them. The government puts them away."

"That's a pretty convenient line of thinking," I took a drink of water. "So you don't know anyone that has tried it, which means you don't really have a clue."

"Sounds like bullshit to me," Trout said.

We finished day one without finding that six-inch pipe. The trench was about four feet deep, two feet wide, and seven feet long.

On the second day, I couldn't stop thinking about Flat Earth Nick's crazy ideas, so while we struggled and dug the ditch deeper, wider, and longer, I kept asking questions.

"Okay, so there's a ring of ice all around the edges of the map, and the government won't let you go there. But how does that control you?"

"It just does! They don't want us to know the truth!"

"But why? Would we riot and overthrow the government and stop following traffic laws? I don't get this control part. I think the way they control us is with jails and police. I feel more controlled by my girlfriend than by the government."

"Listen, man, if the world found out the truth about what's really out there, everything would change. That's why they invented all this crap about moon landings and stuff. All of that was filmed in the desert. Just look at how weird the American flag looked in those videos!"

"I just can't see how that would be worth all the time and money. You know you can go to Cape Canaveral and watch them launch into space, right? Do you think those giant rockets are all just for show? Just to make you think the Earth is round while they waste all that fuel?"

But I was arguing with a brick wall. Nick was convinced that the Earth was flat and the moon landings were faked to make us think that the Earth was round. It was all part of a plot to keep us under the thumb of "The Man." Nick wasn't sure what they did with all of this power, but he was sure that it made those in control super-rich. That was why we were forced to dig ditches. Because the Earth was flat, and they didn't want us to know.

At the start of day three, our foreman came to see what we were up to. He was getting impatient. He stood at the edge of our excavation and looked in. We had a trench almost fifteen feet long, three feet wide, and five feet deep. There was no sign of that hotline yet. It was deeply disappointing for all of us.

"The problem is you guys aren't deep enough. You need to go down, don't stop until you find it! Trout! Quit screwing around and get digging."

Trout smiled and spit tobacco nectar on the ground. "Okay."

We got to it. To go deeper, we had to make our existing ditch wider too. That felt like going backward instead of forward. Cutting the walls back meant partially filling our hard-won hole back in, only to shovel it out again.

It took us through the stages of ditch-digging grief.

Denial: " Digging is easy! We won't be here very long at all."

Anger: "Why the fuck is this taking so long? Nick, shut up about your flat earth bullshit and get digging!I don't need this shitty job! I should quit."

Bargaining: "Trout, I'll trade you a peanut butter and jelly for a couple of those smokes."

Depression: "We're never gonna find this piece of shit line. And Nick is never going to shut up."

Acceptance: "This is my life now. I'll just dig until my body gives out."

At the end of day three, we were over seven feet down. It was really hard to get the dirt out of that hole. We hadn't stacked it far enough from the edge, so anything new we threw up there tended to roll back in. One of us had to stay up top and move the dirt back farther.

It was day four. We kept trying all morning, but our hearts weren't in it. We were all convinced we must be digging in the wrong spot, so we started extending our trench. Nick and I worked on the south end. I moved most of the dirt while Nick kept up a constant flow of bitching, moaning, and whining. He interspersed actual work with water breaks and motionlessness, standing there leaning on his shovel and watching me.

Trout was a machine. Scoop, throw, scoop, throw, spit, scoop, throw. He must have had a lot of ditch-digging practice to be so efficient.

All three of us were in a sour mood, to the point where Nick finally shut up. Trout's spitting even sounded angry.

The hour-long truck ride back to town was silent. Trout dumped us off in the yard beside our cars, and we went home to consider the life choices that led us to this horrible situation.

If only I had joined the circus or became a telephone solicitor, or even started selling my body on a street corner for cheeseburgers like Randy from The Trailer Park Boys. A man's gotta eat, Mr. Lahey.

It was now day five. We didn't realize that anyone besides the foreman was keeping tabs on us. The rest of the pipeliners kept far away from our location, probably so they wouldn't have to help dig. But a welding rig drove by a few times. The driver would slow down and check out our progress at least once a day. I didn't know the welder's real name, but Trout called him Rabbit. The two of them waved at each other when Rabbit went by.

Today, Rabbit slowed down and parked his welding rig on the side of the road. He got out and opened a toolbox. Grabbing a couple of welding rods out of the cabinet, he bent them at one end. Apparently, this was to make handles because he held the rods in front of himself by the short piece. Then he walked over to where we were excavating.

"What are you guys up to?" he asked.

"Feels like we're digging our own graves," Nick said as he leaned on the shovel.

"Maybe I can witch the line and narrow it down a bit for you," Rabbit said, showing us the bent welding rods.

"Come on. Water witching isn't even real. How could you pipeline witch?" Nick laughed.

"You think the Earth is flat, but you don't believe in water witching?" Trout asked. He spat a big gob of brown juice right in front of

Nick. I was surprised that Trout broke his silence, but it just goes to show how fed up he was with Nick's babbling.

The welder didn't seem to care that Nick thought witching was dumb. Rabbit came over to one end of our ditch from hell, held up the rods, and walked with them pointing out. He slowly moved about 40 feet in a straight line away from the ditch end. Nothing happened. We all just stared silently. Trout was nodding to himself. I had no idea what to expect.

Rabbit walked around to the other end of our ditch, whistling to himself. He set up the welding rods, both pointing away from his body, parallel. Then he walked slowly away from our excavation, and about twenty feet out, the welding rods crossed over each other.

"Right here," he said. He bent down and jabbed the two rods in the ground as a marker. "It's five feet down right here."

Trout, Nick, and I looked at each other and instantly came to the realization that we had nothing to lose. We grabbed our shovels and climbed out of our trench, abandoning all of that work. We went over and started a new hole where the welder had put those rods in the ground. Rabbit drove off, still whistling tunelessly.

Two hours later, we had found the line, right where Rabbit had said it would be. We tidied up the new hole, put some plywood over it, and were packing up our shovels when Rabbit came back.

"Did you find it? Not surprised. I'm gonna let you in on a secret. See that 'Pipeline Crossing' sign here by the road? That's for this line you were looking for. Now, see that oilfield shack over there? That's where the line goes."

"So?" Nick said with almost a snarl. Not too grateful for the help, I noticed.

"Well, if you draw a line between the two, you see that your second ditch, where you found it, is located on that line. And your first ditch, where you failed to find it, is way over there." We looked and could clearly see that our first massive excavation was not between the line crossing and the shack. It was way off to one side.

This was a facepalm moment.

"So you're saying if we had used our brains, we woulda known the stakes the line locator put in must've been wrong," I guessed.

"No, I'm saying I'm a genius, and I know how to witch lines with a couple of welding rods." The welder started walking back to his truck.

"And by the way, I helped install this line about ten years ago."

With that, Rabbit jumped in his welding rig and drove off whistling.

Chapter 11

Safety Sideshow Bob Shows Me How To Break a Windshield

The welding shop I apprenticed in had a lot of crew turnover. Good welders wouldn't stay in a place like that any longer than they had to. In the four years I stayed to finish my apprenticeship, I saw about twenty misfits come and go. Only Randy, the shop foreman, myself, and Bob were there all that time.

I saw Randy push one loser out the door because he got so drunk by morning coffee that he was slurring his words. His lunch bag was full of empty beer cans. It seemed like he was slipping into the bathroom to chug a brew in between welds. There were guys using a variety of other substances, too. The company never had to do any drug testing unless there was an incident, so most of the time, we never found out what welders were high on. But I could tell by looking into their eyes and watching their shaky movements when they were really out of it.

One day one of these lowlifes was so out of it that he amputated a finger from his left hand and barely felt it. We had a big machine called an Ironworker that we used to shear flat bars and angle iron into smaller bits. When you pushed on the foot pedal, every single part of the machine moved whether you were using it or not, and a shear blade moved across the opening. This machine had a slot halfway up the side for cutting round-bar. Our poor stoned welder was using the round bar slot as a handy gripping spot while he positioned his chunk of two-inch flat bar on a lower cutting bed. When he pressed the foot pedal, his flat bar cut off and fell to the floor - right beside his pointer finger.

The blood was a bitch to clean off of that worn, old concrete.

We repaired broken industrial machinery where the metal had ripped apart, broken farm machinery where the farmer had ripped it apart, and broken oilfield machinery wherever that got ripped apart. Sometimes we made a new custom item, but mostly it was all repair work. A load of broken shit would arrive, we would grind and weld until it was almost good again, and then ship it back out.

"Stoned or drunk, we'll fix your junk!" was our motto.

We toiled away in a shop filled with ancient tools and leftover bits of plate steel and angle iron. If it was even remotely possible that someday we could use that two-inch-long scrap of flat bar, we were gonna squirrel it away and save it for a rainy day.

Randy, the shop foreman, was crude and hairy, and he used guilt as a motivational tool. He liked me because I didn't talk back, and I worked non-stop to keep from getting guilted into submission. I watched Randy yell, humiliate and guilt-trip more than one guy until the poor bastard quit.

Randy would sit down at lunchtime and chat with me about his passion — tomato gardening. He had this greenhouse packed with tomato plants, and he brought me big red tomatoes to take home. I pictured big, hairy Randy carefully tending his prized tomatoes with gentle, loving hands.

"You gotta plant the right types of tomato," Randy told me. "The beefsteaks are great for burgers and salads. But I really like the way the Roma tomatoes taste, and who doesn't like cherry tomatoes for snacks? Here, try these cherry tomatoes. I just picked them this morning, right off the vine. I planted these seeds myself back when there was still snow on the ground. I don't like buying those seedlings from Canadian Tire. Who knows what you're getting?"

Yeah, Randy loved his tomatoes. But he loved to hate Bob even more. Bob thought he was God's gift to farming and welding. Every time Randy was really pissed at Bob, he would come over to where I was working and vent about it.

A lot of the work required two guys because we had to carry a lot of heavy things around.

Since I was one of the few regular workers in this joint, I got a lot of grunt work that took the special shop knowledge, like how to get the electric hoist to turn on, and the trick to starting our piece-of-shit forklift. Because I got all these dumb jobs, day in and day out, I was partnered up with Bob, the only other steady guy; a part-time farmer who thought he could weld.

Bob was a mid-forties weekend farmer who could one-up you on anything. Any story someone told Bob would tell them how he did it better, how much worse he had it, or how much better his idea was.

He combined all the worst traits parts of farmers and welders. This guy was a major contrarian. He would argue if someone claimed that gravity existed.

I got along with Bob by not talking too much and pretending to let him tell me what to do while I did it my way anyway.

To go with his contrariness, Bob wouldn't follow any safety rules or use appropriate safety gear. This shop was pretty lenient to start with, but we were expected to follow the basics. Keep your eyes, skull, and nuts safe so you can limp home at the end of the day.

Bob went out of his way to break any rule, whether it caused him grief or not. I guess you can do whatever you want on the farm, but that doesn't always fly when you're working around a bunch of potentially stoned or drunk welders. There had to be rules.

The last year I worked at that shop, Randy was at his wit's end with this guy. He was yelling at him all day long.

Bob walked around with his laces undone every morning on purpose, just to provoke Randy. And it worked every time.

"Bob! Tie up your boots, for fuck sake! If you trip on laces and fall in the lathe head first, I'm gonna kill you!"

Bob routinely took the covers and guards off equipment to change blades or grinding disks and wouldn't put them back on because they were "in the way." The bandsaw guts were on view to the world, just begging for someone to put their fingers into the meat saw. After the incident with the Ironworker, we were all a little gun-shy about ever seeing fingers lying on the floor. So I couldn't blame Randy for screaming at Bob.

"Bob! You know what kind of numb-nut lowlifes we got around here. Do you want to be responsible for one of these guys cutting off a finger? How are they gonna roll a joint with only one hand?"

One time after removing the handle and guard off a six-inch grinder, Bob managed to get the tool to kick back. As he forceful-ly worked that grinder like a starving man with a steak knife on a porkchop, he got the disc in the wrong position. The tool flipped back and dug a four-inch line through his skin. The grinder disc was still spinning at full speed when it bit into the back of his hand. Of course, he wasn't wearing gloves. The only good thing was that the blade cauterized the wound. It sliced him like butter, and he didn't even bleed.

Bob got drug tested and passed with flying colors. It wasn't drugs that made him a danger; it was his innate stupidity. He walked around proudly, flaunting his wound and playing it up for sympathy. When he told the epic story of his injury, it was as if the equipment malfunctioned and nearly killed him before he valiantly got it under control. Even after he got the bandages off, I would see him working with all the safety parts stripped off the tool.

This drove Randy into a frenzy. "Bob, for crying out loud, can you put the guard on that grinder before you slice yourself wide open AGAIN?"

One day Randy lost his shit on Bob about the face shield he was supposed to wear while grinding.

Randy shoved it at him and stood there with his hands on his hips while he barked at Bob.

"Put it on and keep it on, or I'm sending you home. Try me and see what happens!"

Red-faced, Bob put it on. I thought that was the end of it, and we all went back to work.

I started cutting up a big pile of rusty old plate into parts for our next job. After I was done, I looked over at Bob's work area. He had a big shit-eating grin on his face, grinding away. He was wearing the face shield on his head backward, with the shield part guarding the back of his head. I guess when you're low on brains, there isn't much up there worth protecting.

Bob never cleaned his truck. The passenger seat was packed with empty chip bags and old Coke bottles. The last time it had been to the car wash was when the previous owner was getting it ready to sell, so it was a muddy brown color instead of white. There was no way Bob could see properly through that dirty windshield. Someone once scratched "wash me" on the endgate, but eventually, new dirt covered it up.

Bob never washed his hands either, no matter how filthy they got at work. He just wiped them on his pants. Every day at lunchtime, we watched Bob get out a sandwich and eat it. Sometimes we could see the rust or grease fingerprints on the bread.

Bob didn't believe in condoms, I bet. He didn't like safety guards on dangerous equipment. The very idea of Bob reproducing was surely one of the most dangerous to humans.

Needless to say, he wouldn't wear a seatbelt in a work truck.

The shop wasn't all repair work. Sometimes we got to build new things. Randy picked up a contract to build and install for a big farm. I was pretty excited to be working on something that would break the monotony of fixing broken shit.

The entire crew spent a week welding up some custom horse fencing for this ranch. We used up a lot of steel scraps and a fresh load of metal to build some fine-looking panels. We even painted them dark blue in front of the shop before we loaded them up on a twenty-four-foot trailer. Such a large stack of steel panels should have been hauled in two trailer loads, but we made them all fit onto one load anyway.

Randy came out to check out the load.

"You and numbnuts over there are gonna take this to the customer tomorrow morning and unload it," Randy told me, pointing over at Bob. "Don't fuck this up."

The next morning I got to work. No sign of Bob. I hooked the welding truck to the trailer alone.

This old beast was a Ford with a cracked windshield, a big steel deck, and a Lincoln welding machine on the back. It was heavy, and the trailer was too much for it. I figured I would make Bob drive because I had only pulled a trailer a couple of times before.

I waited for another fifteen minutes. Finally, the old dirty Chevy drove in, with Bob peering out through his crusty windshield. He got out and slowly walked over to the loaded truck and trailer. He looked like he had just woken up in a ditch. He smelled like he had slept with a goat, too.

Randy came out of the office and stomped over. He got right in Bob's face, hands on his hips, as his big hairy body leaned over intimidatingly.

"On the one day that you got a delivery, you show up late? Where were you? What's your excuse this time, couldn't find your purse?"

Bob licked his chapped lips. "A buddy was over for a few beers. We watched the game. Then we went down to the pub. We didn't wrap it up until real late."

Randy caught a good whiff of Bob's morning aroma. "Jesus Christ, are you still drunk?" He turned to me. "I want you driving today. This loser smells like a brewery!" He turned on his heel and stomped away, slamming the office door.

I winced. I was scared to pilot such a big pile of iron on the highway. The trailer was overloaded and the truck was a piece of shit. This morning was starting great.

We got in the truck. Since I didn't really have much faith in my ability to get us there in one piece, I put my seatbelt on. Then I got the old beast lurching into action down the road.

The truck kept dinging every few seconds. "What's that piece of shit beeping for?" Bob snarled. His antique farm truck didn't have modern conveniences like a working dash, let alone seatbelt warning indicators.

"It wants you to put on your seat belt."

"I don't wear those. You're more likely to die if you got one on. I'd rather be thrown to safety through the windshield than get trapped in a burning wreck or drown if we hit a lake."

"What if there's a front-end collision? Won't you fly out and hit the other vehicle's windshield like a bug?"

"Then I guess it's my time to go!" With that, he pulled the belt behind his back and buckled it in. The truck quit worrying about Bob, tricked into thinking the passenger had his belt on, and Bob settled in, happy that he got to circumvent the rules yet again.

Soon enough, unbelted Bob was leaning on the passenger window, passed out cold. With a week's worth of scruff, unbrushed hair, and a dirty old ball cap, he looked like a homeless guy that I had picked up on the edge of the road. He smelled like one too.

I had my lunch bag with me since I figured the unloading and setup were going to take all day. As I drove, I grabbed a baloney cheese sandwich and took a couple of bites. It was the breakfast of champions.

There were some busy intersections ahead. I knew this trailer would make the truck hard to slow down very fast. I kept to the speed limit since I was nervous about traffic and didn't want to rear-end someone. When we got to our "date with destiny," I was clipping along at about seventy kilometers an hour. I saw a pickup truck coming up to a stop sign on my left. It was a big white one ton.

It didn't stop at the light.

It just plowed right on through.

I locked up the brakes, but there was no chance of avoiding it. The front of the welding rig hit the white truck on the rear wheels and fender of the passenger side. We stopped almost dead, dragged to the right until we hit the curb.

This old beast had already used up its God-given allotment of crash fun bags, so those didn't deploy.

The other truck spun in a big one-hundred-eighty-degree arc and ended up facing right back at us about a hundred yards down.

It all happened so fast. I slammed into the seat belt and hit the steering wheel with my left arm while punching my thumb right through that baloney sandwich as my hand punched the dash. Meanwhile, Bob shot like a rocket right into the windshield head-first. He damn near went right through. Then he bounced back and fell in a heap into the footwell.

Bob wasn't bleeding, but he was going to have a nice goose egg on his skull. I figured he was gonna live because he was using every bad word I'd ever heard.

I took off my seat belt, got out of the truck, and walked around the front. I stood there with a dumb expression on my face, looking at the destruction, still wearing a sandwich on my thumb.

From out of nowhere, a cop car pulled up with its lights on.

It seemed like a good time for a snack. I ate the sandwich off of my hand, then licked the mustard from my palm.

The cop asked if I was okay. "I said, "I think so?" He went to check on Bob. The other driver wasn't stirring yet.

Our truck wasn't going anywhere soon. The radiator was leaking, and the grille and headlights were smashed. The front passenger tire was turned all funny because the tie-rod was broken.

As I stood out on the highway, stunned and banged up, the cops looked at my credentials and such. All of them were in order. They had an ambulance coming for Bob because he most likely had a concussion. The other driver, who also wasn't wearing his seatbelt, was in even worse shape.

The cop told me a little bit about the other guy. "It looks like he stole this truck from work. His girlfriend in Calgary was breaking up with him and taking his kids away with her. So he was in a big hurry to get down there. Looks like he's not gonna make it to Calgary today," he said with a smirk.

As the paramedics were getting ready to put Bob in the ambulance, the cop said, "Excuse me, sir. I have something for you." He handed over a yellow piece of official-looking cop paper.

"What's this?" Bob asked. He was hung over, beat up, and totally confused by the concussion.

"It's your ticket for not wearing a seatbelt. Have a nice day!"

Chapter 12

The Night We Won the Bored Guy Mischief Lottery

I am a disposable pipefitter mercenary.

    I got into this line of work years ago and haven't been able to break myself out of it. For those that don't know, I am a Journeyman Pipefitter, dispatched by the company I usually work for to whatever job and whatever location the work happens to be at. Once one of the older guys I had worked with told me that being a 'Journeyman' literally meant you pack your bags and go where the work is.

    The pay is sensational while you're working. The jobs usually only last thirty days or less, as the plants we are working at need to be entirely shut off while we fix all the major items that can't be done while the plant is online. There is a lot of overtime pay, and with all the extra hours, I can usually make enough in five months to carry me for the year.

If I had to pick one downside to working the shutdown circuit, it would be that I never know where and when the next job is. I've had long stretches where I was off for a few months more than I wanted to be and wound up running out of money.

Another downside to the shutdown circuit is that things can get a little boring at times. There is a lot of sitting around and waiting. We wait for hot piping systems to cool down, we wait for operations to fix their fuckups, and we wait for building materials to arrive. Disorganization is always the cause of waiting. I sound like a whiner, but waiting pays the same as working, and the boredom generated by these long wait times can sometimes lead to strange things happening.

Once again, I found myself working the night shift at another disorganized circus, dropped into a small lunch trailer full of folding tables and uncomfortable wooden chairs. We were smack in the middle of Northern Alberta and about as far from civilization as most civilized people would be comfortable with.

We were not civilized people.

In the trailer with me was John, a young Journeyman like me. Danny, a big guy from the next Province over. He seemed a little out of his element. Leo, the wise old-timer who would boast that he built the current plant that we were working on, way back in the old days. And there was Nathan, the quiet and wide-eyed apprentice.

John's smartphone began to ring about midnight on the third night (a Friday), breaking Leo out of his hand-on-cheek slumber with its loud ringtone. "Who the fuck?" John said, squinting at the number. "Edmonton number. I have no idea who this is." He answered it on speakerphone.

"Hello?"

"Shawn," said a raspy female voice on the other side, "It's Amy. I'm looking for pickup. Do you have anything?"

John looked at us, surprised. We had just won the bored guy mischief lottery. John straightened up in his chair, alert with the thrill of a reverse prank call. Danny leaned in, curious.

"Sure," John said. "How much are you looking for?"

"A half-ounce," Amy said. "Same as last time."

"A half ounce of weed?" John asked.

"Fuck weed," Amy said, annoyed. "A half ounce of hard!"

Danny's eyes widened.

"Listen, I'm out of town right now," John said. "Even if I was in town, I'm tapped out."

"Fuuuck! Come on, man! There's nothing you can do?"

"I'm afraid not," John said.

"You don't know anyone else holding?"

John thought for a couple of seconds. "Let me get back to you. Is this a number where I can reach you?"

"Yeah, it's my husband's cell."

We could hear the flint of her lighter as she lit up a cigarette.

"Okay," John said. "Give me about half an hour, and I'll get back to you."

"Oh, thank you, Shawn! Thank you!" Amy said.

"No trouble. Stay tuned." He hung up the phone.

John looked at us, and we all had a good laugh. I had no idea what 'hard' meant. Crack? Meth? I didn't want to ask. I didn't want to come off as naïve. We all went back to our regularly scheduled boredom.

After the call we were called out to the plant for a quick job, dropping off a load of piping in the laydown yard. We were out of the trailer for an hour. When we returned, John noticed that there was a message on his phone. He played it back over the speaker.

"Hey Shawn, it's Amy," rasped the voice on the other end of the phone. "Just wondering if you've had a chance to talk to your hookup yet. Call me back."

"Holy shit," John said. "What should we tell her?"

"Tell her to call me," Danny said. "I'll pretend I'm your friend, 'Tony."

John called the number back over the speaker. It only rang once before Amy picked up.

"Shawn," Amy wheezed on the other end, "Tell me you have something. I've called around, and everyone in town is dry."

"I can't do anything for you," John said. "But I can put you in touch with another guy I know. His name is Tony."

"Tony huh? He's a friend of yours?" Amy asked.

"I know the guy," John replied. "I wouldn't exactly call us friends, but seeing as the whole town is 'dry,' as you said, Tony will be your best option."

"Well, tell him to get a fucking move on!" Amy said—a wild twinge of desperation in her voice.

"I'll get him to call you if that's all right."

"Yeah, I mean, whatever you have to, man! Jesus!"

"Okay," John said as Amy hung up.

"I got this," Danny said. He went to the bathroom, poured himself a coffee, and looked at his watch. When ten minutes had passed, he called Amy back.

"Hello?"

"Hey, is this Amy?"

"Yeah. You're Tony?"

"You know it. I talked to Shawn. He said you're looking for some hard? How much are we talking here?"

"A half-ounce," Amy said.

"That's not a whole lot. It's a forty-five-minute drive into the city from where I live."

"Shit, man! Forty-five minutes? Where the hell are you coming from?"

"Best we don't get into specifics over the phone," Danny-Tony said. "You never know who's listening."

"Well, I think I can get enough together for three-quarters," Amy said. She sounded a little bit unsure.

"That's a little more worth my time, "Danny-Tony said. "But it sounds to me like you're talking money. That's not what I'm after."

There was a long pause on the other end.

"Well, what the fuck are you after?"

"Shawn didn't let you know? I guess it's been a while since he and I did business together. Long story short here, Amy, I have as much cash as I need right now. The last thing I want is your cash. If I have to drive all the way to where you are, I want to get laid. You get hard if you make me hard. You get what I'm saying?"

"Well, my husband is going to be here. I'm not fucking you!"

"It doesn't matter if you do it or he does it. I'm coming there with the hard and dumping my load. If it's in you or your husband, I don't care."

"Well, he isn't fucking you either!"

"Of course not. I'll be the one doing the fucking." Danny-Tony shot back.

"Like fuck you will!" Amy ranted. "Look, my sister's here too. Maybe she will fuck you. Otherwise you'll have to be okay with cash, and I don't think that she's going to go for it!"

"Amy! I think we're at a stalemate." Danny-Tony winked at us as we tried to stifle our laughter. "Anyway, you have my number. If you change your mind, let me know. I'm only an hour or so away."

"You know what, I don't need your shit anyway! Get FUCKED you creep!" Amy roared and hung up.

The whole room broke up as Danny ended the call. Leo looked at us from his sleepy corner at the back of the lunchroom.

"You guys are a bunch of mean fucks," Leo said before he put his head down and tried to sleep.

The rest of us returned to what we were doing before the call. I hunkered down into my book, John into his phone, and Danny, James, and Nathan into several games of Crib. An hour later, Danny's phone began to buzz on the table, waking us all from our nighttime daydreams. He sprang to life when he saw the number, exclaiming, "Guys! Guys! Guys!" before he flipped the phone open and answered it.

"All right," wheezed a defeated Amy on the other end. "I'll do it. I'll fuck you."

"Who is this?" Danny asked, plugging his nose to change his voice.

"Tony?" Amy asked.

"You don't sound like a Tony," Danny said.

"You're not Tony?" Amy asked.

"I'm afraid you got the wrong number, lady!"

She hung up without another word. We were all dying of laughter.

I have never been addicted to much other than cigarettes and coffee. I reflected on what must have been a lifetime of low moments that got someone like Amy to the point where she was willing to do something awful and humiliating to feed her addiction. What started as a seemingly spontaneous joke soured in my mind. What kind of desperate machinations had we set in motion with our reverse prank call? What if Amy's husband were a violent lout? Would he be furious over Amy's failure to secure him some drugs? If he was the kind of fella who was okay with his wife renting out her body for a fix, what else was he okay with? What we had done was cruel, but we were bored out of our minds. I felt a little better about the whole prank knowing that in any case, Amy wouldn't be getting drugs that could hurt or kill her.

I looked around the room. For a prank we had all found so funny moments before, there was a somber tone to the room now. Was everyone else feeling as dirty about this as I was?

I looked at the clock, suddenly wanting the night to be over so I could go back to camp and sleep. Two hours left. Shit. I poured a coffee and went for a smoke, thankful that my addictions to caffeine and nicotine weren't as bad as what Amy was hooked on.

Chapter 13

All Hail The Condiment King

My fourteen-day shift was over, and it was time to fly back home. Two weeks on, one week off. Guys were excited as we flooded towards the flight check-in building and queued up. At the front of the long line, we could see the security checkpoint.

The line was moving slowly but surely toward the x-ray station. We had our carry-on bags scanned and had the old metal detection wand waved around our bodies. The company was worried that we might be smuggling out tools and such, but that's not all they were looking for. No one was allowed to take home any of the items supplied to us while we were working on their property, even something as small as a ketchup packet.

I finally got to the front of the queue. More waiting awaited me: once I got scanned, I would sit in the waiting area for at least half an hour. Then we would all get loaded onto buses to go to the airport, a half-hour drive. At the airport, we would wait some more until we could finally get on a plane. Including boarding, takeoff, flying, landing, disembarkment, and luggage claim, another three hours would go by. And finally, the hour-long drive through city traffic to my apartment.

These were the joys of remote fly-in camp jobs. All this time was off the clock. We had stopped getting paid hours ago, so this travel was my donation to the corporation's bottom line.

A guy two people in front of me, short and dark-haired, was throwing his big overstuffed duffle bag on the scanner belt. He put his baseball cap, coat, and belt in a tray and stepped up to get wanded by the security guard. The lady waved him through without a problem.

His bag came through the conveyor belt on the other side of the station. He moved to get it, but the security guard grabbed it first. The worker was surprised, and he looked nervous. It seemed like he was starting to sweat.

With a funny glare, the guard took the duffle over to a side table and opened it.

For a few moments, I lost track of what was going on because it was my turn at the scanner. Backpack on the conveyor, coat off, belt off, cap off, and walk up to the metal detection area. Some coins in my pocket made the wand beep, and I pulled them out. The female security guard smiled and let me through. I moved to retrieve my backpack and other items.

As I went past the bag-searching table, I saw that the guard was pulling food out of the dark-haired guy's bag. A big stack of sandwiches, all wrapped in plastic. Maybe four bananas, some yogurt containers, a handful of ketchup packets, mustard packets, mayonnaise packets, and hot sauce packets. A little pile of granola bars. A few of those microwave burritos. Water bottles, a couple of little boxes of Rice Crispies.

"Please follow me, sir," The guard said as he led the condiment thief into another room in the back. Shit just got real. He would lose his job over this, guaranteed, and end up on the blacklist. No one up here would be able to hire him back for at least a year. I'd bet he'd miss his plane, too.

I walked to the back of the waiting area and saw Mark sitting against the wall. The joint was packed, but there was still a spot by him, so I headed over and sat down on the cheap plastic airport chair. It was attached to the whole line of them, which wobbled alarmingly as it accepted my fat arse with a groan. Everyone else on the line wobbled when I sat down.

"Sorry, sorry," I said to the guy next to me. He just shrugged and kept staring at Tic Toc videos on his phone.

"Hey, Mark. Did you see that sad excuse for a thief get busted up there?"

"Yeah, that guy must've had at least twelve sandwiches. I guess he was trying to sneak out enough food to last until he flew back up here," Mark said.

"They don't like it when you steal from the camp, do they?"

"Nope. They're really cracking down on stuff like that. But who would want those sandwiches anyway? Stale bread, low-quality meat, packaged three days ago. I'm just glad to get out of here and eat real food."

"Me too. But some people just can't help themselves. It's like a mental illness. I know this one guy. He's the condiment king. He didn't steal anything but condiments. Well, and toilet paper."

"Really?" Mark asked.

"Yeah. We were on this one job where you drive in and out in your own truck. He took ridiculous amounts of stuff. We were allowed to take two paper lunch bags of food each day from the lunch area in the camp kitchen for free. He always brought one with his sandwiches. The other one was loaded with little packets of ketchup, mustard, relish, and hot sauce. And mayonnaise."

"What? Why?"

"Well, it all started when he lost $60,000 on penny stocks. These guys were trading stock tips and buying cheap stocks online. But this guy started thinking if he got a line of credit on his house, he could make some serious cash. So he basically bet the farm and lost!"

"No way! Did he have a wife? What did she think of that?"

"I don't think he told her what happened. But he was worried about money. So he started trying to cut costs. He made his wife and kids squeeze all their mustard and ketchup out of those shitty little packets to save money."

"Yuck. I hate the mustard from those things. It's gone weird."

"Uh-huh. But only the best for this guy's family. They had to pay for his stock market gambling. Right? He took those little honey and jam packets and those little paper sacks of salt and pepper. And a big pile of those individually wrapped herbal teabags. He put them in this big cardboard box in the back seat of his truck, with some gas monitors on top to cover them up in case security looked in the back window."

"Crazy."

"Yeah, the honey and jam must've been squeezing out the bottom by the time he got that box home."

"You said he was taking shit paper too?"

"Yeah, he went to every bathroom and stole all those giant rolls of paper and had those in a big garbage bag. He got away with this for months."

"What happened? Did he get caught?"

"Of course. One day he was going through the security gate, and they did a spot check. You know, where they take everything out of your truck and put a drug dog in the cab? The guards found his condiment stash and confiscated it. And it got reported to the company, so they sent him packing."

"You mean he lost a job because he was smuggling asswipe? Wow. Time to re-evaluate your life choices."

I adjusted my ass in the stupid plastic bucket seat. The entire line of chairs wiggled too, and the stranger on my other side banged his head on the wall. "Sorry," I said. "These chairs are torture for big boys like me."

Mark grimaced and leaned forward. "They actually take it easy on us over here in North America, you know. I talked to one guy who worked in Zimbabwe. He grew up over there. Nice guy and a hard worker. He said they have a lot more rules over there, and if you don't follow them, you might go missing."

"No shit?"

"Yeah, they just toss you in a ditch or something. Everyone brings their own tools too, nothing supplied. You load up your toolbox, you bring it to work on the first day, and they weigh it to see how much you brought. And when you take it out, they check the records to see if it weighs the same or less. And if it doesn't weigh the same or less, they shoot you. He said he saw them execute a guy over a pipe wrench."

"Wow! Harsh. I bet some of these companies in Canada wish they could shoot us for stealing shit paper."

"Yeah, no doubt. And he said one day, he went to work, and everybody was rioting. They were crashing company trucks into the buildings, lighting stuff on fire. They were lighting the work vehicles on fire, the buildings, everything. So he went straight over to where his tools were, loaded them up, and got the fuck out of there."

"Wow, you're right. I've never seen anyone shot for stealing, and so far, the workers have never burned down one of these shitholes. We really have got it easy over here."

We still had a long wait ahead of us, and I was getting hungry. I couldn't help but look over at the stack of confiscated food. We had hours to go before we were back in Edmonton.

"You think those guards are gonna eat the sandwiches?"

Chapter 14

Why You Never Want Ants in Your Pants

A nts in your pants. It's one of those hidden perks of being an equipment operator that they never tell you about when they put you through orientation.

In 2013, I took a job at a company moving dirt. Since I had previously worked in a mill running loaders, that's where they put me. Mostly I used grapple forks to move around rig mats and a big bucket to move gravel and dirt. It was a busy job. We moved from place to place a lot.

My boss called me one afternoon. "Curtis, can you go to that job we did two weeks ago and help the trucker out? Cam's coming tomorrow to pick up the loader we left behind there and move it to the next spot, but he won't put it on the lowboy. You know how chickenshit he is about putting anything with rubber tires on the trailer. He's a good trucker, but he sure isn't good at loading the equipment."

There was a reason they didn't let Cam load the rubber-tired stuff anymore.

A couple of months before, he had been trying to get a backhoe on a trailer deck, and he forgot which control was which. Cam had it revved up too high and went off the edge of the trailer. The machine ended up lying door-side-down, with the engine running and Cam knocked out cold behind the wheel. He hit his head on the side window, and no one could get in until they broke the glass. Cam said it had nothing to do with the big joint he had smoked right before the incident, but I had my doubts.

I remembered where they left that loader that the boss wanted me to move. "What time do you need me there?" I asked.

"9:00. Then, after you get that job done, head back to your regular spot."

The next morning, I stopped at the gas station to pick up my usual snacks: A double-double coffee (two cream and two sugar), a bag of sunflower seeds, and a couple of cans of Pepsi. That was what got me through the day in the cab. Sunflower seeds and sugar were what I lived for, the perfect mix of salt and sweetness.

After getting in shit so many times for leaving sunflower seed husks in the equipment cabs, I got the message. No one liked being surrounded by someone else's disgusting seed husks. These days I spit them in a used coffee cup instead of onto the floor. But my foreman had yelled at me more than once for the empty snack containers and garbage I left behind in the cabs. What can I say? I was a bit of a messy slacker.

By the time I got to where we had left the loader, it was ten o'clock.

It was a much busier place than the last time I was there. A construction crew from a different company had moved in and started their work.

The loader was sitting beside several crew trucks and a couple of porta-potties. Everyone had stopped for coffee and was sitting in their trucks, about eight guys and gals.

Just then, Cam pulled in with his big truck and lowboy. He came to a halt in the middle of the open area, right in front of all those crew trucks, ready to unhook the trailer for loading.

Cam was quite the character. His big belly, combined with saggy jeans and tiny hips, meant his jeans were always trying to get down to his ankles. But somehow, those jeans never quite made it. It was some sort of wizardry that kept them hovering just above his privates.

His eating habits were a mess too. He was always chowing down on something that dropped crumbs all over him or dripped goop on his shirt. He was a stained, hairy mess. He often walked around with one pantleg in his rubber boot and one out.

I climbed up into the cab of the machine I was there to move.

With a big cloud of diesel fumes, I got the old loader fired up so the engine could get warm. As soon as I figured it would stay running without the engine stalling, I drove over and lined up on the ramp. Time to get this old girl on the deck.

I was starting up the ramp part of the trailer when I felt a funny pinch right around my balls. I wiggled a bit in the seat, assuming that my shorts had bunched up. The loader kept creeping onto the trailer.

There was a jab on my left leg, then two more on my right. What the hell? Something was very wrong here.

Those jabs were starting to sting and burn. There were more and more little pinches. I could feel motion down there. Something was crawling around in my ginch!

Make that hundreds of somethings.

All hell had broke loose in my pants. I couldn't figure out what the fuck was going on as I was dancing around on the seat.

I remembered how Cam had gone off the side of that trailer. *Don't fuck this up!* I had to hold her steady.

After some tense maneuvering that got the machine right up on the deck of the truck, I took her out of gear and put the brake on. I was living in hell. Whatever it was, it was in my pants and was stinging me all over the place. I was in some serious pain, dancing around like a crazy man in the cab. But I managed to drop the loader bucket down and shut the machine off.

I bailed out of that cab straight off the side of the deck and landed on the ground. I took my boots off. I was shaking as I dropped my drawers and kicked off the clothes. I took it all off.

I was covered in ants. I couldn't figure out how or why. They crawled right up my pant legs and got everywhere. Those ants were swarming all over my legs and belly. I stripped naked right there. Trust me, if this ever happens to you, you won't give a shit about proprieties either.

The ants were the half-black, half-red variety. Not that it matters when they swarm your junk.

Those guys were sitting in their trucks watching, but I didn't care at all as I ripped my clothes right off my body.

To me, it was horrifying. To everyone watching, it was hilarious. As I frantically brushed ants off my junk, I looked over at Cam. He was bent over with his hands on his knees, laughing his guts out.

He had tears in his eyes and drool coming out of his mouth from laughing so hard.

He wasn't the only one who was enjoying the show. A couple of pipeliners had come out of their trucks and were holding up their phones, filming the action. Everyone was laughing except me.

After I killed about a million ants, I put my underwear back on, grabbed my clothes, and fled the cameras to get covered up.

Later, I learned that the video was an instant online success. Cam got a copy of that video. He showed it to co-workers, who put it on the group chat that our crew used to communicate. My foreman thought it was extra funny, considering how he had told me to clean up the cabs.

I don't know how it got to him, but my brother got a copy of the video somehow. After that, even my girlfriend had a good laugh.

Isn't technology wonderful? It was a couple of weeks before I got the video taken down.

Eventually, I crawled back up on the trailer and into the cab to see what had gone wrong. Why in the world would ants be hanging out in the loader?

It turned out that I was the culprit.

Whoever ran this machine last (that would be me) had left a bottle of Pepsi tipped over on the floor in the cab. The cap had been loose, and the sweet contents must've dripped straight down through the floor where the machine was parked. Unfortunately, there was a huge anthill nearby. The ants crawled up the loader's undercarriage because they were after the Pepsi. The sunflower seeds and leftover sandwich were just a bonus. They had hit the jackpot, and the whole ant colony had mobilized to gather up the bounty.

I had left the cab a complete pigsty, and it came back to bite me in the ass.

Literally.

Chapter 15

You're Going the Wrong Way!

It's hard to look back and admit how dumb I was when I was 18. All I thought about was video games and girls. I didn't have a clue what to do with my life. When most of my friends went off to college I realized I had no plan, no goals.

I was a bit scatterbrained. My friends say nothing's changed, but it was a lot worse back then. I couldn't remember where I'd put my phone down most of the time and could barely keep track of what hour it was. If we made plans to meet up, I would probably forget.

I didn't have much ambition, but I needed to start making some cash and get on with my life. I asked around and filed out some applications. Even 7-11 wouldn't hire me. I spent weeks moping around my parent's house, wishing I could get a job, but not really doing much about it.

My family came to the rescue. When all else fails, use nepotism to get ahead. My first job was a construction job my uncle lined up for me. He stopped by to tell me about it on a Sunday evening.

"Be at the diner on Main Street at seven o'clock, and the guys will lead you to the work yard. Wear your steel-toed boots."

He also told me the name of the guy I was supposed to meet. I didn't write the name down, so of course, I forgot it in about 4.6 seconds. I had a job! That's all my tiny brain could process.

The next morning I got up early. I was going to be on time no matter what! I drove the old farm pickup downtown and parked it on the main street. I went into the diner and saw several tables full of guys eating breakfast. Which ones were the right bunch? I went to the first table. I thought one of them looked familiar.

"Hi, are you expecting a new guy? I'm supposed to follow you out to the yard."

They look at each other uncertainly. Then, a big balding guy holding a forkful of hash browns smiled and said, "Pull up a chair, have a coffee. We leave in ten minutes."

They introduced themselves as Curtis, James, Harold, and Mikey. I tried to remember who my uncle had told me to meet. I figured these might be the right guys. They said they were expecting someone, didn't they?

After they hoovered up breakfast into their mouths and took a coffee to go, we all traipsed out the door.

They jumped into their pickup trucks, a maroon Dodge and a black Chevy, and I jumped in my old beat-up Ford. I followed them out of town to this yard full of equipment. We all parked off to the side.

Curtis took me over to the foreman's truck. "We got a new guy here."

"Really? No one told me."

"He says his uncle lined it up. Who's your uncle again?"

I stepped up. "My uncle Jim told me to meet in the diner."

"Oh, Jimmy sent you. Ok, I got some papers for you to fill out. Curtis, get him a hard hat!"

I filled out some basic tax forms and the emergency contact info sheet. Someone handed me a hard hat with the name of the outfit on it. I noticed the company logo was different from the one on Uncle Jim's truck. XYZ Corp. Was I at the right place?

It didn't seem to matter. They put me to work. So I stopped worrying about it.

I helped load up trucks, swept out the shop, stacked new deliveries in shipping containers, and otherwise slaved away all day. Everywhere I looked, the company logo was prominently displayed, and it was the wrong one.

I never really paid attention to the name of the company that my Uncle worked for. But I knew this wasn't it. I had a job now, though.

I went back in to work the next day and just kept on going.

Uncle Jim called me after my third day at work.

"Hey! How's the job going? Did you have any trouble finding the guys that morning? I'm coming into the yard tomorrow to pick up some stuff. I'll see you there."

"Uh, no, you won't."

"Why? Did you quit?"

"No, You see, I screwed up and went to work for the wrong outfit."

When I explained what had happened to Uncle Jim, he started laughing and laughing until I thought he was gonna pass out from lack of oxygen. This wasn't the reaction I thought I'd get.

"You're working at XYZ! Hahahaha! That's our competition! Well, you might as well stay there for a while. You can always come over to my crew if it doesn't work out. But maybe you should start paying more attention to your surroundings! You don't want to try to pet a nice kitty and find out it's a skunk!"

So, I stayed at XYZ Corp. for a few weeks. I ended up getting assigned to the truck washing bays. All day long, I wore rubber boots and a rain suit so I wouldn't get completely soaked. Using the wash wand to get all the mud and grease off of the equipment was a hard job, and I didn't like it.

A grubby mechanic came out to yell at me. "Listen, you dumbass! You have to get ALL the grease off this stuff so I can work on it! It needs to be way cleaner when you're done. Stop slacking off!"

I did my best, but I hated that wash bay. There was no one to talk to all day, and it was wet and steamy in there.

One morning, it came to a merciful end.

I looked up when the door opened to see a guy wearing a white button-up office shirt and dress pants.

"Who the hell are you?" he asked.

"I'm Travis," I said uneasily.

"Well, I'm Jim, and I own this company. One of the foremen told me my nephew was down here washing trucks and doing a really shitty job. Since I don't have a nephew, I came to see who you were! Who are you, and why are you claiming to be my nephew?" He looked disgusted, annoyed, and mean.

"I can explain," I told him.

"You lied to get this job, asshole, so don't bother. Just leave."

Jim the company owner turned on his heel and left.

It was a big relief. I didn't want to stay in this hellhole a minute longer, anyway. I took off the rain suit and dropped it on the wash bay floor. Then I grabbed my lunch bag out of the break trailer and got out of there. What a happy moment, when you leave a job you hate.

I texted my Uncle Jim and asked him if that spot was still open.

The next morning I went back to the diner to meet some guys and follow them out to work. I walked past Curtis, James, Harold, and Mikey with a nod. They all smirked.

"Leaving for work in ten minutes," Curtis said. "Need a ride?" Mikey chuckled at the lame dig.

"No," I answered. "Thanks, though."

In the back corner were Uncle Jim and his buddies. No mistakes this time.

"You made it!" Uncle Jim stood up and welcomed me to the table. "Everyone, this is my nephew, Travis. He's coming over from the dark side at XYZ." Uncle Jim looked over his shoulder and said, "Right, Curtis?"

"You bet," Curtis said, smiling. "Good luck, Travis."

Everyone at Uncle Jim's table greeted me with smiles and nods. I took a seat, and one of them handed me a breakfast menu.

That was when I realized I forgot my lunch and my phone.

Chapter 16

I Needed to Go Back to Work to Recover From the Vacation in Hell

M y relationship was in trouble. That's what happens when you work away from home for most of the year. You aren't there to do the things a guy has to do.

I should have tried a little harder to keep my girlfriend happy, but I can't take all the blame. Vanessa didn't come to visit me. She expected me to listen to all of her problems when we talked on the phone, but none of my problems ever got any air time. She never once asked me how I was holding up living so far away. I didn't feel like we were on the same team.

But we had been a couple for two years and had some good times together. Vanessa kept me out of trouble. And the sex was great.

Lately, she had been distant and untalkative. I knew we couldn't go on like this. I wanted to make things better between us, but I didn't know how.

My best bud at work told me I should take Vanessa on a trip to get away from it all.

"You need to suck up and show her you care. Why not head down to Cancun for a week and spend some of that cash you've been banking? Get her some of that cheap Mexican jewelry, go on a few tours, and go bar hopping. It's a good way to see if you want to keep her around."

His advice sounded solid.

"Let's go to Cancun," I suggested the next time we were on the phone. "There are some good all-inclusive deals if we book ahead. Whaddya think?"

"I don't know. I'll have to get someone to cover for me at the salon."

"C'mon, it's now or never. I have to go to that shutdown next month, and then I'm stuck at Fort Mac till Christmas!"

"All right, but you're paying for everything."

I almost asked, "So what else is new?" Instead, I clamped my jaw shut and rolled with it.

I went online, double-checked schedules, and booked a trip. We were going to Mexico.

Our tickets were for separate locations on the plane. I couldn't get seats together because I booked so late. Across the aisle was the best I could do.

"But we won't be sitting together!" Vanessa said, upset.

"It'll be okay. We're right across from each other. Let's go with it. Whatever it takes to get to Cancun, right?"

"Okay, you're right," she said.

Two weeks later, we were at the airport in the security lineup.

As the line snaked forward, I saw everyone taking everything out of their pockets and putting change, wallets, and such in trays to send through the x-ray machine. I had a horrible thought.

The day before we left for the trip, I was over at my friend Jon's house target practicing. I always put a bunch of bullets in my jacket pocket instead of carrying around the whole box.

Had I gotten rid of all those extra .22 shells?

I searched in my pockets. A sinking feeling shot through my stomach as I felt a couple of live rounds in there.

"What's wrong?" Vanessa asked as I frantically looked around. Yes! A garbage can on the other side of the rope line. I quickly ducked under, pushed my way through the waiting people, and dumped the bullets. There was a lot of angry muttering from the other travelers as I shoved and jostled my way back to Vanessa. When I got back to her side, she looked at me with a frown and said, "What are you doing?"

"Nothing. Just needed a garbage can," I muttered. My face felt hot and red.

Then we hit the front of the line. Vanessa passed through easily as she placed her items in the trays like a pro.

It was my turn as I fumbled with my stuff. All I could think about was whether or not I had gunpowder residue on me. Could they actually tell? A crazy urge to blurt out, "I don't have a bomb!" seized me, and it was all I could do to lurch forward silently.

I put my wallet, my belt, and all the other junk in the tray. I shoved it forward to the security lady. She scanned my passport and waved me toward the metal detector. As I raised my arms and walked through the detector, it beeped loudly. The guard on the other side stepped forward with a wand and passed it over me, only to have it beep annoyingly. I could feel beads of sweat running down my back. I was in full-on panic mode now.

"What is that on your right side, sir?" He asked with deep suspicion. I reached down. Shit! My favorite folding knife was still clipped there. I pulled it up and said, "Oops!"

When I pulled out the knife, the guard had stepped back. All of the security personnel in the vicinity went on alert.

"I'm afraid I'll have to confiscate that, sir," the guard said with a steely expression on his face. "Please step over here." He was looking at me like a criminal.

Two of his guard buddies were waiting in the frisking area.

"But that's my favorite knife."

"I'm sorry, you should have left it at home. Please step over here."

As everyone else watched, My entire body was patted down as the guards looked for anything else suspicious.

"Have you used any illegal substances lately?" one guard asked with a serious look on his face. His left hand was on my back, and his right was on my side. It was unnerving.

"No," I said untruthfully.

After being thoroughly patted down by three large dudes, they let me go with a warning.

I bolted away from security. Vanessa was red-faced and upset.

"That was dumb," she fumed. "Who brings a knife to the airport? Now we barely have time to get to the plane. Hurry up!" She speed-walked away from me as I struggled to get my belt back through my pant loops and put my hoodie and cap back on.

We made it to the boarding gate and straight onto the plane. At least we didn't have to sit around waiting.

We boarded the plane, and everything seemed fine. I sat down all alone on my aisle spot. My seat row mates hadn't gotten on yet. Vanessa's seat was right across the aisle from me.

We looked into each other's eyes and smiled. We were officially on vacation. I congratulated myself for being such a stud.

A middle-aged couple came down the aisle toward us. "Can you let us in, please?" The guy gestured to the seat beside me. I caught a whiff of something stale and unwashed as I jumped up and let them get settled.

When I sat down beside the lady, who took the middle seat, all I could smell was yuck. It was the worst body odor I had ever experienced, like a dirty gym sock left in an ogre's armpit, then sautéed in a pipefitter's gloves.

Why did this couple reek so bad? Their clothes appeared clean. He was clean-shaven, and she had on makeup.

They looked totally normal, but they smelled like homeless people.

Everyone else boarded and sat down.

I stopped breathing through my nose. It was only a five-and-a-half-hour flight. I could do this. Whatever it takes to get to Cancun.

Vanessa held my hand as we taxied down the runway, accelerated, and took off. We grinned at each other. These Canadians were headed to Mexico! Soon the plane leveled out, and Vanessa let go of the death grip she had on my hand. I could see how relieved she was that, so far, we hadn't died in a dazzling ball of flame on the ground.

The odor seemed like it was starting to fade. It's okay, I thought. I'm getting used to it.

Then the man took off his jacket and opened the gates of smell.

He undid the zipper and wiggled around to get his arms out of his sleeves. As he slipped off his top layer, new waves of stench rolled over me. My brain was shutting down. My eyes watered. It was hard to believe that anything could be so bad.

He chatted with his wife. They were both happy-go-lucky and relaxed.

It was unfair that anyone who stank so bad could be that happy while I hunkered down and suffered.

I looked over at Vanessa. I could tell she was suffering from the smell, too, although she wasn't so close to it. She reached up and turned the air on, blowing it right down at her face.

I quickly did the same. It helped a tiny amount. But every time the couple moved around, a fresh batch of stinky particles seemed to shoot off of them. Even a steady stream of air blowing in my face wasn't cutting it.

I looked over at the stench culprits. I couldn't figure it out. What was the deal?

Were they on the run from spies and had to sleep in a dumpster to evade capture? Or maybe they were allergic to water?

The man noticed me looking his way and smiled at me, the unconcerned smile of a social simpleton. Just a friendly, smelly, inconsiderate beast.

There was no escape. Just when I thought things couldn't get any worse, the couple brought out the cheese. A fancy one, the kind that doesn't smell good.

This can't be happening!

But it was.

How can you bring stinky cheese on a plane? Isn't there a law?

They laughed and enjoyed the shit out of their snack, joking and bantering. I sunk further into a tortured state of doom.

I leaned over to Vanessa. "Forget Snakes on a Plane," I whispered. "I feel like I'm in a movie about homeless people with cheese on a plane."

She laughed quietly and then coughed as she breathed in cheese fumes.

I turned my head away and pretended to sleep. This, too, shall pass.

It seemed like days, but it was only a few hours later. The plane started descending into paradise. I was that guy who stood up in the aisle immediately. The air was a little better up higher. Then, we were moving toward the door, and I was finally free!

I sprinted away from that rude-smelling dude into the airport, almost leaving Vanessa in the dust. We queued up to get through customs. I noticed the smells of normal people and normal things. I was relieved. Customs never smelled so good. The whole flight, I had been worried that the stench would burn my sense of smell right out and ruin my trip.

We stepped out of the airport into the hot sun.

Vanessa sniffed loudly. "It's hot out here. Take off that stupid hoodie. It smells now anyway."

I did so. She grabbed it out of my hands and walked over to the garbage can. "This thing is contaminated," she said as she tossed it in.

First, I lost my favorite knife, and now my favorite hoodie. I was starting to get a bad feeling about this trip.

We got a cab to the resort and checked in. The weather was perfect. We spent a bunch of time at the pool and at the bar, soaking up the sun and the tequila.

We decided to go into town and see the sights. A cab ride got us down to the marina, where all the restaurants and shops were located.

Vanessa went into one of the many gift shops. I waited outside and looked across the water. It was a gorgeous day, and tourists on jetskis zipped across the water.

A scruffy-looking Mexican guy covered in tattoos sauntered over. "Hey, man, you want something to smoke?"

" You bet I do!" I answered.

He sold me a little bit of weed for what seemed like a lot of money. But I figured, what the hell.

I didn't mention the transaction to Vanessa when she came back out with a big smile on her face, carrying a bag. We walked down the block.

Ahead there were a couple of Mexican police officers, complete with bulletproof vests and shotguns. They stepped in front of me.

"Excuse me, sir," One of them asked loudly. "Do you have any illegal substances in your possession?" He held his shotgun with both hands like he was ready to use it.

"Uh, no?" I said weakly.

"Don't be ridiculous!" Vanessa snapped. "Tell them you don't have anything!"

"I'm sorry, miss, but we witnessed your husband taking a suspicious package," the other officer said with a big grin. "But no se preocupe, por favor. If he pays the fine and hands it over, we will let you go. But, it's up to you," he told me. "We can go to the station and file some forms."

Vanessa turned to me with an exasperated look. "What did you do?"

"I just tried to buy us a little fun for back at the resort," I said.

"Well, how much fun are you having now?" she asked.

She had me there.

I turned back to the cop. "Officer, how much is the fine?"

"Five hundred American dollars," he told me.

I got out my wallet and gave him five hundred dollars. Then I turned to go.

"Hey, wait a minute. Aren't you forgetting something?" The police officer still had his hand out. I got the baggy out and put it in his hand.

"Gracias, Senor," he said. "Have a nice day!"

As Vanessa gave me shit for being such a dumbass, I watched the cops walk down the street to the guy who sold me the drugs. They laughed and handed him back the weed to sell to the next sucker.

To make it up to Vanessa, I decided to take her on a tour of the countryside. I knew she wanted to see Tulum and Playa del Carmen, so I mentioned renting a car and going south. Vanessa was all for it.

The guy at the car rental company insisted on selling me the premium insurance package.

"Senor, we suggest to you the deluxe insurance. It covers anything that could happen to you. You want to make sure you are safe."

"Okay," I said. "How much more is the insurance?"

"It's two hundred dollars," he said with a smile. "Here is the brochure so you can read about all the things that are covered. But trust me! It covers anything that can happen in Mexico."

I paid for the insurance. But I never read the brochure.

The road trip was a blast. We rented a room down the coast so we wouldn't have to drive back that first night. Everything went so well.

It made me remember the other times I had spent with Vanessa. We were good together. I was happy.

The next day we got up extra late. I always sleep in when I'm hung over. Too many margaritas!

It was pouring rain and miserable. After we checked out of the room, we wandered about for a few hours. We planned to get back to Cancun that evening. We headed back a little late in the day.

Halfway back to Cancun, Vanessa told me she needed a bathroom break really badly. We were on a highway that only had the occasional run-down old shack bordering it. It was still raining cats and dogs. I drove for a while, and we saw nothing that could help her out of her misery.

"I'll pull over, and you can just take care of business here," I suggested. "At work, we call that a tailgate meeting."

"No way! Someone will see me," she said. "Don't you know it's illegal to go to the bathroom in public in Mexico?"

"I won't tell anyone," I said. She didn't believe me.

She was desperate, but she just stared at me in disgust when I offered her a plastic shopping bag as a makeshift in-car solution. I started looking for an exit that might lead to el bano. Unfortunately, we really were in the middle of Mexican Buttfuck Nowhere, and it was getting dark.

Ahead of me, I saw a car turn off the road towards some lights.

"Maybe those lights are a town," I said. I turned and followed the car.

Shortly, the pavement ended, and the road turned to muddy dirt. This wasn't good, and alarm bells went off in my head. Unfortunately, I'm terrible at listening to alarm bells.

"Stop, don't go down here!" Vanessa urged.

But there was no room to turn around, so I had to keep going. "I'm gonna find you that bathroom."

The car in front of us splashed through the biggest puddle I had ever seen. It kept on motoring right through and disappeared around a corner. I went after it.

The rental car made it to the middle when a wheel got stuck, and it started spinning. I looked out at the water, which was pretty high and rising. I gave it more gas, and we listed to the side a bit as the wheels spun. The car sank down in the front as we slipped off the high part of the road. The water had risen up past the bottom of the door, and it started seeping into the car.

We were stuck. Then the engine quit. I struggled to get it started again. No dice.

"We have to get out of the car!" I told Vanessa. I pushed open my door. She screamed when the cold water splashed into the car and onto her feet. She scrambled towards my side, and I pulled on her arm. We splashed out into the puddle, which was rapidly turning into a river.

As she left the car, her phone fell out of her hand straight into the drink.

"My phone!" she wailed.

"Forget it! We have to get to the bank!" I grabbed her hand and pulled her toward the edge.

We slipped and splashed toward safety.

Soaked and muddy, we followed the road. Soon we came to a small house with a car in front. I knocked on the door. A moment later, a Mexican lady opened it.

She didn't speak any English. Then a male teenager who knew some English came to the door. I told him what had happened, and the two of them had a quick conference in Spanish. They laughed and Spanished some more. I'm sure they said something like, "Stupid tourists." Then they let us in. The woman vanished for a moment and came back with a blanket. Vanessa was shivering so badly she couldn't talk.

The boy asked me where I rented the car, then pulled out his cell phone and made a call for a tow truck.

Vanessa finally got to use the bathroom. The woman brought us cups of hot tea.

In a while, a truck showed up in their yard to give us a ride and retrieve the car.

I thanked the family and tried to give them some cash, but they wouldn't accept it. They even made Vanessa keep the blanket since she was still shivering.

The tow truck driver didn't speak any English, but that didn't stop him from communicating with hand gestures and good-natured laughs. After he dragged the car out of the water, he jumped back in the truck where we were keeping dry. He pointed at a sign on the edge of the road that we hadn't noticed.

"Cuidado con el caimán!" He said with a laugh.

"What does it mean?" Vanessa asked.

"Alligators! Watch out!" he yelled. He put his forearms together like a pair of scissors and clapped his hands shut with a slap. Alligator! Hahaha!" Then he started driving.

"Vanessa clutched at my jacket, eyes wide with fear. "We could have been eaten! You almost got us killed!"

"I'm sorry, babe. I didn't know," I said. "But look on the bright side. You always said you wanted to meet the locals, right? And you got this authentic Mexican blanket."

The next day I went to the car rental place to find out how much this adventure was going to cost me. I hoped that the deluxe insurance I had paid for would cover the damages.

"I'm sorry, senor," the man behind the counter told me. "You were not insured for rising water. We will have to charge you replacement value for the car."

"What?" I asked in shock. "You told me the insurance would cover anything that could happen in Mexico."

He got out the insurance brochure. "You didn't want to read this. It says right here that water damage isn't insured."

I was getting angry. "You said, ANYTHING that could happen in Mexico! Don't you have water in Mexico?"

There was no way around it. I now owed them for a five-year-old Toyota Corolla that had water damage and wouldn't start. I went out to their back lot to look at it with them.

It was never going to run again.

"All right," I said. " How much?"

"Twenty thousand dollars," He said with a grin. "But do not worry. We already put it on your credit card."

I went back to the resort in a bad mood. For the rest of the day, I drank too many beers and tequila shots, trying to drown my sorrows in all-inclusive drinks.

Vanessa and I weren't getting along very well the next day when we packed up the room. I was sulking about the twenty grand. She was sulking about her phone and the alligator.

"Don't forget to clean everything out of the safe and grab my passport too, please," she said from the bathroom as she did her makeup and packed her essential items.

"Okay," I said. I opened the safe and swept everything out of it into my carry-on bag. I was so hungover I was barely functional.

We took the shuttle to the airport. When we got to the counter to check our bags, Vanessa asked me for her passport. I looked in my carry-on and realized I hadn't packed them. Fuck!

This time she lost her temper. I have never seen anyone so angry.

"You are such an idiot! I asked you to bring my passport, and you couldn't even do that right! What else should I expect after you nearly got us killed yesterday? I wish I had never gone on this trip with you, loser!"

Everyone else at the airport was staring. The lady behind the counter was embarrassed. I wanted to crawl away and die.

After screaming at me and stomping off, she phoned the resort and got them to go check the safe. The passports were there, and the staff sent them to us in another cab. There would be exactly enough time to get them before boarding.

"How much money do you have?" she snapped at me. I got out my wallet and opened it. There were three hundred American dollars and about a thousand pesos. She grabbed it all and went to stand outside to wait for the cabbie. When the guy arrived, he got the best tip of his life.

She came back inside and shoved my passport at me, then stomped over to the counter to get processed. I followed with my tail between my legs.

We made it back to Canada with no further incident.

We barely said goodbye to each other when we went our separate ways at the airport. I thought about how much this trip set me back.

The resort and flights, $3,200. A vintage Buck folding knife, $80. Fine for illegal weed, $500. Buying girlfriend a new phone, $400. Replacement value of the car, $20,000.

This vacation from hell had cost me a fortune.

But on the other hand, I had decided that Vanessa and I were done. I couldn't keep going out with someone who never had my back and would treat me like that.

I called Vanessa's number. There was no answer. So I left a message.

"It's over. Have a nice life."

There was one more thing to take care of. I dialed the number on the back of my credit card.

"Customer service, how can I help you?"

"Hi, I was a victim of credit card fraud in Mexico. I need to reverse the charges."

" Certainly, sir. What was the amount?"

"Twenty thousand dollars."

Chapter 17

Things Always Get Weird When I Go to Strip Clubs

'The Titty Bar.' 'The Knocker Locker.' 'The Rippers.' 'The Peelers.' 'The Ballet.' There are so many names for strip clubs. I don't know how I feel about strip clubs. I don't go out of my way to visit them, but every so often, I have found my way into one. Usually when I have gone, it has been with a group of other dirty construction workers, and almost always after everyone had too many drinks and wanted to crank a dull party to eleven.

The first time I visited one was in Dawson Creek, British Columbia, with a bunch of forty-something-year-old guys I was working with. I might have been nineteen or twenty years old. It was January of 1998, and we had been snowed and frozen out of the site we were working at, and with the weather forecast showing several days of extreme cold, we all got bored and went to the strippers. The older guys I was with didn't want to sit on 'Pervert Row' – the seating area around the perimeter of the stage - and opted instead for a table at the back of the smoky bar. I wore glasses at the time, which had broken in a bizarre Ford Aerostar mobile wrestling ring accident during a night out with friends. I couldn't yet afford a new pair, so my first titty bar experience consisted of overpriced drinks, music I wasn't into, and the blurry forms of nekkid ladies cavorting on a stage in the distance. I immediately felt like a pervert.

I left the strip club that night, and the experience left little impression. We did all the same things I'd done at regular bars. We drank beer and had wild conversations. The only differences were that the music was louder, the drinks were way more expensive, and there were faraway boobies.

The thought of going again did not cross my mind after that. There was this new commodity back then called 'The Internet.' The forty-somethings I was hanging with didn't know what it was, but I knew that you could see naked ladies there whenever you wanted, and you didn't have to show your face to the world while you were peeping.

It wasn't until my first year of trade school a year later that I revisited a strip club. A group of people from our class went to the nearest nudie bar after our mid-term exams.

"It's a tradition," I was told.

I thought that was odd, as we were all at school for the first time, but I went anyway, not wanting to seem like a prude. This time, I had glasses but didn't need them. The twenty-somethings that made up my first-year class had no scruples about sitting as close to the stage as possible. Again, the drinks were expensive, and the music was lousy.

One of the guys from my class, Jeremy, was way too into the experience. His eyes exhibited his rabid fascination as soon as we entered the place. I watched in amazement as he shoveled money generously at the first two dancers. In Canada, dollar bills were retired in 1987 and replaced with brass-colored coins with a picture of a loon on them. A loon is just a fancy duck. We Canucks affectionately know these coins as 'loonies.' The strip clubs in Alberta are known for their coin toss games. Testosterone-crazed spectators take turns tossing 'loonies' at rolled-up posters of the dancer onstage. A dancer would balance the rolled-up poster on her asshole, squeeze it between her breasts, or grip it with her labia, while 'gentlemen' would try and knock the poster off by throwing a loonie at it. Jeremy was a crack shot. He won a poster on his second try.

The second dancer wore high, tight leather boots that laced up the front. Jeremy waved a fifty-dollar bill at her, which immediately caught her attention. She tried to grab it, but he pulled it away before she could get it. "Nuh-uhh!" he said, shaking his head at her. "You're going to have to go the extra mile for this. You're going to have to show me your toes!"

"My tits?" she asked.

"No. I'll see those later. I want to see your toes."

"Are you fucking serious?"

"Serious," Jeremy replied. "I just have to see them wiggle them for me."

"Fuck you!" the stripper shot back. "You know how hard it is to take these things off?"

Jeremy waved the fifty-dollar bill back and forth like a lighter at a Pearl Jam concert. The stripper rolled her eyes, then finally relented. She unlaced her boots – the whole process taking several awkward minutes while a couple of bouncers watched nervously from the back of the stage. Once her boots were off, she wiggled her toes for Jeremy, and he handed her the money.

"Do you like women's feet that much?" one of the guys asked Jeremy.

"No," Jeremy replied. "I just like knowing I've inconvenienced her."

The barefooted dancer completed her round onstage, and the music dropped to a low level. The bootless dancer was now picking up the coins that littered the stage. She walked the perimeter of the stage. Now partially clothed but still shoeless, she used a saucer-sized industrial-strength magnet fixed to an extendable pole to snap the coins up. It reminded me of the guys at the beach who comb through the sand with metal detectors.

By the third dancer, most of the class had trickled out. All that was left of the group was me and another guy, Paul, who had been my ride there. The thought of walking six blocks through a light-industrial park with no sidewalks in an Edmonton February was not top of my list of things to do that day, so I stayed with Paul for one more dancer.

The next lady that danced was a master of her craft. She was extremely fit and muscled in a way that was sexy as hell. She had steely blue eyes and jet-black hair. All her moves were expertly timed to punch with every beat of her chosen songs – all eighties stuff. As each song finished, she would stalk the perimeter of 'pervert row' like a panther, using her stark blue eyes and graceful moves to entice any nearby man. There weren't many to choose from, so she fixed her gaze on Paul.

He was happy to have her attention.

For two songs, I watched as she locked eyes and gyrated just for him. She was flat-out seducing him with her eyes and body. It worked like magic. Paul's wallet opened up, and twenty-dollar bills flowed out. She spent more and more time at Paul's beck and call, and he had given her more than two hundred dollars. I went to square up my tab, wanting to leave.

When I glanced back at Paul, the dancer was now squatting right in front of where he was sitting, her legs spread and her long fingers parting her lady bits for his viewing pleasure.

Paul wasn't interested.

He was locked in on her eyes, a zombified look of awe - paralyzing his face into a stupid, slack-jawed gaze. I paid my tab and went to get him. He'd run out of twenties and was begging her for her phone number, which she was not about to give him.

I had to pull him out of there, mostly because I was sick of the place and wanted to get home.

"Come on, man!" Paul begged. "We can't leave now! She's totally into me!"

She had sunk her well-manicured talons in his heart, and I marveled at both the skill she exhibited and my friend's foolish belief that out of all the pervs she'd seen in her profession, some pipefitter apprentice with too much gel in his hair would be the man she'd always been dreaming of. I pulled him through the bar and out the door.

"Dude, let me back in!" Paul protested as the gray light of an Edmonton afternoon hit us. "She was totally into me!"

"Sure she was, Romeo," I said.

"We have to go back!" Paul was delusional.

"You're out of twenties, and she was leaving the stage," I told him. "You'd have to fight the bouncers to get to her. You're a nineteen-year-old guy with about a hundred and forty pounds on your frame. You're never going to win that fight."

"I'll drive you back, buddy," Paul said, and he finally got me back to my car.

It seemed surreal the more I thought about it. I had been smitten before, but I don't remember all reason leaving me as quickly as Paul's had. I had never seen anything like it. That dancer had confidence in her skills that was so powerful and purposeful. The whole scene reminded me what simple creatures we men are when our base instincts start running the software. If she had zoned in on me instead of Paul, would I have turned mush like Paul? I liked to think I wouldn't have, but I didn't want to test it out. I made a pact with myself to stay away from those places.

It was a pact that I was quick to break.

Shortly after finishing my second year of Trade School, I got a job working on a small expansion at a pumping station north of Fort McMurray as a welder's helper. I had opted to leave my car at home and was catching rides to work with my foreman, Hugh. We would bomb our way north on Highway sixty-three in his little white '89 Tercel that would fart out some smoke occasionally. It wasn't the most reliable vehicle, but it did the job.

By September, the upcoming prospect of working outside in the winter made me not want to be there anymore.

My attitude started to slide right into the shitter.

I started going to the bars with the guys, coming to work every other day hungover as all hell.

My conscience had taken a vacation.

The last day of every ten-day stint fell on a Wednesday. We worked an extra half-hour every day of the shift to get out at noon on our travel day.

As usual, I had traveled up with Hugh, but at some point that week, he had been driving around town in his rickety Tercel, and the alternator gave out on him. Hugh had the car towed into the shop on the Tuesday night before our last day, and he and I got a lift from the job site to town from one of the other foremen.

Hugh had him drop us off at a mechanics shop on Franklin Avenue at the mechanic shop. The mechanic took us into the garage and showed us the progress. It was close to being done, but it still needed some time. The mechanic snapped a mounting bolt while pulling the old alternator off.

"Come back in two hours," the Mechanic said. "I'll have it done by then."

On foot, we set off on the mean streets of Fort McMurray at one o'clock on a Wednesday. "I'll buy you lunch," Hugh said, and we popped into the Plaza 2 mall and hit up the diner in that dingy building for some mid-day comfort food. I crushed a pretty decent plate of fish'n'chips.

We managed to kill forty-five minutes over lunch. We hit the pavement again and made it a few blocks before Hugh started getting thirsty.

"Let's go get a beer," Hugh suggested.

"Sure," I said. "Where do you want to go?"

"Let's try the Oil Can."

I knew The Oil Can was a legendary Fort McMurray stripper shit-hole.

"That's a strip club," I said.

"Yeah," Hugh said. "My wife doesn't like it when I go to them, but I don't see her anywhere."

"It's two in the afternoon," I said, remembering my pact with myself.

"You want to walk home?" Hugh joked. "Come on, you pussy!"

I deflated a bit but went along with it. Hugh seemed to have his heart set on it. I knew it was ultimately because I was weak-willed and easily led.

We passed two other bars that served beer on the walk there.

We walked to the Oil Can in relative silence, and I steeled myself for another weird experience. As we got closer, I could sense Hugh's nervous energy as he fidgeted with the coins in his pockets and checked his watch too frequently. He had become weirdly quiet. He was likely stepping way outside his comfort zone, probably breaking a significant rule of his wife's. The approaching reality of setting foot in one of those forbidden places had given Hugh a last-minute attack of conscience.

"Your wife keeps you on a short leash, huh?" I poked.

"Huh?" Hugh asked. His attention was elsewhere.

"Your wife," I repeated. "She's got you by the short and curlies?"

"Oh, fuck off!"

This was his suggestion in the first place. I wasn't about to let him back out now.

We were standing under the piss-yellow awning sign that led to condemnation. I swung the door open with gusto and ushered Hugh inside. Age before beauty, as they say.

We entered the bar. There was soft music playing, and as we came in. As soon as our feet touched the musty red carpet, the music kicked on, pumping Chumbawamba's 'Tubthumping' with punchy bass-heavy gusto.

My eyes adjusted to the light as we walked in. I could see a man working behind the bar - probably pulling double duty as the bouncer - and a waitress. They both sprung to life as we walked in. The show's star was onstage, a tall blonde goddess in her early twenties. As the music got louder, she grabbed the brass pole in the middle of the stage and twirled around it with great skill.

Hugh stopped in his tracks, looking around the room. We were the only customers in the place.

"Where do you think we should sit?" he asked. His eyes were nervously darting around the empty room. Did Hugh actually think there would be more people in a strip club at noon on a Wednesday?

"She knows we're looking," I said. "Might as well sit up front." I chose a seat along the edge of the stage, right in the center. Hugh nervously sat beside me.

"I've never sat this close before," Hugh whispered.

He was twisting in his chair nervously as the first dance started. He might have been acting nervous, but the shit-eating grin on his face told me everything I needed to know.

We ordered a couple of beers and watched the show, applauding the hot blonde dancer as she performed several gravity-defying moves on the pole for her first song, 'Money For Nothing.'

"I love Dire Straits," Hugh said.

"Uh-huh," I said, transfixed. I didn't want to admit it, but something grabbed me. I was in. I wished I was as calm and wise as Hugh, but my lizard brain was not responding. There would have to be an explosion to make me look anywhere else.

As the song faded, the dancer, still mostly clothed then, sashayed over to where we were sitting. "You boys like what you're seeing?" she asked. She smiled brightly at the two of us. I genuinely felt that she was happy we were there.

I had become Paul.

Hugh gave her an awkward smile. I gave her a thumbs-up like a fucking idiot.

She returned to the center of the stage for the next song, 'She Sells Sanctuary.' Hugh ordered more beers. Hugh handed the waitress a twenty for a roll of loonies. I knew what that meant. We were going to be tossing loonies. Hugh wanted to win a poster.

Not wanting to be a cheap fuck, I got some loonies too.

Mid-way through the song, our dancer, sweaty and glowing, made her way back to where we were still gawking like a pair of perverted mouth breathers. Her hands were at her breasts, cupping her bikini top with her long fingers as she squatted down, spreading her legs suggestively. Hugh and I were hypnotized.

"It doesn't look like those beers are doing much for your thirst," she purred. "Looks like you could use a little milk!" With that, she unleashed her magnificently augmented boobies, giving them a good shake for us at close range, then she returned to the stage, finishing the song topless. I was suddenly impressed by the sheer athleticism it took to do that job.

The final song began. 'In the Air Tonight.'

She did another sexy squat in front of us and teased us with the prospect of exposing the Full Monty. Hugh reached into his pockets, pulled out a five-dollar bill, and laid it on the stage. She pulled one string loose on her bikini bottom before looking at me suggestively.

I knew what she wanted me to do.

I dug some change out of my pocket and placed it on the stage. She smiled at me and pulled the string on her left side, her right hand holding the fabric flat against her hot zone. She sat back on the stage with smooth grace, keeping her legs spread, and removed the material. The big reveal! She grabbed a rolled-up poster, held it in the shape of a funnel in front of her vagina, and invited us to throw coins into it.

Hugh unrolled his loonies, and we threw a few each before Hugh hit the bullseye, winning the game. She handed him the rolled-up treasure.

She then turned around, pushed her ass up, and shook her booty for us. She took another rolled-up poster and clenched it in her butt cheeks. Hugh and I resumed the coin toss. After only two throws, my aim was true, and the poster spun wildly out of her bum and onto the stage. She sat back up and handed me the poster.

We still had coins left, and she took a plastic restaurant glass and some keychains from her stack of prizes. She propped the glass up in front of her cooch, angling it towards us, and we tossed more coins, trying to land one in the glass. This game seemed harder, but I got a couple of them in. Hugh missed five of them before he took some reading glasses out of his jacket pocket and fumbled them onto his middle-aged face. His next two were bullseyes. When we had thrown our last coins, the dancer sat in a more modest pose and engaged us in conversation.

"So, where are you guys from?"

"Okotoks," Hugh said.

"Calgary," I told her.

"Some southern guys, huh? We don't see too many of you in here. Most everyone is from the East Coast."

"I'm from Antigonish, Nova Scotia originally," Hugh said. "I'm learning the fiddle and everything."

"No way!" She said. "My dad played the accordion!"

"Nice!" said Hugh. "Does he still play?"

"He died when I was twelve," she replied, shoulders slumping.

Fuck, I thought. *This went south fast.*

I held up my beer in a toast. "Here's to the music!" I said, trying to take the conversation out of the mausoleum.

"Hear here!" Hugh said.

"Cheers, guys," our dancing queen said before getting up and retrieving her discarded bikini. She retreated to the back of the stage where her bag was stashed and pulled out her magnet on an extendable pole, using it to pick up the coins we threw from the stage floor.

"Huh. That's neat," Hugh observed, sipping his beer, "It's good that she doesn't have to crawl around and pick them up."

"I guess you haven't been to one of these places since they got rid of dollar bills, huh?" I joked.

"Yeah," admitted Hugh. "I've been on a short leash since the eighties."

After picking up the coins, the dancer withdrew behind the stage curtain. Show over.

Hugh and I finished up our beers, and he picked up the tab. "Well," Hugh said as he stood up, "We'd better get back to the garage. The car should be done by now."

I downed my beer too.

Hugh and I headed out the door, squinting as our eyes adjusted to the light. We headed toward the garage, stripper posters in hand. Hugh unrolled his. It was a heavily airbrushed picture of the early afternoon entertainer we'd just seen. She was wearing a different bikini and posing on the hood of a hot-pink Plymouth Barracuda. Hugh nodded in approval as we stopped at the first intersection, waiting for the light to change.

That was when I heard a pair of heeled shoes behind me and turned to see who it was behind us. Wouldn't you know, it was the dancer we'd just seen. She was dressed in civilian clothes. She lit up a cigarette, and I saw her eyes dart over to Hugh, who was oblivious. I felt awkward and thought I would deal with the unexpected encounter by being casual and friendly.

"So, how's it going?" I asked her.

"Better now. I didn't think I was going to make any money this afternoon. Then you guys showed up."

"Glad to have been of service," I said.

"I haven't been at this for very long," she admitted. "They put the new ladies on in the afternoons to test our mettle. I still have to earn my stripes, I guess."

"Sounds a bit like what I do," I said.

She laughed. "I doubt that."

"I'll catch you later," I said.

I turned my attention back to Hugh, nudging him to cross the street when the light changed. He put the poster away. The dancer waited to cross to the other side of the road and walked in the same direction we were traveling, all the way along Franklin Avenue to the mechanic's shop. She walked into the garage just ahead of us and held the door for Hugh as we walked in. It turned out that her car was in the shop too.

I watched her dig all the loonies we had just tossed at her from her purse. She handed them over as payment, along with a heap of five-dollar bills.

That was my last day at that job. I found another one closer to home before the winter came. It was the last time I visited the strip club too. I decided to restart my old pact with myself and stay the hell away from those places. It always got weird when I went, and I can't figure out why anyone would still go to them these days. The drinks are too expensive, and since everyone is carrying around a phone these days, we all have limitless access to any smut a person can think of. I sometimes wonder how they've managed to stay in business.

Okay, maybe I've been back once or twice since.

Chapter 18

Welder's Helper Blues

If there's one thing everyone knows, it's that welders are a cantankerous bunch. They always have to do things their way, and they will take every opportunity to cut a corner. I mean, sure, Hashtag, Not All Welders. But in general, welders are a pain in the ass.

I think it's learned behavior. They saw welders acting that way when they were apprentices, and it infected them like a bad virus. If that weld isn't sliding together like an effortless, fun ride? Welders might scream at their helper, throw their stinger, or toss a grinder. But even when things are going well, they bitch about everything under the sun and complain that they aren't getting enough jump hours. Meanwhile, everyone around them has to deal with their bullshit. But for less pay, and usually, NO jump hours. (For you non-oilfield workers, a jump hour is an hour that you get paid for even though you didn't work it.) Welders can be prima donna pains in the butt.

As part of my karmic debt, I was a welder's helper for a guy named Brant. Apparently, I had done terrible, no-good, ugly-bad things in a previous life. To pay off my sins, I had to endure Brant and his daily abusive rants.

Brant was always in a bad mood. It might have been because he was going through a divorce. Or maybe he was just a dick.

To be fair, the working conditions were terrible. We were putting together forty-eight-inch diameter pipes in some pretty muddy ditches. The mud got on everything, and at some point every day, Brant had to stand in it or lie down in it to get the welding done. Mud got on the tools and packed the wheel rims full too. This would get Brant so wound up that I thought he was going to have an aneurysm.

All I knew was he was a nasty guy to work for. I was just gonna tough out this one gig and then move on.

The job had two client inspectors in charge of welding, Ian and James. Everyone called them The Cutout Brothers because they loved to watch a crew work all day and then reject welds and have guys cut them back out.

A cutout is what happens when a welded pipe joint has to be removed because it either isn't high enough quality or it's no longer needed. The welders work for hours to finish the weld, and then they have to cut all of that hard work out and throw it away.

James was no-nonsense and stern, but Ian would call a cutout with a big grin on his face. He would make a snipping gesture with invisible scissors and say, "Looks like that one's a cutout!"

Every time this happened, morale went right into the shitter. But no one took it as hard as Brant, and guess what? Bad moods roll downhill. He'd take it out on me.

We always drove to work in complete silence. There was no "good morning" and definitely no friendly banter. When we would get to work, he would send me out of the truck so he could sit in there by himself. "Nothing personal, it's just personal," he'd tell me. So I would find somewhere to go. I'd sit in a crew truck or hang out by the ditch on my own.

"If you play stupid games, you win stupid prizes."

Andrew Beers

Once we started a weld, he would use hand signals to tell me to turn the amps up or down on the remote, but the signals never made any sense. I had to guess. He'd wave his hand, so I'd turn the dial and say, "Up!" and he would lose his shit under that helmet.

"No! Down! Down!"

I was always in trouble with this guy. He loved to yell at me and make me feel like a piece of shit.

After a few weeks, I decided to fight back.

I always figured that the reason some welders turned sour was that they were trapped with their own thoughts while focusing hard on a weld. They flipped the lid down on their welding helmet and concentrated on the blinding light. And while they did that, they repeated a mantra made up of whatever they were thinking about or heard recently. This would change their mood for good or bad.

Here are a few of Brant's daily mantras.

"I'm not getting paid enough!"

"I can't believe this shit. I get no respect around here."

"We should get to go home early. We work harder than anyone else out here!"

"This tie-in ditch is dug all wrong. Fuckin' equipment operators don't have a clue."

"We work harder than all of these other guys. They just stand around pulling their puds and watching us weld."

"That other company gives all their welders two jump hours a day, and we only get one. Bullshit is what that is."

"The road to this job is too rough, and my truck is getting destroyed! I'm going to need to buy new tires now."

"My helper is a piece of shit."

"These welding rods are garbage! That's why that last weld was a cutout. Fucking shitty welding rods."

"Can't this company afford pipe clamps that work?"

The road we drove in on, 'The Willow,' was rocky and hard on tires, which was a super sore spot for Brant. He went on and on about how much a set of tires for his welding truck cost and how the company should pay for them.

Because of all this nasty garbage in his head, Brant was constantly throwing his grinder down to show how mad he was and yelling at me like a five-year-old having a tantrum because Mommy asked him to stop poking the cat.

One day, Brant called me a loser one too many times. I couldn't stand the abuse the clown was heaping on me any longer.

It was time to have a little fun. I decided to create a rumor and get Brant going.

Brant was welding. With all of the equipment running, it was really loud. I leaned over the pipe and yelled at the welder's helper on the other side, Mitch. "Hey, Sean just told me that Deadcor welders get two extra jump hours every day."

"Really?" Mitch yelled back. "Sweet!"

"Yeah, and they get new tires for their trucks for free twice a year."

"Hah! I bet Brant wishes he was working at Deadcor!" Mitch said over the noise of the welding.

"Down! Down! Pay attention and quit yacking!" Brant yelled at me. I turned the remote dial.

Soon Mitch and I were working by ourselves while the two welders took a break.

For those who haven't seen a pipeline weld, the welder only does the most critical tasks. He welds. The helpers do all of the grunt work, like grinding and heating the pipe.

As I worked, I could see out of the corner of my eye that Brant was talking loudly and waving his hands around while he raged. He was bitching about jump hours and tires.

The other welder was trying to calm him down, but it didn't work. He stormed back to us, angrier than ever.

Brant was still upset at lunchtime. He had a toaster oven on the back of his truck with a single serving of lasagna heating up, and as he pulled it out with an angry jerk, the lasagna flipped out of the tinfoil tray upside down on the dirt.

"Fucking piece of shit!" Brant yelled as he kicked the lasagna with his boot. He went to sulk in his truck without his lunch.

The boys had another weld lined up for us to work on. I got all the cords strung out in the ditch while Brant sat in his truck.

The inspector, Ian, pulled up in his jacked-up white Dodge. He inspected the pipe ends and stood on the bank. As Brant walked by, Ian said, "What's wrong, Brant? Did someone spill your lunch?"

Brant just mumbled and went into the ditch to start the weld. But I could tell he was extra rattled, stewing about Deadcor welders and jump hours and tires. Now Ian was standing on the ditch bank, ready to call a cutout.

The weld didn't go very well. It's more like an art form than a science. When a welder isn't in the right state of mind, he can make mistakes that will ruin his work.

Brant wasn't able to focus. He had lost his mojo. He struggled with it for a long time, and I knew he was worried there was gonna be a repair. He was so stressed he even stopped yelling at me.

He finally finished the weld and left the ditch. I rolled up the cables and put away the tools.

Brant sat in his truck. I took my phone and my lunch kit over to the crew truck to wait.

The ultrasound testers rolled up, scanned the weld, and hung a blue ribbon. There was a repair, and Brant had to try to fix it. Ian was ecstatic.

As I expected, Brant's attempt to repair the weld failed.

Ian came over with a big grin and made his scissors signal. "Nice try, boys! But I'm afraid that's a cutout!" Ian was never happier than when he was ruining a welder's day.

I was cleaning mud off of the welding cables with a rag. Brant walked over to me. He was shaking with anger.

"I'm blaming this on you!" he yelled. "If you weren't such a shitty helper, I wouldn't have been in such a bad mood, and I would have got this one."

I stopped wiping mud off the cords and put down the rag. Then I took a step toward Brant and looked him in the eye.

"You know, I heard about a welder's helper on a job down by Drumheller," I said. "His welder kept yelling at him and abusing him. One day, he snapped. He waited until the welder was burning welding rods with his lid down. Then he wound up and walloped him in the back of the head so hard that the idiot's head bounced off the pipe."

"Are you threatening me?"

I took a step closer. "I'm just saying it's hard to blame a guy who gets abused by an asshole every day if he snaps and punches that asshole in the back of the head. Maybe you ought to stop yelling at me."

Brant must have seen a look in my eye that made him think twice. Because instead of insulting me or yelling, he shut up and walked away.

It turned out that the foreman saw the whole confrontation. The next day, I got moved to skid hustling. He decided it was time to get me out of there before things went south.

I enjoyed the shit out of throwing skids all day. Not a welder in sight.

Chapter 19

Stick With Your Pack

I was a lone wolf. I had started a new job at a site I had never been to, north of Fort McMurray, working with a crew I didn't know. I wanted a place to escape the drama that had infected the shop where I had worked for the last couple of years. You'd think a hundred dudes stuffed into a dusty, loud fabrication shop wouldn't be much of a setting for a soap opera, but dammit, men can be catty and bitchy too, and I had had enough of it! One day, I just quit. I packed my locker up and left without a word.

It wasn't long before I found my next gig. When I got to the new job, the superintendent gave me the option to work days or nights, and I chose the night shift. Forty people were working the day shift, and only six were on the night shift. I was lucky number seven.

On the seventh day of our eight-day rotation, my foreman, Jordan, popped into the changing room as I was getting my coveralls on for the night. "Hey, I've got something for you guys," he said. "Get as many as you can into a truck and meet me at the pond."

"Sure," I said.

Having never worked at this plant, I had yet to learn where the pond was. I turned to my colleagues.

"Any of you know where the pond is?" I asked.

"It's one road south of the tank farm," Chris replied.

"Right. Let's get enough guys to fill the truck and head down."

Matt, Brian, Scott, and Vic volunteered. Chris stayed behind to guard the lunchroom.

We drove past the tank farm to the pond. The pond was set in a low-lying area that was accessible after driving over a steep gravel hill that crested a retaining wall. The route then meandered downhill to a nightmare landscape of putrid, glistening water.

Near the water's edge was a massive pressure vessel that looked like s stubby missile with several different-sized nozzles protruding from it like a pincushion. It had been laid out atop wooden timbers. We stopped the truck there, using the illumination from the headlights to light up as much of the landscape as possible. Though we hadn't received specific instructions, it was obvious that we would be doing something with this vessel.

I looked around. There was a double-decker trailer set back along the edge of the dirty water line that likely had bathroom and lunch facilities for the poor sons of bitches who worked down here. It was about seven hundred feet from where we were.

Not too far to walk, but I'd be driving if I had to shit in a hurry, I thought.

Small bushes dotted the banks of the pond. They had no leaves even though it was the middle of summer. In the dark, it was hard to tell if they were dead or a weird mutation that had adapted to slurp this horror pond's dirty, damp soil.

Jordan's truck crested the hill over the barrier wall, bouncing along the uneven grassy ground. Jordan got out of his pickup and lit a smoke, giving the rest of us, who also smoked, permission to do the same.

"Welcome to the pond, boys!" Jordan said. "I see you all found our job for the night." He clicked on a flashlight and illuminated the pressure vessel we had gathered around.

"This is a 'treater' vessel," Jordan explained. "I guess they want us to roll it over so they can cut some of the nozzles off and weld on bigger ones. The smaller ones keep getting clogged with slugs of sand or some shit like that. I figured you guys could handle it. I brought some big lifting straps and some shackles for the job."

Vic and I walked around the giant metal tube, trying to devise a plan for flipping the thing over while Brian and Scott got the straps — big pink Kevlar-covered loops that looked like elephant intestines when they plopped them in a pile on the ground. Once they unloaded the shackles out of the truck, Jordan hopped back in the cab.

"You guys going to be good here? The crane should get here soon." Jordan asked.

"I think so," I said.

"Right on! I'll be on the radio if you need me," Jordan said, already driving away.

We watched his truck crest the barrier wall before we started appraising the scope of work we were about to take on.

"How the fuck are we going to flip this thing?" Vic wondered aloud.

"You're the senior guy on the crew. I figured you might know," Scott said.

"Shit," Vic said, "You young guys think everyone over forty has been everywhere and done everything? I've never lifted anything this big before."

I looked at the rigging that had been dumped on the ground. The straps looked like they would be long enough if we looped them together with a shackle.

Rolling was going to be difficult. The straps would likely contact the attached metal pipe supports as we rolled the vessel over. We'd have to ensure we had some softeners – thick chunks of nylon that would keep our straps from being cut. It was an easy fix, but we would have to visit the tool crib.

"We'll shackle two slings together, run them under the sheet, and make sure they bite at the top. We can tie a rope to one of the slings and keep it from wandering away when the crane takes the weight. We'll need softeners, in any case. Jordan didn't bring any."

The guys all nodded their heads in agreement.

"Brian and I can take the truck and run to the tool crib for some." Vic volunteered.

"Sure," I said, "Scott and I will stay here and set up the slings while we watch for the crane. Might as well be ready when it gets here."

"Sounds like a plan," Vic said, three strides closer to the truck.

Scott and I got to work on the slings and shackles, throwing a length of rope under the vessel so that we could pull one of the slings under it. We got the first one looped together when Scott stood up and dusted himself off. "Well, nature is calling." Scott said, "I have to shit."

"My God, man. Can't you hold it?"

Scott looked behind him to the double-decker trailer off in the distance. "No."

"I guess," I said, "If you have to go, you have to go."

I took off my radio and tossed it to him. "In case you get into trouble."

Scott stomped off into the darkness that engulfed the space between our work area and the faraway trailer. I returned to hooking up the rigging under the vessel.

Alone at last, I was working with my best friend – me. I loved it.

Once Scott had moved off into the distance, I noticed how quiet it was without the clanking of shackles, the thump of work boots on the dirt, and the general conversation. I could hear the low hum of the plant in the distance, the low-pitched inhalation of fluid movement. And the exhaling buzz of metal moving against metal.

Above all that noise, I noticed a high-pitched yipping coming from nearby. I stopped what I was doing and looked around. One of the small bushes along the edge of the obsidian waters was shaking. I took a few steps to investigate and saw a small mangy-looking dog emerge from the bush. I could not tell you what species it was. It might have been a coyote or a fox, but with its patchy coat, evil-looking murky eyes, and rib-exposed, thin build — it was impossible to tell.

The animal sprang up when it saw me, a peacock dance that looked funny but was probably intended to frighten a threat — me — away. I suddenly understood what was going on in the bush. Whatever species of dog this was, there was a litter of pups in there somewhere. I didn't think momma was happy to have me around.

"Keep jumping, you mangy thing," I told the dog. "I'm bigger than you."

I returned to work, taking a few steps from the vessel to check the spacing between the lifting straps. As I stepped backward, I heard a feral growl behind me. I spun around to find another dog with darker, thicker fur than the one that had emerged from the bushes. It had taken position behind me and was offended by my two backward steps. The dog's gleaming fangs were exposed in a menacing grimace.

I froze in place, alarmed at the sudden appearance of the freaky-looking dog. I looked back at the bush. The first dog was still there. It was no longer bouncing wildly but was now on all fours, keeping its space-black eyes locked on me while giving off the odd yip.

I looked toward the faraway trailer where Scott had gone. There was no sign of him. I looked to the entrance to the pond, and there was no sign of Vic and Brian in the truck either. The darkness between me and the ramp was moving. The night revealed one dog, then another. Like Gremlins, each had unique and sinister characteristics.

I spun myself in a frantic circle, attempting to figure out how many dogs were around me. Seven of them had come out of the darkness. They had made a ring thirty feet around me, and I had nowhere to go. I was surrounded. My hands shot toward my coverall pockets, searching for anything I could use to defend myself. I had nothing but a lighter and a pocket level. I held the level out in front of me like it was a knife. The dogs didn't seem to care. The ones at my back moved closer when I wasn't looking - like the ghosts in Mario Bros. I could hear their paws shuffling in the grass as they approached, and I would spin around to face them, waving the level in front of me. It wasn't working. The circle was closing.

There were nine dogs now.

"This is it. This is how you go—taken down by a pack of diseased mutts." I said to myself.

These fuckers weren't going to take me without a fight.

I found the first dog I had seen, the original shit starter. I took two steps toward that one, swinging the level at it to see if I could break their ranks. She jumped back as I approached, but the two that flanked her closed the gap quicker than I could get outside their circle. They were growling at me now, all gnashing teeth and evil eyes inching their way ever closer. I caught one in my peripheral vision trying to skip closer to me, and I reached out with my right foot, pushing it back by shoving the sole of my work boot close to its angry face.

"Get any closer fucker, and I'll make you taste my composite-toed boot!"

The circle was now eight feet. They no longer needed every dog to keep me penned in. Three dogs held back outside the ring, pacing back and forth to pick me off if I managed to get out of the circle. I was panicking now as they closed to within striking distance. My heart was pounding, and my mouth had gone dry. I was hyper-alert to every sound and movement.

The dogs closed the circle tighter. I again zoned in on that first dog, setting my right leg back a half-step to get myself ready to kick it or try to run if I had to. I thought about the pups in the bush. I knew she was protecting her babies, but she and I were both scared animals now. She would do what she thought she had to, and if I wanted to live, I would have to also. I felt one of the mutts nip at my leg as I swept it forward, kicking it at the dogs in front of me. They jumped back, avoiding a boot to the teeth. I quickly used the extra real estate I gained to hop forward a couple of feet and swept my leg behind me to ensure the beasts to the rear couldn't make any headway. I was keeping them back but knew I couldn't do it for long.

I thought about how many of them I could break up with my work boot before they took me down and finished the job. None of them were huge, but what they lacked in size, they seemed to make up with in ferocity. I didn't think my chances were good.

I looked again at the trailer, but there was no sign of Scott.

I swept my completely non-threatening pocket level at the dogs. "Come on, you fuckers! I'll show you what your fucking teeth taste like!"

I had decided to go on the attack as my last stand. Yelling, I charged forward, kicking my legs in a spastic roundhouse goosestep. The dogs backed away as I charged forward, roaring like a war-hungry marine. At that moment, the landscape lit up, and all attention — mine and the dogs' — was directed to the road entrance to the pond. Vic and Brian had crested the hill in the truck.

The dogs scattered. I was safe.

I tried to catch my breath, bending over with my hands on my knees. Brian and Vic parked the truck. Brian got out of the driver's side. "Dude, what the fuck was that? Were those coyotes?"

"I have no idea what kind of dogs those were, but I think I was about to be killed and eaten by them!"

"Where's Scott?" Vic asked.

There was still no sight of him. "He went for a shit over there in the trailer just after you guys left."

"Jesus Christ," Vic huffed, throwing his hands up. "Why the hell didn't you go with him? Where's your radio?"

"I gave the radio to Scott. I wanted to wait for the crane and get the rigging hooked up."

"You don't work alone, ever!" Vic said sternly. He was right. I knew that working alone could be dangerous, but I hadn't even registered that I was working alone. It was unfamiliar territory to me. The lone wolf in me liked doing things on my own. Besides, I had no idea feral dogs would set upon me.

But I knew Vic was right.

"Shit," I said.

I faced the fact that I had fucked up by staying behind alone.

"I'll go get Scott with the truck. You two stay here." Vic said as he hopped in the truck's driver's seat and sped off. He returned quickly with Scott, who had taken his dump and then had directed his attentlon to a stash of porn magazines that had been leisurely left on a table. He'd been leafing through when Vic found him.

We rolled the pressure vessel without incident and returned to the lunchroom for a break.

After that, I noticed that I was a lot more friendly with the other guys. Instead of sitting by myself in the corner, I joined the other guys where they were all sitting and got to know them better over games of crib and discussions about kids, family, and movies we all liked.

I've since learned to ignore my lone-wolf tendencies, and I've gotten better at working with a team. I've been to several other jobs since the pond incident, and now I'm the first to introduce myself to a new pack. I look for the other lone wolves and try and bring them into the fold. And I never work alone.

Chapter 20

How a Pipefitter Named Pig-Boy Put the Boss in His Place

P igboy was a big guy. Messy, too.

When we first met him, he was a laborer named Donny. He worked hard, and everyone liked the guy. He was big enough to handle the toughest jobs, and maybe he wasn't fast-moving, but he was always on the go.

We were working for a really fussy foreman. Al was an ex-army dude in his fifties, and he liked to yell at us like we were in basic training. We all thought it was hilarious and mostly did what he told us to do.

Al kept his truck spic and span, and he bitched like you wouldn't believe if the crew trucks or the equipment weren't clean enough. He had a rag on his dash that he used to wipe off even the smallest bit of dust, and he used spray-on truck polish liberally. That was the cleanest company truck anyone had ever seen.

At least until Donny got ahold of it.

Al's truck was in the way one day, blocking the path so we couldn't get the dozer past. Donny went to move it.

If he hadn't just been moving water pump hoses in a muddy ditch, that would've been fine. But his gloves were covered in slimy, sticky clay, and he'd leaned on the muddy bank with his whole back. Donny was covered in mud.

He jumped in the truck and grabbed the steering wheel, muddy gloves on his big hands, and moved the truck so the dozer could go by.

When Al returned to his truck, he stopped short when he saw mud on the door handle and running board. Then he opened the truck door. Mud on the floormat. Mud on the seat. Mud on the inside door handle.

Mud on the steering wheel.

Al stormed over to us and yelled, "Who the hell messed up my truck?" Everyone just stared at him, surprised.

"I did," Donny said.

"You wore your muddy gloves and *touched the steering wheel*? What are you, some kind of pig boy?"

Pigboy could clean up, though. Every week, he put on clean clothes and showed up at the closest town's Karaoke night. Pigboy could belt out almost everything the DJ brought. He'd go on stage and kick ass at Karaoke, then drink too much and show up barely alive the next day.

We needed someone to run the pipefitting truck. Before we knew it, Pigboy took the job. He was threading two-inch pipes and gooping them up with that black dope.

For those of you who don't know, pipe dope is the lubricant that you put on the threads to keep the pipe from leaking after you screw it together.

You couldn't go near anything that Pigboy assembled without getting that black shit on you. Al or the client inspector would come to look at his work and walk away pissed off. Their hands or sleeves always got that black stuff on them, and it would find its way into their trucks or onto their faces.

"Pigboy, quit smearing so much of that black shit on everything!" Al would yell. "You only need a tiny bit. It keeps getting on my gloves, you messy excuse for a pipefitter!"

Pigboy just smiled, said, "I'll try, Al," and kept doing exactly what he wanted to do.

His truck cab was a big greasy mess, cluttered with thread-cutting fluid and pipe dope and sweat and leftover lunches. If you needed to take a ride with Pigboy, you were going to get dirty.

Pigboy was a hard worker, but he liked to party. Then he liked to sleep in.

One morning, he was extra late. Al went to Pigboy's camp room and banged on the door.

When Pigboy let him in, Al said, "We need you at work. We got to get that meter shack hooked up to the line today. Get your act together and get dressed!"

"Okay, Al," Pigboy said.

When Al went out into the hallway, Pigboy shut and locked the door, then went back to bed.

He slouched in a few hours later as if nothing had happened.

After that, Al was on the warpath. That old army vet was determined to make a better man out of Pigboy.

He harassed Pigboy daily.

Truck inspections. Safety paperwork. Calling Pigboy out at tailgate meetings. Spot checks on his work followed by lots of yelling, as if we were in basic army training. Al was micromanaging all day long.

We felt sorry for Pigboy, but he just soldiered on through everything Al threw at him without much of a complaint. It went on for weeks.

Pigboy was a stoic kind of guy. He took things as they came and had more mental toughness than you'd think. But even a quiet guy has his breaking point.

One day, Pigboy had just plumbed in a small separator shack, and he was wrapping up his tools. The rest of the crew was nearby, breaking down a boom to load it on the low-bed trailer.

Al pulled up at high speed with his meticulously polished truck. He waited for the dust to settle before he opened the door. He wasn't getting dust get on that dash!

Pigboy's shoulders slumped. He knew Al was going to pin him to the wall again.

Al jumped out with a smirk on his face and stomped over to the door of the shack Pigboy had been working on. With a flourish, he pulled a white rag out of his jeans pocket and wiped it across the door and then the handle. He inspected the rag, then turned it to show Pigboy.

"Look at that! Dope all over the door handle. You're going to have to stay late and fix this mess."

Pigboy grimaced. "Come on, man. I've cleaned up my act. Check out my truck, I even cleaned the cab!"

It was true. Pigboy had put in some effort, and the shack was actually in pretty good shape.

But Al just wouldn't let up.

It was already after six on a Karaoke night, too.

"Can I just take care of it in the morning?" Pigboy asked. "It's late."

"Nope, you can do it now, slacker!"

With a smirk, Al jumped in his truck and headed for town.

Pigboy looked thoughtful.

"You guys got any spare ratchet straps?" he asked us.

"Sure, in the driver-side toolbox," I said. Pigboy grabbed a bunch of them.

The next day, Al missed the morning meeting. This was unheard of.

We all got to the line ahead of him and got to work. A half-hour later, he came flying in at high speed. He got out of his truck without even waiting for the dust to settle.

"Which one of you jerks did it?" He screamed. He stomped around so red-faced that I was worried he was gonna have a coronary event.

None of us had any idea what he was talking about.

Pigboy had a quirky smile on his face. Al stomped over and pointed at him. "You sonofabitch! It was you!"

"Me what?" Pigboy asked quietly.

Al ran back to his truck and opened the tailgate. He dragged out a wadded-up bunch of two-inch ratchet straps and threw them on the ground. "Who did this?"

None of us would say a word. We all knew who had borrowed those straps, but we weren't going to rat Pigboy out. Al closed his tailgate, jumped in his truck, and sped off.

Then we got the story out of Pigboy.

Al had been staying in his trailer down at the campground. Pigboy snuck up on him in the middle of the night and quietly slipped the straps around the trailer, right over the front and back door, and even the emergency exit window. He was sure Al was gonna wake up and catch him, but the old guy was snoring so loud that a bomb could have gone off without bothering him.

When Al got up, he couldn't tell why his doors wouldn't open. He had no choice but to call for help, but by the time he did, everyone else was at the foreman's meeting. All he could do was sit in his trailer and rage.

> "I learned long ago, never to wrestle with a pig. You get dirty, and besides, the pig likes it."
>
> George Bernard Shaw

Later that afternoon, Pigboy was bolting up some flanges at a riser when Al rolled in. He waited for the dust to settle out of the air before he opened his door. He strode over to Pigboy's work and bent down to examine the lineup.

"This flange is out of line!"

"No, it isn't," Pigboy said.

"Yes, it is! You need to take this back apart and put it together right, you big slob!"

"I'm not changing that flange," Pigboy said. "You need to stop picking on me."

Pigboy walked over to his truck and reached into the toolbox. He grabbed a yellow two-inch strap and unrolled it.

"What are you going to do with that?" Al asked.

"Strap down this pipe on the back of my truck," Pigboy said with a smile, throwing the strap over the deck. He looked Al right in the eye, and neither one said a word.

After that, Al left Pigboy alone — for a few days.

Chapter 21

The Lumberjack Effect

W hen Paul the timber beast left the bunkhouse that morning, he had no idea he would disrupt the lives of two innocents. He had to get that logging truck on the road and head North. Those logs weren't gonna haul themselves!

Before he headed out, he took care of a little grooming.

Whistling Johnny Cash tunes while he combed his beard, Paul thought of the many manly activities the day would bring. He was a busy beaver, not a blanket head.

The first order of business was a visit to the Cougar's Den for a stiff shot of black coffee and a plate of pancakes. His friend Susan ran the local diner, and she knew how to feed a lumberjack. Paul grabbed his trusty axe, put on his plaid, and set out to start his day.

Down the street walked an unsuspecting couple. It was River Rose and her hockey player wife, Moxie. These lovebird Canucks were out for a stroll. That's when they fell afoul of the Lumberjack Effect.

"There's only two types of manly men left in this
world. Lumberjacks and Liam Neeson."

Daniel Tosh

Everyone knows that lumberjacks are irresistible. Scientific studies have shown that 98% of the population will fall for a lumberjack faster than a lumberjack can knock down trees.

No one can help themselves around a man who sports a beard, wears plaid, and knows how to use an axe.

Moxie took one glance at Paul's lip lettuce and burly beard, and she was a goner.

She had to have this man.

River Rose hadn't noticed Paul. She was talking to Moxie and enjoying the scenery.

Moxie wasn't listening to her wife. She had her attention firmly on Paul's bearded masculinity.

Moxie chirped at the lumberjack, "Is your dad Liam Neeson? Because I'm 'Taken' with you!"

"Hello, ladies," Paul said. He gave them a wide berth as he passed them.

Moxie couldn't resist taking a good long gander at the lumberjack's booty as he headed away.

"I can't believe this!" River Rose said, tears in her eyes. "This is how you behave on our anniversary?"

"I'm sorry, honey," Moxie mumbled. "I don't know what came over me. You're the only one for me!"

As the couple headed home, Moxie knew she was in for it. She would spend a long week in the Sin Bin for her indiscretion.

She just couldn't help herself, though. She loved a lumberjack with an axe.

Paul shrugged and kept walking. What was he, a piece of meat or a human being that just happens to have a beard and an axe?

I caught up with Paul at the Cougar's Den a while later. He was chowing down on a plate of pancakes and fried eggs. He told me all about what had happened.

"It's the Lumberjack Effect," he said. "People see me and want to get in my plaid. To be honest, it's kinda annoying. I don't like being objectified. Doesn't anyone want to love me for who I am?"

At that moment, a waiter spilled coffee all over the counter, his eyes glued to the woodsman instead of his work.

"I'm so sorry," the waiter said as he wiped up the drink.

His boss, Susan, patted the waiter on the shoulder.

"Don't be hard on yourself," she told him. "I don't expect you to be able to hold up under this kind of stress." She nodded toward Paul. "It's his fault. The Lumberjack Effect makes everyone lose their cool."

"See, this is what I mean," Paul said. He shook his head sadly.

I had another question for Paul. " But what about this ax-ccessory trend? Even you savage lumberjacks need to be civilized. Do you think it's safe to pack an axe everywhere you go?"

Paul stared at me in disbelief. "You know this is Canada, eh? I'm not leaving it where I parked my moose."

The door to the diner opened, and we all glanced over.

It was a lady in plaid. Her long blonde hair, her smile, and the spring in her step mesmerized every man and woman in the joint.

She went to a table by the window, leaned her axe against the wall, and had a seat.

Only one kind of person would wear plaid and carry an axe.

The new girl was a lumberjill.

Paul didn't waste a minute. He went straight over to introduce himself.

"Hi, I'm Paul," he said smoothly.

"I'm Holly," the lumberjill said. She looked him over with a smirk. "Wow, you're my kind of man."

"If I were a tree in the forest, would you hear me falling for you?" Paul asked.

"I sure wood!" She said with a smile. "Join me for coffee?"

Chapter 22

How I Survived The Danger Crew

I know I'm a competent worker. I can do my job just as well as anyone, but one hard fact about working in oilfield maintenance and construction is that none of the work is permanent. Unless I'm working at a job full of people who already know me, I sometimes get frustrated that I have to start from the ground floor – convincing everyone I know what I'm doing. It can be exhausting, considering the barrier for entry for most of the supervision on these sites comes down to being drinking buddies with someone who can pump you a little higher on the food chain. The supervisors never have to convince us grunts working the wrenches that they are competent.

It's impossible to know what you're walking into sometimes, and whenever one of these types of jobs comes along, I keep my head down and try not to get noticed. The types of guys who run these jobs are always looking to make an example of someone else. It hides their shortcomings.

Again, I found myself at one of these gigs.

After three weeks of working night shift maintenance at the refinery, I could tell it wasn't going well. I could tell Kyle, my foreman, had no use for me, a judgment call on his part that automatically extended to the fresh-faced apprentice named Jake I had been paired with. Jake and I had never met each other until this job, but to a guy like Kyle, that didn't matter.

"Tomorrow, you and Jake are going to the bolt-up crew."

I knew this meant that he wanted to get rid of us. I knew the tactic. A foreman who couldn't deal with conflict would bump guys he didn't like to another crew –usually with a surly prick for a foreman who was good at making people's lives hard.

"I don't want to work on another crew," I told Kyle.

"You're going to work with Daryl tomorrow. He's a friend of mine and a pretty good guy. It should be a better fit for you guys."

"Sure," I relented.

Jake and I grouped back up with the bolt-up crew the next night. We waited outside the foreman's shack for Daryl to meet with us.

Daryl bounded down the foreman's shack's stairs while addressing Kyle's radio call.

"Yeah, Kyle, I'm looking at them right now," Daryl said over the radio. "Thanks a lot."

I introduced myself and the rest of the guys to Daryl. He was a short guy with a mullet and mustache. He seemed nice enough.

"We have an easy couple of jobs for you guys tonight," he told us. 'We're having some trouble breaking some old pipes in the rack in Plant Seventeen. We've got all the gear already set there for you guys to use. You'll see when you get there, but we want you to saw all the bolts off. We're trying to do it without making any sparks. Operations have had a few close calls with fires in the plant. Getting a permit for anything that involves open sparks or fire is a massive ordeal around here. Jump in that pickup, and I'll take you over."

We hopped into his truck, and he drove us to the base of a large structure. Once there, we got out of the truck and wound our way through a maze of pipe racks until we reached a large opening at the foot of two ominous towers. We snaked our way up several flights of winding, rusted staircases until we got to a main deck that could not be seen from the ground. The deck was a sprawling platform with several large pipes- big enough that if they were open, a person could crawl through them. The lines ran horizontally five feet from the floor, and each section of the piping was joined at bulky bolted sections, the flanges we had to unbolt.

Daryl pointed to one large pipe and flange scaffolded with a generously large deck that would easily accommodate a couple of workers and the required tools. He asked me and Jake to get on that deck while he got his other guys going first. Jake and I heard their tools scream to life as they got down to business.

Daryl climbed the short ladder to our deck, and once he found his footing, he went to work. He checked the tag hanging off the flanged connection we were about to break against a drawing and tag list in his clipboard.

This guy looked like he gave a shit. I thought we were off to a good start.

The flange bolts all looked like they had seen some shit. Their extended length of threads was scaled and gray, and the nuts looked like nature had decided to weld them to the bolts themselves. The bolting was large, with nuts the size of my fist and bolts two inches in diameter and as long as my forearm. A solid chunk of metal that we call a spacer ring was placed between the mating surfaces known as 'flanges' where the two pipes bolt together.

Daryl directed me to a large reciprocating saw that had been left for us on the deck. "That's what you will be using to cut these bolts off," Daryl assured us.

"That thing is fucking HUGE!" I said.

The saw was three feet long and had a six-inch blade attached to the end that would pump back and forth with a piston-like action. I've used them before, but the ones I'd used in the past were the smaller electric types. The saw was obviously too big for the job and not the right tool for this application. It was the 'Rambo' model. The pipefitter equivalent of Sylvester Stallone's belt-fed M-60 rifle in 'First Blood. There was a circular hole near the end of the saw where it was typically mounted on a stationary vise, as the sonofabitch was too big for most people to handle. You needed a pivot point and a fulcrum. The weight of the tool was supposed to do the cutting.

I had no idea how I would hang on to this thing.

"Holy shit," I said to Daryl. "Why is it so small?"

Daryl's sarcasm detector might have been broken that night. "It's the biggest one we could find. Do you think it will get through those bolts?" He asked with a flattened seriousness.

I let the joke fly over his head and picked the tool up, keeping my hands off the switch. The swath of destruction this thing could cause was monumental. I imagined what an instrument of this size could do if someone deployed it in a horror movie.

When I held the blade up to one of the studs we needed to cut, I realized that cutting would be awkward.

"Shit," I said to Daryl. "I don't know if this will work. I don't think there's enough room between the bolts once the saw blade gets through. Can't we grind them off?"

"We asked that already," Daryl said. "The client doesn't want any sparks in the unit. This line is normally full of butane. Cold cutting only."

"You're the boss," I said.

Jake climbed onto the scaffold with me as Daryl swapped places with him on the short ladder that tied our deck to the central platform and put on our face shields. Those were a must with any tool that would make small metal particles fly around. This big bastard of a saw was sure to make a mess. I looked at Jake and nodded. He nodded back. I laid the saw blade against a bolt and pulled the trigger. The tool fired up, and the blade started its seismic back-and-forth action.

As soon as the edge began to cut through the threaded side of the bolt, it seized.

I lifted the tool to dislodge the blade. The saw came back to life once it was free of the bolt, then slammed the blade into the side of the spacer ring, bending it and rendering the tool useless.

I swore, put the saw down, and looked for a stash of replacement blades. There were none, so Jake climbed off the scaffold and flagged Daryl down to see if more were nearby. There weren't.

We waited for one of the laborers to run up to our deck from the tool crib with one blade. "Just one?" I asked. "We're going to need them all. Is there a full box of these at the tool crib?"

"Yeah," the laborer affirmed, "But Dougie's only going to let you have one at a time."

"Don't go anywhere," I said.

I changed the blade using the quick release, flopped my face shield down, and found the groove in the bolt I had already started cutting. I hit the actuator on the saw and got the same results. I got maybe a millimeter further into the bolt when the saw blade hit the spacer ring and bent the brand-new saw blade into a cartoonish 'Z' shape.

"You better tell Dougie we need the whole box," I said.

"You've got that right!" the laborer said before leaving the deck to get more saw blades.

The laborer returned after twenty minutes with a box of saw blades for us, with a stern warning from Dougie.

"Dougie says that there ain't too many jobs out there that need more than one saw blade."

"Sounds like Dougie should go fuck himself."

"Well, there's no need to be such a prick about it," she sneered before flipping me the finger.

I put a new saw blade on the reciprocating saw and went to work. I was at least three millimeters into the bolt I had started to cut. "At this rate, we'll be done in a month!" I shouted to Jake over the sound of the saw.

I tried to keep the blade angled away from the spacer ring to try and minimize the number I bent. A new problem presented itself. The saw blade was getting hot enough to bind on the bolt we were trying to hack through. Once the serrated edges of the saw blade got hot enough, the blade would bite into the steel and the saw would violently shake me around like a rag doll as I hung on.

"Holy shit!" said Jake, "You okay, man?"

"I'm fine. But there's no way I can keep cutting through these bolts with this saw. Jesus." I was frustrated.

"Would it help if I pushed on your back?" Jake asked.

"Sure, it's worth a try."

Jake stood behind me and put his hands on my shoulders. He braced his back against a horizontal scaffold tube. I got myself ready for action, turning my head to see how Jake was doing. "Ready?" I asked.

"Fuckin' hit 'er!"

I pulled the trigger on the saw, and the blade started back up. Having Jake's extra weight pushing my back seemed to do the trick. The saw was beginning to sink into the hardened bolt, and a good cascade of metal flakes was falling from between the flanges, catching the artificial moonlight generated by the nearby diesel-powered light plants. The air was sparkling with magic fairy dust. It looked like we were finally winning against the stubborn bolt.

"That's right, baby! I always win!" I bragged over the pneumatic chug of the saw.

The minute I started gloating, the saw blade got too hot and bit into the bolt again. I shook violently as Jake tried his hardest to push my shoulders forward. His arms couldn't overcome the saw's power. My back began slamming into his torso, bashing Jake against the scaffold tube. The poor bastard was getting some CPR chest compressions. I could hear him yelling, "Fuck! Stop! Stop! Stop!" I laid off the trigger, and the saw wound down.

"Fuck this," I said to Jake. "This sucks. We can't do it with this piece of shit saw."

"What should we do?"

"Daryl will have to make that decision. Go find him and tell him they might have to rent a nut-buster."

"You're making that up to fuck with me. I'm not falling for that."

Jake was right to be suspicious. We tradesmen had a habit of sending the younger guys on joke quests for items that didn't exist. Things like 'skyhooks,' 'petty files,' and 'level fluid.' But in this instance, there was no need for him to worry. A nut-buster is a tool I've used for this purpose in the past. It was a heavy hydraulic tool that drove a hardened wedge into the side of the big nuts, splitting them so they could be removed without undoing the threads. It was the exact tool they needed here.

"Don't worry. It's a real thing." I could tell he didn't believe me.

"I'll go with you," I said.

We pushed 'The Saw of Doom' away from the entrance to the scaffold. I wanted to make sure no one would stumble on it if they climbed up before we descended to ground level, where we found Daryl sitting in his truck.

"What are you guys doing down here? Are those bolts cut?"

"We can't cut them," I said.

"Why not?" Daryl snapped. His face turned from a slack-jawed grin to an annoyed sneer. He reared in his seat, tilted his head down, and looked at us with a sinister upward gaze.

I braced myself. This looked like it was going to go downhill.

"The saw isn't working," I told him. "We either bend blades, or it seizes up, and I can't hang on to it."

"Can't hang on to it?" Daryl scoffed. "It's a reciprocating saw. You've never used one before?"

"I have. But not one meant to be mounted on a bench. It's the wrong tool for the job. You need a nut splitter."

Daryl hopped out of his truck, throwing his hard hat and safety glasses on as he made his way around the side of the truck to where we stood. He dug his still-clean gloves out of his pockets and rammed his hands into them in a fashion that seemed a little too aggressive for the gesture.

"It's shutdown season. We tried to get a nut splitter, but they're rented out everywhere. The nearest one is in Saskatoon."

"Saskatoon is only a day's drive away," I said. "I'm sure you can have a hot shot truck bring one here for tomorrow night, and we can get back at this then. Jake and I are happy to do whatever else you have for us."

"Yeah," Jake agreed.

Daryl was having none of what we were selling. He glared at us and walked to the stairs, taking them two at a time.

"Come on," Daryl said without turning back. "I guess I'll have to show you two pussies how to get shit done."

Daryl shot us a pissed-off look before he climbed the ladder to the scaffold deck where Jake and I had been working. He hefted the saw in his hand, checked the blade, and got to work on the stud. He got three strokes out of the saw before the blade bent.

"Fuck!" he spat. "Change it!"

Jake obliged him and inserted a fresh saw blade into the end of the saw.

Daryl wheeled the hulking tool back around for another go. He tried to angle the saw blade away from the spacer ring. The blade quickly seized as the friction heat expanded the blade and the bolt. Daryl tried to hold on to the saw, but it was useless. He convulsed violently as his arms fought to maintain his grip on the saw. Eventually, the saw dislodged itself, and Daryl was caught off balance. He fell with the saw in his hand and let go of the handle as he hit the deck. The saw was still stuck in the stud and pumped until the attached air line emptied itself.

"Whoa!" I heard Jake yell.

We both lurched into action to help Daryl out. He was a little slow to get up. Daryl climbed from the deck, rubbing his elbow where he fell.

"You going to be okay?" I asked.

"I'll be fine," Daryl said. "We won't say anything about this to the safety fucks now, will we?"

"I'll leave that up to you," I replied.

Daryl paced the deck, pumping his arm to get the pain out of his elbow. After a minute, grab the radio speaker attached to his lapel.

"Hello, tool crib?"

"Go for the tool crib."

"Dougie, It's Daryl here. Do you have any big angle grinders in there?"

"Hang on. I'll check."

"You have to be fucking kidding me," I quietly told Jake.

There was silence for thirty seconds before the radio came back to life.

"We'll have to blow the dust off 'em, but I have two nine-inch grinders here for you," Dougie said. "You sure you want 'em? They're too big for most people."

"Thanks, Dougie. I'll have some guys come and pick them up shortly."

Daryl looked at me and Jake.

First, this guy didn't want us to make sparks, and now he was okay with us grinding these bolts off?

"You guys good with this? We'll have you guys cut the studs off. We can get one of you on each side of the pipe."

"No, Daryl. I'm not doing it. And Jake isn't either."

"The fuck?" Daryl said, "Is this insubordination?"

"Not at all," I tried to assure him. "But we'll need a new permit for hot work now that we're going to be making sparks, which means we'll have to have one hundred percent spark containment. You'll have to get the scaffolders up here to tarp the scaffolding to contain the sparks."

He knew I was right, but he stayed mad anyway. He hung his head and paced the deck, hanging on to his radio.

"Hello, scaffolders."

"Go ahead."

"It's Daryl. I'm up in Plant Seventeen. We're going to need a scaffold tarped in. Can you have a couple of people come over here to bust out a quick spark containment?"

"It's your lucky day! I have a couple of people who just finished a job. They'll be there in ten."

"Right on! Thank you."

Daryl turned his gaze back to Jake and me. "You two stay here, He told us. "I'm going to grab the grinder and a new permit. Show the scaffolders what you need."

Daryl bounded down the stairs. I looked at my watch. It was getting late in the shift for all of this to happen without trying to ram the job to completion.

"How do you feel about this?" I asked Jake.

"I don't know, man. I'm just an apprentice."

"That's not what I asked," I pressed. "If you let everyone make your decisions for you, you'll get railroaded by guys like our friend Daryl here. If you can't have an opinion, you'll wind up getting fucked. Some guy like Daryl could be steering you toward an accident. So what do you think?"

"It does seem a little fucked-up," Jake admitted.

My mind was made up.

"Daryl might have to get told he can get fucked." I said.

The scaffolders took forty-five minutes to get there, not ten. When they arrived, the pace wasn't as quick as Daryl had been promised. The scaffolders had to complete a hazard assessment for the new work area. That took another twenty minutes.

Red tape was killing Daryl's plan.

It took Daryl over an hour and a half to get back. He returned with two nine-inch grinders, a few lengths of extension cord slung over his shoulders, and the salmon-colored paper of a new hot work permit.

He was huffing and puffing from the long climb up the stairs. He noticed the scaffolders had not made any progress on the containment and wasn't happy.

"That's as far as they got?"

"That's as far as they got," I said.

"Fuck me! Can you guys stay and work until the dayshift shows up?"

"No," I said.

"You have something better to do?"

"I don't know what to say, man. I'm not doing this job unless you get a nut splitter. It just isn't safe."

"What now?"

"I'm not doing it," I insisted. "And I'm not staying late to watch the scaffolders put up a tarp. It's the end of the shift. Instead of acting like an asshole, you should focus on handing this over to the dayshift so they can get the proper tool here and do the work safely."

"You're calling me an asshole?" Daryl said. He was fighting to keep his cool. "Goddamn it, man! How about making things easy? You're the one acting like a prick!"

"And you're trying to get us killed," I answered.

"Just... fucking hang out here for the night, then! I'll figure this out." Daryl stormed off.

Daryl didn't return for the rest of the night. Jake and I returned to the lunchroom and hopped on the bus back to camp.

The next day, the bus had to stop along the shoulder of the highway. Someone asked the bus driver what was going on.

"Fire in Seventeen," the driver said. "No traffic in until they finish the investigation."

"Was anyone hurt?" I asked the driver.

"You know as much as I do. All I know is there was a fire. They're tight-lipped when there's an accident or a fire in the plant."

We sat on the bus along the shoulder of the road for three hours. The curve of the road allowed us to see the line of vehicles waiting to get into the plant. It had to stretch a mile in either direction. I was sure that the flanges that Jake and I had been working on were the source of the fire, and I worried that someone had been burned. The scaffolders' containment would have made it harder to get off the deck if there was an emergency.

Eventually, the buses started moving, and our bus crept into the plant. Kyle was waiting for Jake and me in the lunchroom.

"You guys were working for Daryl last night in Plant Seventeen?" Kyle asked.

"Yeah."

"They want you guys back to assist in the investigation."

"Holy shit," I said. "Tell me no one got hurt."

"No one was hurt," Kyle said. "But there's a fuck-ton of damage. They have a couple of safety liaisons there who want to get your version of events."

Jake and I suited up, and Kyle drove us over to the stairs where we had been working the night before. The area had been cordoned off with DANGER tape. The two safety officers for The Company were waiting there for us. Both were young, but they seemed knowledgeable and professional. They let us into the red-taped area and then up to the deck where we had been working.

We got there, and I was immediately gobsmacked by what I saw.

The flange we had been working on, one of the safety investigators told us, had been in the process of having the studs cut with the nine-inch grinders. The blades on the grinders were not quite long enough to get through the studs, as the disc was depleted as the studs were cut. The guys doing the grinding had decided to get as many of the studs cut as deep as they could with the grinders before they brought in an oxyacetylene cutting torch to finish the job.

The cutting had gone well until the last stud. When the pipes were initially bolted up, someone likely forced them together. There must have been a large gap between them, and one bolt was holding all the tension and stress associated with forcing the two massive pipes together. The last bolt to be cut snapped apart and both sides of the piping spread apart violently. Once the line was broken, the piping contents were agitated and a slug of inflammable butane was released. The released gases caught fire on the open flame of the acetylene torch, causing a small explosion.

The fireball rose into an electrical cable tray overhead, melting all the wiring above them while the pipe contents continued to burn. The two fitters on the deck were able to leap to safety without getting burned.

"We've had issues lately with the contractors getting sloppy on the lockouts," One of the safety officers said.

"No shit," I said.

I looked above as they pointed out the damage. It looked like a bombing. Melted electrical cables hung from the structure like stalactites. The beams and columns that held up the decks above us had been covered with soot. The aluminum cable trays had all either melted or sagged with the heat.

I marveled at the damage and lack of casualties as the two safety officers quizzed us about what had happened the night before, and we walked them through the events as we remembered them. They commended Jake and me for not proceeding with the job.

"You guys did the right thing by refusing the work," one of the safety officers said. "It would have been much worse if it had happened at night. We only have half the fire crew here for night shifts, and we would have had to call the Fire Department from town to help put this out. We got lucky."

"That's good to hear," I said.

"Jesus," Jake said. "I'll be asking more questions about things from now on. Daryl acted like a real dickhead. Are there lots of guys out there like him?"

"You wouldn't believe how many," I said. "But now you know how to spot them."

The next night on Daryl's crew was no better. Daryl had us working with two maniacs, Dion and Wheeler – two guys who were known 'yes' men. Daryl had them breaking open a piping system that might be full of toxic gasses that would kill anyone who breathed it. Dion and Wheeler were to be under fully Self Contained Breathing Apparatus that consisted of an air tank and full-face mask with a breathing regulator. It was just like a SCUBA diving setup but without the water.

While Dion and Wheeler opened the pipe above us, Jake and I were supposed to work directly below the open grating floor they would be on.

I refused to do the work unless we went under SCBA too, or unless we could wait until Dion and Wheeler were done. Daryl flipped out on me.

"Why the fuck does everything have to be a deal with you, huh?"

"They're cracking open a sour gas line, right?"

"Yeah," Daryl said. "So?"

"Hydrogen Sulphide. You know, the deadly nerve agent? It's heavier than air."

"Yeah," said Daryl. "That's why Wheeler and Dion have the SCBA masks."

"What about me and Jake? You have us working five feet under them on an open deck. Whatever's in their pipe is going to hit us."

"You ever consider that there's probably nothing in there?" Daryl said. His dial had been cranked to eleven, and there was no turning it down.

"Probably nothing?" I asked. "Like there was nothing in that butane line that exploded last week? You can get us masks, or I'm not doing it. Not until Dion and Wheeler get finished anyway."

Dion and Wheeler stood at the ready with their SCBAs buckled on and wrenches in their hands.

Daryl paced for a few seconds, deep in thought.

"You know what, you fucking clown?" Daryl raged at me. "You're fucking done here! Get the fuck BACK to the lunchroom and park your ass there with the rest of the fucking rejects! I'll figure out what to do with you later, but you'd better hope I don't fucking see you again!"

"Or what?"

He had nothing. I started walking. Jake

"This will be the last fucking time you work with me, you lazy bastard!"

I thought about turning around and punching Daryl in the teeth. Instead, I reminded myself there was zero violence tolerance on any oilsands site. If there was a fight, both parties got terminated without any tribunal. Fighting also came with a ban from all locations and companies in the area.

In other words, if you wanted to kick the shit out of someone, you would have to square that thought against a lifetime of lost opportunities and wages. Still, as I got further away from Daryl, a great feeling swelled in me to slap the words he was continuing to yell at me - 'cocksucker,' 'cunt,' and 'fuckhead' — out of his stupid, rotten-toothed mouth.

I noticed a smoking area up ahead.

I walked in and lit one up. There was no one else there, and I enjoyed the silence. The midnight sun was low on the horizon, and I marveled at it as I smoked alone.

The silence did not last. I was soon joined by one of the operators, a long-haired metal head looking guy. The name tag on his coveralls said "CHAD." He was a twitchy-looking dude. He looked like he wanted to say something but might have been waiting for me to say something. I didn't mind the awkward silence. Chad, however, did.

"Man," Chad said, looking up at the lights of the high structures surrounding us. "Only a couple of years ago I was driving around this place high on crack, thinking these lights were helicopters chasing me down."

I was amazed. Was there anyone on this job site that wasn't completely fucked?

"Sounds like something right out of 'Goodfellas.'" I said.

"You know it," Chad told me through a smoky exhale. "I used to write safe work permits for people while I was blitzed on crack. Thank fuck no one got hurt."

This whole place had an explanation, and its name was Chad.

"Good thing," I replied.

"I'm glad every day that I was able to get through it," Chad continued. "I almost lost everything. Now I own two houses, one paid off and making me some rental money. I met a nice lady. Life has turned right around for me."

"That's great, man. You have yourself a great night. Stay out of the light and off the radar." I tossed my lit smoke into the long gray ashtray tube, hoping it would spontaneously combust.

I took the twenty-minute walk back to the lunchroom, following the soot-covered structural steel columns down the walking path. I thought about what was going on here, every messed-up interaction. I wondered if I would one day be one of these guys, detached from reality by drug addiction or just too much time away from the real world. I questioned if I wanted to be there and thought about quitting the trade altogether.

I could get bees and spend my days keeping them. Harvest some honey and sell it at farmer's markets. Could I go back to school and do…. something? Anything? Maybe I could re-train as a police officer and shake down Daryl. I would cuff him in front of his wife and punch him in the stomach when he bent over to take his shoelaces out before I threw him in a holding cell, tears in his eyes and snot dripping off his face. I decided that becoming a cop to kick the shit out of Daryl was too much trouble.

I talked myself out of my 'Lethal Weapon' fantasy as the lights of the lunchroom appeared around the next corner. I sat there alone, leafing through old newspapers. I wanted to go home. I wanted to start looking for somewhere else I could work. Staying here and fighting with Daryl was pointless.

After a couple of hours, the crew filed into the lunchroom, including Jake.

"What happened out there?" I asked.

"I just waited for those guys to finish both jobs," Jake said. "Daryl was pretty pissed. He spent a bunch of time bad-mouthing you to anyone who would listen. The superintendent came by, and he laid into him about you."

"I figured as much," I said.

"What do you think they're going to do with you?"

"Probably shitcan me? I couldn't say."

They didn't shitcan me. The next night, after we all had our pre-job talk in the lunchroom, Daryl instructed me to wait for the superintendent.

No one came. The next night, Daryl seemed shocked that I was in there.

"What the fuck are you doing here?" he asked.

"You tell me," I answered.

"The superintendent was supposed to come in and talk to you."

"Well," I said. "He didn't."

"Just stay here," Daryl told me. "I have shit to do. I'll get him to come in and talk to you."

"We don't have to wait for him," I said. "If you need to say something, I can handle it."

That option didn't make Daryl happy. He walked out without a word and returned an hour later with the Superintendent, a slim older gent with a white handlebar mustache and sun-leathered skin. His hard hat said "RORY."

"Let's figure this out," said Rory. "I have stuff to do. Why won't you do what your foreman is telling you?"

"Because he's asking me to do unsafe things."

"Like fuck I did!" Protested Daryl.

Rory waved his hands to settle Daryl down. It worked.

"One at a time here, fellas," Rory said. "What was he asking you to do?"

"He wanted me to work underneath a couple of other guys opening a sour gas pipe simultaneously with no masks. I didn't refuse. I just asked for a mask or to wait until the other guys were done."

"Is that right?" Rory asked Daryl.

"Technically," Daryl admitted.

"Technically?" Rory scoffed. "Either you did, or you didn't."

"I did," admitted Daryl. At least he wasn't a liar.

Rory deliberated for a few seconds, rubbing his mustache.

"Well," Rory said, "I can't have you two jokers working together anymore. Daryl, you have to stop being such an asshole. I've warned you about this before."

Daryl looked down at the floor. His plan had not gone how he had hoped it would.

"You," Rory said to me, "I have a friend looking to put together a group of guys at another site. He likes guys like you with an eye for detail. You'd be one of the first guys there, setting everything up. It's good for about a year. You interested?"

Anything was better than another day with Daryl Danger.

"I'm interested," I said.

"Great, said Rory. "I'll pay you for the night. Go back to camp and pack up your stuff. You have to be there in two days."

I did as Rory told me.

I was at the next job for a solid year, and it went fantastically. I was made a supervisor almost right away and was lucky to get a great bunch of guys working with me. About eight months into the job, Daryl showed up onsite. His project had finished, and he was transferred to my site. There were no supervisor jobs for him, and he was on the tools. I was his foreman now.

I could tell he was nervous. He probably thought that I was going to fuck with him the same way he fucked with me. I wanted to, at first. My 'Lethal Weapon' scenario I had concocted before popped into my head. I didn't do anything to him, I just gave him work to do, and he did it.

He was pretty good at it too.

Two weeks after he started, he came up and apologized to me.

"I was wrong," he told me. "I had been going through some personal stuff when we worked together before. My dad was sick, and I might have been drinking too much."

"Hey man, it's okay," I said.

"It's not, though," said Daryl. "After you left, a guy got hurt. He got his hand pinched when we set down some heavy equipment with a crane and lost two of his fingers. If I weren't such an asshole, I probably wouldn't have put him on that job. He told me before we started that he was unfamiliar with that type of work and uncomfortable with heavy lifts. So, I called him a pussy and made him do it anyway. I had to put his crushed fingers in a plastic bag."

I felt terrible for the guy who lost his fingers and I felt bad for Daryl too. I could tell he had never factored hurting someone into his career plan.

We got along after that. We weren't exactly best friends, but we had an understanding, and no one got hurt on our watch.

Chapter 23

The Liar, the Dicks, and the Shitshow

They say that sociopaths are drawn to positions of power. That's why you shouldn't be surprised when you find them in the upper echelons of government, patrolling your streets with badges and guns, or supervising a multi-million-dollar job at one of the country's largest oil and gas facilities.

He went by the name of George, but we all called him 'Big George' not so much due to his physical stature but because of the size of his ego. He was a big bastard of a guy, maybe in his late forties then. He managed to piss me off before I even started working for him.

It was a union job. I had 'pulled a slip' for the Pipefitters Union Hall in Edmonton. After finishing a year-long stint at a major construction project close to Edmonton, I took on a nightshift shutdown at a refinery. It was a tough one in the 'alkylation unit.' It was three weeks in full rubber suits and full-face protection, required to protect you from the sneaky rot of accidental exposure to the hydrofluoric acid used in the final stages of refining gasoline. The rubber suits were a misery known to anyone who worked in those nightmare zones. They were a necessity. You didn't want to go home with some HF acid splashed on you. If you did, you could rapidly lose a large part of your body and maybe even die.

After the Alky Unit shut down, I was looking for something a little easier on the body. I wanted to ensure that I would have a few weeks in August off before picking up another shutdown slip in the fall. A 'special project' in a tank farm sounded like an easy win. The only catch was that I had planned a camping weekend in British Columbia with my wife and kids at the time the job was supposed to start.

Usually, this kind of scheduling conflict could be easily handled. Most superintendents were decent and accommodating guys. With the unpredictable nature of our trade, if you needed a day or two with the family in late July, they were pretty good about giving it to you.

Big George was not one of those guys.

I called the number on the slip and asked Big George if I could come up two days after the start date, but he insisted that I get to the job right away because he was too busy and needed the manpower. I kissed my wife and kids goodbye and drove five hours north on the 'Highway of Death.' Several hard hat markers had been laid on the side of the road where workers had died on their travels. I had driven this highway last seven years ago, but I didn't remember there being so many. It was a somber omen to start a new job.

This site had a strict security policy. The other new hires and I were warned that the security clearance process would take a long time. It took three days in camp before my security clearance was activated, days that could have been spent with my family as I had originally planned.

On our first night on the job, all the new guys waited until Big George summoned us all to his office for his unofficial orientation.

The group was a mishmash of individuals. In the room with me was a large Bosnian plumber named Luka. Cody was a wide-eyed second-year apprentice who was jittery and nervous. Gerry was the older guy in the group. James was a nonchalant journeyman who had just gotten his ticket and came off as a bit of a dickhead. And finally, Ian, a quiet guy who struck me as a little hard to read.

We crowded into the cluttered and grimy office. Big George's desk was a disaster and was jumbled with paperwork, old coffee cups, and pens that didn't work. He sat behind his desk staring at us.

I looked around the room in those moments of awkward silence. I noticed that the body language in the room was reflecting how I felt. Luka bumped the back of his head against the wall in an erratic rhythm. Cody chewed the inside of his cheek, and Gerry rolled his eyes. Ian was taking a cue from James and looking up at the ceiling, both admiring the dust that had gathered to hang in long strands over the years.

He began to take us through his rules on the job in the most alpha-male way possible.

"I want to get one thing straight before we do anything else," Big George said, locking eyes with Cody, who immediately began to fidget.

"This is my job," he snarled, jabbing his thumb into his chest with every syllable. "If you have a problem with anything, you come to me before anybody else. You don't go to a job steward. You don't talk to anyone with the client unless you have come to me first. If I see one of you talking to someone you shouldn't be, we will have a big problem. I need to know you understand this."

Big George looked around at us all again, "I want to see heads nodding."

Cody nodded first. "Okay. I get it." He said.

We all followed suit and pledged obedience to Big George's way. I had to choke the words out, as the whole thing, a bunch of grown men repeating back words to another adult, made me feel like I was in kindergarten again, but I didn't want to rock the boat. As the words left my mouth, I looked over at Ian. He was steely-eyed and was having none of this bullshit. His lips stayed sealed. Big George zoned in on him right away.

"What's your name," he asked Ian.

"Ian."

"You have a problem with any of this, Ian? You going to be a problem for me?" Big George asked, from his low throne, arms still crossed defensively. Ian stood steadfast. His gaze never left Big George. He stood at the wall, not leaning, not at attention, but not relaxed.

"I don't make problems," Ian said.

"Good," Big George broke the eye contact and swiveled to his desk, punching in the password to his desktop. "Now you guys have to get a load of this!"

For the next two hours, we were treated to a slideshow of Big George's most recent visit with his wife to a Caribbean resort known for swinging sex and raunchy behavior. He bragged about how he could walk around, feeling women's asses and breasts as he pleased, and talked up all the crazy sex with strangers he'd had there. He bragged about how his wife was banging a couple of younger dudes in a hot tub while he and a bunch of other sun worshipers huddled around the side of the tub to watch.

I couldn't help but notice that the slides didn't match the stories.

He showed us a few pictures that amounted to nothing more than a couple on a beach vacation, nothing too raunchy. He explained that away.

"They don't encourage you to take pictures of the sex that happens there. What happens there stays there, if you know what I mean."

Big George went into vivid detail about the other sights he saw during his many visits with his wife to the red-light resort. Someone getting bathed in human fluids from multiple sources on the dance floor area while onlookers cheered, spit roasts galore—not the luau kind—the kind with a dude on either end of a lady.

He told us his blowjob stories – the ones he received anyway. He regaled us with outstanding eyewitness accounts of lesbian orgies, bisexual orgies, naked food fights, and tattoos on taboo body locations. On and on and on, Big George spoke in vivid, moist detail. I'm not a person who would generally rush to judgment about a person's sexual habits, but Big George's need to tell us all about every gory detail seemed a bit weird, even by tradesman standards. I imagined it was all supposed to prove that Big George's life was so much better than ours. I mean, what could be better than watching your wife get double-teamed before breakfast at an all-inclusive resort? Mimosa anybody?

Once Big George had finished telling us the last of his sticky sex stories, I noticed Ian looked slightly annoyed that we were all still there. Like me, he was probably hoping we had heard the end of Big George's exploits and might get some details about the job.

Big George shifted his focus to his former bodybuilding career. He did have photo documentation to back that up.

From his desk drawer, he produced a stack of Polaroid and instant camera pictures of him in multiple bodybuilding competitions in the nineties. Indeed, he had once been pretty ripped. He explained his present saggy appearance was due to his improperly coming off the steroid and hormone cycles due to a knee injury. That required a lengthy recovery period where he could not work out to maintain his physique and could not afford the high cost of proper meals, drugs, and hormones. The results of which were the lumpy, flappy-titted man before us.

If only that had been where the stories ended with Big George. He went into his time in the mob wars in the province he was originally from. He boasted of his involvement in the illicit drug trade. He had moved mountains out east – mountains of cocaine, that is.

He was known for intimidating and beating captive policemen. He participated in something called 'blanket parties.' He and a few co-horts would wait outside an unsuspecting victim's house late at night. One of them would smash the window of the victim's car, setting off the alarm. A few others would lie in wait near the front door. When the unsuspecting victim came outside to check the damage to confront the vandal, the assailants would cover him with a heavy blanket and bind the unfortunate bastard's arms under the blanket with a loop of rope. They would then go to town on the poor sonofabitch with baseball bats, chains, hockey sticks, feet, and fists.

A blanket party, of course, was only done to 'lowlifes' and 'junkies' that could not pay the tab they owed.

Big George lamented the friends he had lost in the large-scale war between rival sects in his home province. They were all struggling to be on top of the mountain, fighting the police, politicians, and local officials, and many had been fatally shot, stabbed to death, or bombed to smithereens in the process.

He described how he had suffered several gunshot wounds to his torso and legs, and my mind immediately went to the pictures we had just seen of Big George in his royal blue ball-hugger shorts, tanned and oiled like a new baseball glove. I didn't remember seeing any bullet wounds in the photos.

He went on to talk about his criminal past until a meeting notification popped up on his computer. When he ran out of stories about how awesome he was, he jumped out of his desk chair and shooed us out of his office.

"Go up to the lunchroom, fellas," Big George told us. "I have a meeting to get to. I'll send the other coordinator, Sam, up to get you guys going in a bit. Just hang tight up there until he comes to get you."

We did what we were told and waited in the lunchroom.

Sam did come by. He was a short guy who looked tired. The first and last words of every sentence he said came with a hint of a whistle, like he was about to call in some songbirds. Sam seemed flummoxed that we were all there.

"You're George's guys?" Sam asked.

"Yeah," replied Ian.

"What's he got you guys doing up here? Aren't you supposed to be down at the tank?"

"He told us to sit up here and wait for you," Gerry said.

Sam's face told us all the truth. We had walked right into the middle of a shitshow, and Big George was the star.

"Fuuuck around!" Sam said, frustrated. He took a minute to gather his thoughts. "Well, we can't have you all sitting up here pulling your puds. I'll see if they can take you over on the shutdown."

He raised the radio on his lapel to his whistly lips and called up one of the foremen on the nearby shutdown. "Come in, Carl!"

"Go for Carl!"

"It's Sam from Special Projects. I have some guys here that need a home for the night. Do you think you can find a spot for them?"

"Yeah. I think I can use a few guys to do some blinding up in the structure. Can you send me about four guys?" Car replied.

Sam did a quick headcount, lips moving with a barely audible whistle.

"Yeah, copy that, Carl. I have four for you. Where can they meet up with you?"

"Drop 'em off at the foreman shack."

"Copy that. Thanks, Carl!"

"Thank you!"

"Okay, four of you can head to the shutdown," Sam said, returning his attention to us. He jingled around in one of his pockets, produced a set of keys, and threw them at Gerry. "You know where you're going?" Sam asked Gerry.

"I think so," Gerry replied.

"Okay," said Sam, "Normally, I'd take you guys over there, but there's too much going on trying to get everything lined up. You might've noticed that some folks don't give a shit if things get done around here or not. So, who's all going?" Sam finished, eyeing us up.

"I'll go," I volunteered.

Luka and Cody chimed in next, and Gerry had the keys already, so he volunteered to come along. As we walked through the main hallway, past Big George's office, the big man called out to Sam.

"Hey, Sam! Where are you taking my guys?"

"They're heading over to the shutdown for the night," Sam replied.

Big George got up from his desk and headed out the door to talk with us. "You guys be back here tomorrow night, okay? I just got us approved to work eighteen days straight. We're going to money you guys up!"

Big George then ducked back into his office and hopped onto his computer, making himself look busy.

When we got to the shutdown, I found a familiar face. My old friend Jamie was there running a pipefitters crew. He and I had worked together at the last job I was at until we both quit. That job had been grinding to a halt, and he and I had both decided to jump ship for better-paying and shorter-term gigs. It turned out we'd landed at the same spot. Jamie was a great guy, and we got a quick bullshit session in before the toolbox meeting.

Unfortunately, I was not working for Jamie that night.

As luck would have it, I also recognized two apprentices, Dan and Walt. It was a small world. We would be working with Dan and Walt while we were at the shutdown. They were happy to have me on board with the team for the night.

The four of us from Big George's crew sat around and watched everyone go to work before our new foreman, Carl, showed up and introduced himself. He was a short man with a big, red, veiny nose. The beacon of an accomplished drunk. He never stopped smiling.

"Hey all, I'm Carl," he exclaimed, through a nicotine-stained grin. "I'll take the four of you over to grab tools. We'll be doing some de-blinding up in the higher structures. Dan and Walt can go ahead and walk the lock-out."

Lockouts at an active plant are some of the most important safety precautions. Every place has a different way of doing it, but each lockout must prove that all pressure, electricity, or other hazards from the system have been eliminated. It keeps people from working on a pressurized pipe or electrical system that could kill them.

In this case, we would be working on a previously in-service oil line. Dan and Walt were trusted to walk down the piping system with the operators and make sure that all the valves feeding it were locked closed with chains. This ensures that a primary set of keys to unlock the system is impossible to tamper with. No one can open any part of the system and return it to service without everyone working on it being out of harm's way when the system gets back up.

Dan and Walt drove off, and the rest of us piled into another truck with Carl. We were on the way to the tool crib to pick up the usual assortment of wrenches, flange spreaders, and other tools of the trade. Carl made awkward small talk through the five-minute drive through the plant to the central tool crib.

"You guys working for Big George, huh?" Carl asked through a shifty smile. "He's one to watch, if you know what I mean."

"What do you mean?" Gerry asked.

"Oh, I have a feeling you'll see eventually," Carl said.

Carl bothered me. Intentionally vague people drive me crazy.

As we got to the tool crib, Carl hit the child locks on his door-side console, locking the windows and doors. He cocked his right leg and farted. The smell was absolutely disgusting. A sour milk and dirty sock cocktail. We all winced and pulled our shirts over our noses to keep the stink at bay.

You'd think the truck was full of raw sewage. Carl was a chemical weapon.

"Now listen here, fuckers," Carl grinned from the front seat. "No one gets out until you answer my question. You got that?"

Cody's eyes were closed. He spoke through a pinched nose that made him sound like a cartoon character. "What question, you smelly old fuck?"

"I want to know who in this cab is circumcised and who isn't," Carl replied. "I'll go first."

Carl raised his hand and said, "Circumcised!"

We looked at each other, caught off guard by such a lunatic, weirdo question. Carl cocked his leg and farted again.

What was wrong with this guy? I tried to hold my breath but couldn't. I got a big lungful of Carl's ass gas. Cody did too. His hand shot up as he exclaimed, "Fuck! I'm cut! Open the goddamned window!"

"No can do!" Carl said, grinning like a psychopath. "Consensus has not been reached yet!" He looked at the rest of us.

Luka broke next. His hand shot up. "Uncircumcised!" he choked.

"That's fifty percent!" said Carl. "You last two guys going to bump the numbers?"

"Still have my toque," I told him as I tried to keep from gagging.

Carl looked to Gerry, who was having none of this shit. "Fuck you. Open the door," Gerry said.

"All right, relax, sweetheart," Carl said. "I'll put you in the "cut" column. That makes it fifty-fifty. Nice getting to know you, fellas!"

Carl unlocked the door and let us out. Everyone took big gulps of the air when we got outside. The plant was rich with hydrocarbon flavor—not much better than Carl's cadaver farts, but better nonetheless. Carl laughed as he walked over to a nearby smoke pit that had a few old wooden chairs to sit in while you smoked. There were metal buckets filled with sand for butts, but that didn't stop everyone from just littering the ground with trampled cigarette remains.

The rest of us gathered the tools we would need for the night into four canvas bags. We threw the full bags into the back of Carl's fart wagon. Luka, Cody, and I joined Carl in the smoke pit. Gerry stood outside the truck and rolled the windows down to clear as much of the turd smell as possible before we all had to get back in.

I got up next to Carl in the smoke pit, lit one up, careful not to get too close in case he shat himself again, and asked, "What the hell, man?"

"What?"

"The circumcision shit. What the hell was that all about?"

Carl looked me dead in the eye.

"Well," he said, 'I just wanted to know if any of you would stick out if we all wound up on a nude beach in Israel. I guess you and the big guy wouldn't blend in!" He walked towards the truck and shouted to us without turning around. "Enjoy your smokes, fellas! I'll be in the truck when you're done!"

Luka came up behind me and said, "That Carl is one weird fuck."

"There are a lot of weird fucks here," I told him.

We accompanied circumcised Carl to the work area, a large ominous structure on the edge of the plant. It had to be two-hundred feet tall and was stained a sooty black. At its base was an open bay door, large enough to drive a dump truck through. It was home to about six operations workers who were there to meet us. They greeted Carl with smiles and waves, showing they were familiar and friendly with him.

I wondered if they'd traded circumcision statistics with Carl.

We unloaded the tools from the back of the truck into a large freight elevator. Gerry hit the up button, sending a shiver through the elevator compartment as the pulleys and wires attached to the elevator groaned to life.

The top of the structure was hot, filthy, and humid, and the air was filled with a sharp hydrocarbon reek, like chainsaw fuel. The walls at the top were just as dirty as the floor. Everything was covered in grease and soot. Steam puffed from traps attached to the tubing systems under insulation.

There was a catwalk around the inside of the western perimeter of the structure that led to an outdoor walkway. Standing near the door to the outside was a safety watch lady who was enjoying the cool evening breeze. A network of large pipes was bolted together at staggered intervals at floor level. Tags hung on each flange connection indicating where plates needed to be installed to isolate the down-stream piping from any pressure source. Several other large pipes rose through the floor before they changed direction to a support structure that carried them outside. Tags were hanging on two of those as well. The safety watch had staged several self-contained breathing kits on the catwalk.

An operations lead named Cliff gestured for everyone to come in close for a pre-job talk before we all got down to business.

"Okay," said Cliff, "We have five flanges up here to get to, so we'll start with these at the floor and move on to the vertical ones after. Once you break them, we have Amy up there to watch and do initial gas testing at each flange."

Cliff waved up at Amy, and she waved back.

"Once she gives you the okay, you can break the flanges fully and install the blanks. If anyone needs to take a cool down before we get started, you can get a breather on the outside catwalk before we get going. Good to go?"

Heads nodded in agreement.

"Everyone take a cool-down, grab water from Amy's cooler, pack up, and we'll get started. I want to have pairs of two tackling one flange each. We can finish three at once. Then the first teams finished can move to the next two." Cliff instructed.

We all headed out to the outer deck, a terrifying structure with an open grating floor welded down to the primary framing. It was sturdy, but allowed anyone standing on it a view directly below their feet to the ground two-hundred feet below. I'm not afraid of working at heights, but it was a little unnerving. We hung out for five minutes and opened the front of our coveralls to let the cool summer evening breeze in. We chugged back our bottles of ice-cold water. Then Walt downed his water, crushed the bottle on his forehead, and exclaimed, "Let's get this show on the road!"

We got down to business. Each of us chose a breathing apparatus and masked up. The sharp crack of six breathing air regulators signaled that we were ready to go. Amy also donned a breathing pack and readied her gas detector wand.

I paired up with Luka, and he and I got to work taking the nuts off our flange. It was an oversized flange with heavy bolts and nuts the size of my fist. Luka was a large guy and worked more quickly than me.

Carl's guys had indeed done an excellent job getting everything ready for us. The nuts and bolts came loose for us quickly, and it wasn't long before we had half of the bolts removed from the hulking flange. Luka and I then removed all the nuts from one side of the flange and stuffed the serrated jaws of the flange spreader into the gap between the flanges. Luka gave the handle of the flange spreader a couple of hard pulls, and the flange began to open. Usually—ideally—once you reach this stage, if you have a system that has been sufficiently locked out, nothing should happen.

But that was not the case this time.

We opened the pipe, and a white burst of steam belched from the opening. This wasn't a steam pipe. I guessed that this was purge steam that would typically be pushed through to clean everything out, as it wasn't much hotter than what comes off a pot of boiling water.

What the fuck? This was an oil line, not a steam pipe. There should be nothing in it.

This was going to make the job harder.

Amy came by with her gas detector but couldn't get close enough to deploy the tube end of the device in the open piping. The steam was fogging her mask like it was ours. I could now only see outlines.

A shadow of a person where Luka was, and a streak of royal blue of Amy's coveralls as she moved away from our pipe and over to another.

"What do we do?" asked Luka.

"It's open," I replied. "We have to put it back together now. We'll have to work by feel. Make sure that you keep your hands out from between the flanges in case the spreader lets go. If it closes back up and your hand is in there, you'll lose your fingers."

"Okay," said Luka, his voice muted from behind his fogged facepiece.

Working blind like this increased the chances that one of us might inadvertently trap our hands or fingers in the danger zone.

We returned to the open, steam-belching maw of the pipe. We felt our way through the mist for parts and tools. We jacked the two flanges apart enough to slide the blind - a large circular piece of solid metal about an inch thick - and installed a gasket on each side. We let the flange spreader off, and the flange stayed open with steam still erupting from the opening. I hoped the flange would have closed itself. It would have kept most of the mist at bay. We'd have to keep going by feel until we got at least one bolt tightened.

I passed bolts and nuts to Luka - enough to get his side of the flange filled - and went to work putting mine in. I fumbled in the steam for everything I needed. After a few minutes of frantic effort, we installed and tightened one bolt at the top of the assembly and the steam stopped. We tightened the rest of the bolts and got ourselves out of the work area to the outside catwalk, where we could remove our air breathers safely.

Luka and I got another drink of water and looked back into the steamy room. Walt and Dan were also done and had already removed their breathing packs and were sipping from ice-cold water bottles on the outer catwalk. I joined them.

"You guys confirmed the lockout on this, didn't you?" I asked.

Dan and Walt looked at each other like they didn't understand.

"Well, we checked with operations that it was locked out," Walt told me. "We put Carl's crew lock on the lockbox. It's fine. Why?"

"Did you guys have steam coming out of your pipe?" I asked.

"Yeah," Dan scoffed. "So what?"

"Don't you think it's weird for a locked-out piping system to have steam shooting through it while we're working on it?" I asked. I was starting to get myself worked up.

"Not if they're still flushing it with steam," Dan said.

I was stunned. These two hadn't checked anything. If they had, they would have known that it was still in the process of being internally flushed.

"Why would you give the lock-out the okay if they are still flushing the pipe with steam?" I asked Dan.

Walt interrupted, "Hey, man. This isn't new construction. This is the way things go at a live plant. If you don't like it, you can piss off and join the long line of other guys who couldn't hack it."

Walt and Dan were still apprentices. They had never behaved like this before they came to work here. Dan and I had gone to high school together. I knew him. Something was off, and I thought it might have had something to do with their identical ruddy, scabbed complexions.

These guys look like they've been "mething" around.

"Listen, guys," I told them. "I don't know the lay of the land here, but I do know that if you guys fuck up and hurt someone or yourselves, none of these people you are trying to impress aren't going to go to bat for you. You'll be thrown under the bus. Just be careful."

"Thanks, 'Dad,'" said Walt sarcastically. "We'll take that to heart."

Walt walked away, annoyed because I had dared question his competence at this job. He and Dan had clearly been ordained as the "go-to" guys.

Gerry, Cody, Luka, and I brought the gear down the elevator and back to the truck, where Carl was already waiting for us.

"How'd she go?" asked Carl.

"There was still steam in the lines," Gerry replied. "We couldn't see a fucking thing. I'd say it was kind of a shit show."

Carl laughed it off. "That's operations at this place. Hey, look on the bright side. It's all done, and no one got hurt—well, physically hurt anyway—maybe some hurt feelings by the look of things? Hopefully, you'll all get over it."

"Thanks, that means a lot," Gerry said. "Take me back to our lunchroom."

Carl drove us back to the lunchroom. He tried to engage us in small talk again, but we weren't interested. He dropped us off in the dark. Ian met us as he opened the door to enter the cool night air on his way for a cigarette.

"How was that?" Ian inquired.

"Absolutely fucked," Gerry replied. "These guys are going to kill someone going about like that. I don't think I'll be going back to work with them again, and I might look for a new job when we go out on days off."

"That doesn't sound good," Ian said.

We gave him the rundown about what had happened.

"It looks like I'll be double-checking all the lockouts on this job." Ian agreed.

"How about you?" I asked Ian. "Did you get anything done?"

"This is it," Ian said. "We saw Big George when we were on our way out here, but he just waved us into his office to brag about how many guys he's watched his wife bang. I pretended I had to take a shit and never went back, but I think James got sucked into that black hole. He's probably still in there."

We all sat in the smoke pit chatting. Luka bummed another one. I liked the big guy. He was good company.

After the smoke had cleared, we headed back inside. Sure enough, Big George was in his office with poor James, who looked at us as we walked past with an expression that I imagined might cross the face of any hostage who longed to be rescued from a bad situation. Big George stopped us as we went by.

"How did it go out there, boys?" Big George asked.

"They tried to cook us like lobsters," Luka replied. "There was still steam in the piping when we opened it up."

"Yeah, they tend to get a little 'cowboy' around here," Big George said like it was no big deal. "They don't like to wait for things to cool down. You'll get used to it. One time me and Barry- who's high up in operations now - had to jump up onto a scaffold where a seal had let go on a bitumen line. It was pissing hot oil all over us. We went in there against orders, with alarms ringing all over the plant. Barry and I tightened that bastard up. We both got back to camp that night covered in oil and tired as hell. You could see the imprint of my oily ass on the bedspread when I peeled it off the next morning. They gave us shit the next day and tried to fire us, but Barry and I saved the plant, and they knew it. Since then, they've let us do what needs to be done."

"I'd rather watch this place burn from the highway than gas myself or be lit on fire." Ian said.

"Well, I guess that's why you're pulling wrenches, and I'm pulling in ten more bucks an hour than you," Big George smugly bragged.

Ian's face went red. He wanted to get into it with Big George, but he also wanted to keep his job. Probably recognizing that Ian was about to pop, Big George changed the subject.

"So, I know your guys' slips all say you're working a ten-day shift, but things have changed. We will be working eighteen-day rotations starting now. Twelve-hour shifts each night. You guys are going to make some money!"

My heart sank. My wife and kids had been banking on my only doing a ten-day stretch, and my wife had re-booked the campground in the mountains we had arranged before this job started.

I'd have to call and tell her to cancel the whole thing. Again.

My wife wasn't a fan of the unpredictable nature of my chosen line of work, and this would be rubbing salt in the wound. I had braced myself for that phone call. Everyone else—mostly all single guys— was happy with the news.

"You guys can get out of your coveralls and head to the lunchroom." Big George informed us. We still had five hours left in our shift. He handed Luka a walkie-talkie. "Keep that close by in case I need you. I'm just waiting on permits from operations. We might still get down to the tank tonight."

Gerry was already there, digging into an egg salad sandwich from an overstuffed brown lunch bag. James, happy to have been rescued from Big George's undertow of bullshit, relayed the info to Gerry, who shrugged and said, "Ass time in the lunchroom? Easy money!"

We hunkered in for the rest of the night and only left the lunchroom once the early morning sun rose and it was time to go home. We saw Big George again as we headed out for the bus. "Maybe we'll get out tomorrow night, guys," he said. "Have a great sleep!"

We spent the rest of the nights that shift in the lunchroom. Ten boring hours each night.

It got harder and harder to break the monotony. Countless games of crib were played. After that wore thin, I brought out my sketchbook and drew pictures, practicing for the comic book I wanted to illustrate.

Having borrowed my wife's MP3 player for its Wi-Fi capabilities, I could poll my friends and family on Facebook for drawing challenges. I drew superheroes, cool cars, sexy ladies in skimpy underwear, and my greatest challenge - 'Val Kilmer in his Gonch Listening to Simple Plan.' It was a masterpiece.

We napped a lot, taking shifts like soldiers in case some higher-ups came in to check on us. The only requirement was for us all to stay awake, and sometimes official-looking folks we didn't know would pop their heads into the lunchroom to see what we were up to.

We never did work the eighteen-day stretch. Big George hadn't organized it properly – or cleared it with the management – and after ten days, we all went home.

—-

When we all got back to work, we regrouped in the lunchroom, where Big George met us.

"More of the same," he informed us. "I'm still having trouble getting permits. Everyone's going full tilt on the shutdown. Just stick it out in the lunchroom."

On the way to the bathroom one night, I passed by Big George's office. I was hoping he wouldn't notice me, but he did.

"Oh! Icy, man!" Big George said. He jumped up from his desk to meet me in his doorway. I stopped but didn't say anything.

"I have something for you," he said. Big George extended his hand to me. I didn't want to look at what he was offering.

Please don't be a dildo, I thought.

It was not a dildo. It was worse, much worse. It was a radio. I knew what this meant.

"I was going to give this to Gerry, but I don't think he likes me much. I figure you might be okay with an extra five bucks an hour."

Sonofabitch. He was making me his foreman.

Under any other circumstance, I would have loved the job and the money, but I didn't want to be under this guy's thumb. And I didn't want to stay long-term. But I betrayed my better judgment and said yes. Fuck-a-doodle-doo.

Big George's new thing became leaving us all night in the lunch-room all night and would call us out to the job during the last forty minutes before the end of each shift. It wasn't enough time for anything to be accomplished, and we would just stand around and wait for equipment to show up or wait to meet the dayshift guys for an on-the-job-handover. It was a tactic to make it look like we had been accomplishing things when the more productive dayshift arrived.

The extra time onsite messed with my internal clock. I was getting dark circles under my eyes, my skin looked gray, and I was tired and bitchy.

Big George fucked up all the paychecks. The first payday had arrived, and everyone noticed that their deposits were messed up. Gerry was missing three days off his pay. Ian and Cody were each missing one day of income. Luka and James were short some overtime, and I was missing a few hours.

We took turns filling out the "query forms" that Big George was supposed to forward to payroll to fix the issue.

"Don't worry fellas," the Big Guy said. "I'll make sure these are taken care of."

I noticed Big George was wearing slippers. Slippers. Not work boots. Not running shoes. The motherfucker was wearing comfy, fuzzy, baby blue, loafer-type slippers. The man gave zero fucks.

After four weeks mostly sitting in the lunchroom, I'd decided that I'd had enough. Gerry had taken some extra time off. He mentioned before he left that if his paycheck issue wasn't sorted out before he got back, there was going to be hell to pay. I wanted to be a good foreman and clear up the payroll issues before he got back. I stopped by Big George's office.

"How about those payroll forms? I asked, nodding to the stack. "Gerry is short a lot of money, and it's been over a week."

"Yesh," Big George sighed. "That's gotta suck."

"It sure does," I replied. "I could take them over to wherever they need to go."

"The administration doesn't want anyone in their office below supervisor level. They had an incident with someone yelling and screaming at them a few months ago."

"You should get to them sooner rather than later," I told him. "Gerry isn't a complainer, but he's pissed that he hasn't been paid."

"Yeah, I guess he would be." Big George said. He put his hands up behind his head and leaned way back in his comfy leather chair. "I'll see what I can do."

I let it go a few more nights before I decided to pop into Big George's office while I was in a bad mood. The stack of payroll forms was still on his desk.

"Still haven't sorted the payroll out?" I said, catching him by surprise.

"Shit," Big George said. He scooped up the pile of papers and slipped his feet back into his dirty Crocs.

"Yeah, 'shit' is right. Gerry's going to lose it when he gets back."

Big George was up and out the door. "I'll take these over right now," he said.

Great! I thought. You've only had several weeks.

I watched Big George bound down the hallway and out the door to his truck. I was about twenty feet behind him on my way to the smoke pit and made sure to see him drive away. I stuck around to make sure he came back without the forms. After fifteen minutes, he got back, jumped out of his truck, and gave me a thumbs-up. He had finally done his fucking job.

I went back to work in the lunchroom. I stayed there until forty minutes until the end of the shift – doing nothing until Sam called over the radio.

"What's your twenty, guys?" Sam asked.

"Lunchroom," I replied.

"Okay. I'll be right up to see you guys."

Sam didn't know then, but he was about to have a bad time—courtesy of me.

I looked at Luka and Cody, "He's going to ask us to work overtime for Big George." I told them. "I'm not fucking doing it."

"Can you even do that?" asked Cody.

"Why not?" I shot back. "Our shift is ten hours. We've been here for nine already. Overtime isn't mandatory, and we're not prisoners. Big George can get fucked. He didn't even take our payroll forms in until today."

"The fuck? Are you serious?" Luka said. "They were supposed to be in weeks ago!"

"I know, man. He doesn't care. If he doesn't care if we get paid, why should we care about working overtime for him?"

"Yeah!" an eavesdropping James said.

"What do you think we should do?" Luka asked.

"Easy. He's going to ask us to work another three hours, and we say no. I'm going to tell him I'm doing my laundry tonight. You can tell him anything you want. He can't make you work overtime.

"I don't know, man. I don't want to make waves." Cody said, voice wavering.

"We have barely turned a fucking wrench since we all got here four weeks ago. We don't know how many hours we are supposed to work in a day. Big George can't even tell us how many days we work in a row. He spends his time jacking it to swinger porn and muscle cars in his office. All we do is set up work for dayshift. All of us want to work, but we never get a chance to get anything done. We just sit in the lunchroom like a bunch of chumps. I'm sick of not doing anything, and I'm sick of Big George. Don't you feel like we're being disrespected here, guys?" I looked around the room. I could see they were all thinking about it, and by the looks on their faces, they knew what I had just said was the truth.

"All we have to do," I told them, "is go back to camp. It doesn't have to be a fight. But to make this work, we all have to stick together."

Everyone was nodding their heads.

"I'm in," Luka said.

Sam showed up in the lunchroom ten minutes before the shift was over. I took no pleasure in ruining his night.

"I need three of you to head down with me to the tank and set the crane up again for dayshift." He told us. Sam must have noticed that everyone had their heads down and were too scared to look him in the eye.

"Hey, what's with you guys?" Sam asked.

"We're going back to camp," I said. "All of us." No one else said anything. Cowards!

"Come on, guys, don't do this to me tonight! There's a bunch of bigwigs coming in tomorrow after lunch. If they don't see progress on this job, we're all up shit creek. They might pull the contract from us."

"Cool," I said. "Maybe we can all come back with the new contractor and maybe... I dunno? Do some fucking work?"

I walked away and began taking my boots and coveralls off. Luka and Cody followed me.

"Come on, guys," Sam pleaded, "I get that you want to stick it to Big George, but you don't have to fuck me over too."

Sam didn't seem like too much of a turd, but I'd decided that Big George needed to be taken down a peg, even if that meant Sam was collateral damage. I kept taking my coveralls and boots off, undeterred by Sam's attempt to appeal to my feelings.

Then Sam said something that cemented my decision.

"I didn't want to have to do this, Sam said, "But I'm ordering you to work. You can't get on the bus until the dayshift shows up."

What the fuck did he think this place was? The US Fucking Marine Corps?

"I had no idea overtime was mandatory," I replied.

"It is tonight," Sam said.

Sam was full of shit, and he knew it. I could see it on his face.

"I'm going back to camp right now," I told him. "I'm going to do my laundry. If you can find somewhere that says I have to work your mandatory overtime, you can fire me."

I looked at Cody and Luka. They were wilting like gas station sandwich lettuce. Neither of them would return my gaze. James and Ian had already disappeared.

I was prepared to die on this hill.

I made my way downstairs and outside, and was waiting for the bus that would take me to camp. A moment later, Cody and Luka joined me. They looked sick.

"I don't know about this," Cody said. "Sam's pretty pissed off."

"Who gives a shit?"

"Dude," said Luka, "Aren't you worried about Big George? That guy is a fucking psycho."

"You think so?"

"Yeah. The motherfucker has been shot!"

"You believe that?"

"Why would he lie about all that stuff?" Said Luka.

"Look," I said. "You've seen the bodybuilding pictures he likes to throw around. Did you see any bullet wounds?"

A puzzled look crossed Luka's face. "No. Good point."

"And you guys think that if he had been running drugs and breaking legs for the mob, he'd be shooting his mouth off about it to everyone who crossed his path? I'm not in the know about how those groups operate, but I figure a guy with lips as loose as Big George's would have been told to shut his fucking face by now. Unless he's a poseur.... Which he is."

"You're willing to gamble on that?" Cody asked.

"It's not a gamble," I said matter-of-factly. "Big George is a total douche. Any guy who watches other dudes fuck his wife, and then mouths off about it to total strangers is not running with the mob. Anyone who can oil up and pose in speedos for a bodybuilding competition has never been shot. I'd say the fucker is lying about ninety-nine percent of everything he told us."

"Dude, he's going to come unglued on you tomorrow," Luka said. "Maybe us too."

"I doubt it."

Sam approached. "Guys. Come on. You're really fucking me over here."

"I'm just doing my laundry," I said.

Cody and Luka said nothing.

Not wanting to watch Sam beg pathetically, I walked the five hundred feet to the next bus stop as Cody and Luka followed Sam to the smoke pit. I knew they had folded when I got on the bus, and they weren't on it.

I awoke later that afternoon feeling refreshed and ready for a fight. I packed my lunch as usual, and when it was time, I boarded my regular bus early, getting one of the 'bad kid' seats near the back before the bus filled up.

Big George wasted no time when he heard I had arrived. I was putting my coveralls on in the hallway with the other guys. Gerry had returned to the site that night and was oblivious to what had happened the night before. Ian and Cody were also there when the Big Guy showed up with an angry scowl. He pointed to me and said, "YOU! IN MY OFFICE! NOW!"

Oh no! I was in trouble!

When I got to the office door, he was already sitting at his desk.

"Sit down!" he ordered, shaking with anger.

"I'm good to stand," I said. I knew I had this. All I had to do was stay calm.

"Have it your way," he said. "What the fuck do you think you're doing, pulling that bullshit last night? When we need you to work overtime, you fucking work overtime!"

I stared at him, saying nothing. I could see my silence was bothering him. He fidgeted in his chair and coughed, gripping his chest with each violent breath out. I thought he might have a heart attack, and

I wondered how much effort I would be willing to put out if I had to give him CPR.

"I fucking set you up as my foreman, and this is how you act?" Big George continued, huffing after the brief coughing fit.

"Setting me up as your foreman doesn't mean I will be your lap dog. The other guys are just as annoyed as I am. They just don't have the balls to say anything. We sit in the lunchroom for most of the night, going fucking crazy with boredom because you can't even do your job and find us something to do."

Big George chewed on that truth bomb for a while before he lowered his voice and said, "I'm busting you down. I'm making Gerry the foreman. Give me the radio."

"Not a problem," I said as I handed the radio back to him.

"And I'm switching you to dayshift."

This was the news I had been hoping for. Union rules dictated that he would have to offer me a layoff if he wanted to change my shift, which I was more than happy to take.

"Cool," I said. I might have been smirking. "I'll take a layoff."

Big George shook his head. "No layoffs. You're going to dayshift."

The crew had gathered in the hallway behind me and were listening in.

"I know the rules. If you want to change my shift, you have to offer me a layoff."

"I told you. No layoffs."

"Well, if you have anything else to say to me you'd better do it through a union steward. I'll be in the shop with the guys."

I left his office and marched past the wide-eyed group in the hall. "Good for you," Gerry whispered as I passed him. The guys all followed me into the shop.

"Holy fuck, dude, you're out of your mind!" Luka said. "He's pissed! He's going to wreck your goddamned life!"

"Looks like we're going to find out," I said.

We sat for a few minutes in the shop. It wasn't long before Big George burst through the doors at the far end of the shop. He looked happy and jovial in a way he hadn't before. He didn't look like the arrogant blowhard. He struck me as a completely different guy. His coveralls and work boots were on—a sight 'as rare as rocking horse shit,' as my dad used to say.

"Guys," Big George pleaded, "I had no idea you all thought the job was off the rails. I get it now. You know you all could have come and told me if you had issues about how things were going. My door is always open. What can I do to get things back on track here?"

Attitude: Adjusted.

"You could get us paid," Gerry told him. It hit Big George like a bullet.

"Yeah," he said in his new teddy bear voice, "I fucked that up. Sorry. I took the forms over to the payroll ladies last night."

Yeah, I thought, *Only because I made you, fucker.*

"They're going to put a special deposit in tomorrow for anyone affected." he continued.

"You could let us know what shift we're working," Ian said. "Is it ten days or eighteen?"

"What do you guys want to work?"

Everyone looked around at each other. Eighteen-day shifts were big money.

"Eighteen," James said.

"I'll try and get those for you. No promises, but if I can't get an answer before the fifth day in every shift, we'll stick to a ten. Deal?"

Everyone nodded. That was acceptable.

"Okay. Is there anything else?" Big George asked humbly.

"Hours," Luka said. "Are we doing twelves or tens?"

"What do you guys want to work?"

"Twelves?" Luka asked, looking around at everyone else. They were all nodding in agreement.

"Twelves it is!" Big George said. "Guys, I'm so sorry. Things will be better, I promise. I will grab you guys a permit and walk the work tonight with operations. You guys won't be spending as much time in the lunchroom." He looked around the room. "Are we good?"

Everyone looked at me.

"Yeah," I said. "We're good."

Once he had left, I turned to Luka and Cody. "See? I told you he'd never been shot."

We spent the first half of that shift finally getting things done like we'd wanted to the whole time. We rigged in valves. We bolted up piping.

It was the first steady work we did on the project we'd been hired for. It felt good. Even James and Ian were pulling their weight. I didn't know what Big George was going to do about me. I figured that he would be cooking up some way to fuck me over. I was still hoping for that layoff.

After lunch, I joined Cody and Luka for a cigarette, and Big George himself came for a smoke. He side-eyed me like he wanted to tell me something, but he didn't. His phone rang, and he answered.

"Yeah, this is George. Huh? Yeah. Uh-huh. Uh-huh. What? What? Like fuck they are! Like fuck! Yeah? Well, FUCK YOU TOO!"

He smashed his phone on the ground, locked eyes with me, and flared his nostrils. There was madness on his face. I could tell that he wanted nothing more than to choke the life out of me, but he knew the rules as I did. He could kick my ass if he wanted to, but that meant bye-bye to the overpaid job, adios to the Cessnas, and sayonara to the all-inclusive tropical gangbangs. He'd be banned from the site the same as me.

In my mind, I dared the big sonofabitch. He had a lot more to lose with a lifetime ban than I did.

Big George thought better of kicking my ass and stormed off. Everyone was laughing.

Sam strolled up.

"Was the Big Guy out here?" he asked.

"He was," I said, pointing to the remnants of his phone on the ground.

"Hmm. That would explain why no one can get a hold of him. Was he pissed off?"

"I'd say. The guy went nuts and smashed his phone. What happened?"

"The bigwigs from The Company popped by the tank this afternoon. They looked around and decided that there wasn't enough getting done over there. They started to quiz some dayshift guys about why that was, and the consensus was that nothing ever gets done on night shift. They decided the Big Guy wasn't pulling his weight. They are putting him on dayshift so they can keep watch on him. You probably saw him get the phone call."

"Sure did," I said. "So, what does that mean for my layoff?"

"No layoff," Sam said. "Nightshift is my baby. You're mine now."

"I'm staying on nightshift? Am I still the foreman?"

"After what you just pulled? No. And that horseshit better not be a normal occurrence, or we'll have serious problems."

"Point taken," I replied.

The next few days were a downer. Sam gave me the worst of the jobs. I ran tools back and forth to the tool crib. I did confined-space watch for the guys working in the tank. That meant all I got to do was sit at the entrance to the tank and log when the other guys came in and out on a sheet of paper.

I was in the doghouse and not allowed on the tools. The rest of the guys got chummier with Sam, who made a real effort to treat everyone better than Big George had treated them. He got Gerry his money within a day. We got put on a ten-day schedule, and with the regular shifts at the tank, the last-minute requests for overtime stopped altogether.

Everyone was happy now, except me. I bided my time and kept my neck off the chopping block. I knew Sam had clocked me as a troublemaker and was looking for any excuse to gun me. I wasn't in any hurry to give him one. I kept angling for my layoff, but after I had kicked up the fuss that I did, I knew that they would not go out of the way to do me any favors.

Sure enough, the time came when I wanted to leave. I asked for my layoff, which they rejected. I had to quit, and so I did.

I kept in touch with Luka for a while after I left. He wound up being made foreman – for Big George. Sam had come into work drunk as a sunk one night and backed his company truck into a concrete barrier before he even started work for the night. He refused to take the post-incident drug and alcohol test, and they fired him for refusing to do a piss test. Luka told me everyone still talks about how fucked up things were before I stuck my neck out.

"It's too bad they cut you loose, man," Luka told me. "No one else knows how to keep Big George in his place. He's acting like a jackass again. It's like nothing happened. His sex stories are even worse now."

"You could always tell him to shut the fuck up," I said.

"Nah. He hasn't dicked around with our pay, and he gets us stuff to do. I think your beef with him made a difference."

"Still think he's been shot?" I asked.

"Ha," Luka chuckled. "Yeah. But only the kind of friendly fire he'd find in a hot tub."

I knew what he meant. Gross. I wouldn't miss that place.

Chapter 24

Seven Signs That Your Friend Needs Your Help

I'm writing this in the hope that I can help someone avoid making the same terrible mistake that I did. I wish I could go back and fix it.

We all know people who aren't here anymore because they decided to quit life. But it doesn't have to end like that. Sometimes all they needed was a friend to reach out.

I visited a friend of mine one weekend, and I missed the signs. Shorty wasn't in a good place; things felt off. It wasn't anything specific, but the friendly banter and interest in life seemed missing. He was just sitting there, quietly watching TV. It was eerie.

I couldn't figure out what was going on. I knew something wasn't right, and it was an awkward evening. So I left him to his own devices and went back to my busy life.

A week later, Shorty ended it all.

The last time I saw him, I'd left him sitting by himself when I knew something was wrong. I let him down.

I will always regret that I wasn't more informed or better prepared to help.

It's easy to miss the warning signs that a friend needs you. You have your own struggles, and of course, they take up most of your attention.

That's why it's important to notice any unusual behavior in the people that you care about. One of your friends, family, or co-workers could be slowly inching their way toward the edge of the cliff, and maybe they can't do anything about it on their own. They need a helping hand.

There are parallels between a person drowning and a person going through emotional difficulty. As we go about our noisy lives, someone could be drowning in their anxiety or depression right beside us. Unless we look around, we won't see them start to slip under.

When someone is drowning in water, everyone expects them to splash around and cry for help. It seems like a person drowning would be obvious, something you couldn't miss.

If you don't know to look, you are probably enjoying water sports, the beach, the sun, and the outdoors.

They look like they are treading water just fine. But in fact, in many cases, they are doing just the opposite. Their silence, vertical body, and inability to cry for help don't draw attention. They are actually about to go under.

Sometimes the reason a swimmer silently drowns is the same reason that a person succumbs to emotional distress. They are so focused on keeping up appearances, or dealing with their internal state, or putting out fires in their lives. They don't have time to step back and think it through. It's a lot like drowning.

They might be embarrassed, ashamed, or feel like everything is pointless anyway. The thought of asking for help either didn't occur to them or seemed too hard.

So you need to learn what the signs are and pay attention. Be there for them when they need you.

Disclaimer: The authors are not mental health experts and present this as information only, not advice. If you are worried about your friend, family member, or co-worker, please seek professional help. If you are the one who is struggling, please seek help. Type "mental health hotline" into the browser on your phone or computer, and you will see several options for immediate assistance.

Sign # 1: A Decline in Performance

Has your co-worker recently started turning in substandard work, running late every day, or being rude to customers? This could be a sign of mental distress.

In the construction industry, we talk about guys who start drinking or using too many substances to the point where they are sleeping at work and unable to function. We say they need to stop using so much. But what if this is a last-ditch attempt to keep going when their lives seem to be falling apart? Offer a helping hand.

If your son or daughter seems unable to get out of bed in the morning and their grades are dropping, anxiety and stress may be the culprit. Don't ignore it.

When your girlfriend, boyfriend, or partner struggles to get along in the workplace or is getting poor performance reviews, it's time to care. Be there for them.

Sign #2: Emotional Outbursts, Fights, and Freakouts

Sudden emotional outbursts that are uncharacteristic of a person can be a sign that they are fighting internally. Instead of blaming them and fighting back (it's hard not to!), it's best to realize that this isn't about you or the outside world. What you are seeing is the outward signs of their internal storm.

If they're coming in like a hurricane after long periods of calm weather, try not to take it personally. Step back and assess the situation. What's going on?

Sign #3: Poor Hygiene or Sudden Physical Changes

Showers and clean clothes might fall by the wayside.

I know it can be hard for some guys to tell if one of their coworkers has mental problems or is just a slob. The thing to watch for is changes for the worse. Like a guy who used to shave and style his look, but now he hasn't had a haircut in four months.

So when your friend, who's normally put together well, shows up looking like she slept under a bridge with a goat and three marmots, then you should question it.

Sign #4: Irritable and Easily Frustrated When They Usually Aren't

A sure sign that someone has encountered a run of bad luck or a setback in their personal life is excess anger. Has his fuse shortened so much that everyone is walking on eggshells around someone who used to be a friendly guy? Did she used to be calm and collected, but now is angry at her computer, drawers that won't open properly, or the fact that it's cloudy outside?

Something is causing this change in their personality.

Sign #5: Reduced Interest in Favorite Activities

"Hey, Steve! We haven't gone out together for weeks. Want to meet up at the usual spot?"

"Nah, I'm just going to stay home. Don't feel like doing anything tonight."

"Come on! You never want to go out anymore! What's so exciting at home?"

"Going out just feels like a waste of time."

Did your buddy used to love going hiking or skiing but now hides away like a hermit crab in its shell? This could be a warning sign. Pay attention to what's going on in their internal landscape.

Sure, maybe they are just sick of seeing the same old same old. Or maybe they are barely keeping it together.

Sign #6: Expresses Feelings Of Pointlessness and Uselessness

If your friend frequently mentions that there's no point in trying or that everything is hopeless anyway? Don't ignore this.

They feel defeated and without hope. This isn't a feeling that is easy to get rid of, and they might be in trouble.

When someone tells you that their life is pointless, pay attention. Don't dismiss it as regular complaining.

Sign #7: Withdrawn and Alone

Is there one person at work who always sits alone, forgotten and quiet, while everyone else talks and jokes around?

Does your son retreat to his room and stare silently at the wall instead of taking part in family activities?

Is your mom always off by herself, ignoring what goes on around her?

Maybe depression is the reason. They might come out of it okay all by themselves, or they might not.

How to Reach Out

Reaching out to someone you think needs help can be difficult and awkward, especially in a construction setting. But don't let that stop you! If you are doing better than they are mentally and emotionally, you surely have the energy and ability to make an effort.

Please don't ignore them. If they are struggling, and on top of all that, no one seems even to notice or care, it will be more depressing than anything else that could happen. Not knowing what to say is not an excuse! Say something positive and polite.

Make the first move. Don't make them ask for your help. They might be dying inside and want to reach out SO BADLY. But they probably can't. Offer a specific thing you can do for them. For instance, offer to take your friend out for a coffee to talk.

Be supportive, but don't bombard them with unsolicited advice. Listen to them, but resist solving all their problems or telling them how you would fix things. If it were that easy, they would already be in a different position, wouldn't they? This person is stuck and needs a helping hand, not a know-it-all who thinks they can tell them how to run their lives.

Focus on them. Don't make this all about you. Your lives might be intertwined to the point that their troubles are making a huge impact on you, but for a few minutes, try to see it from their side only. If your daughter is having some major issues at school, but all you can talk about is how messy her room is and how she won't clean up the bathroom? You're headed down the wrong path.

Forget about words of wisdom, and just listen. Don't tell them about the silver lining in their tragic situation; it won't help. Hearing about how much better they've got it than starving children in a third-world country won't do anything and might even make them feel worse.

Let them know they can call you or text you any time — but only if you mean it. And don't wait for them to text — send them one first.

In Conclusion

If you see someone struggling in silence or who just isn't themselves, pay attention to these possible symptoms.

- Emotional outbursts

- Struggling to get work assignments, housework, or school-work done

- Poor hygiene

- Irritable

- No longer interested in their favorite activities

- Tells you that everything is a pointless waste of time

- Withdraws from the world to be alone for extended periods

After my friend died, I wished that I had done something. Anything. Maybe I couldn't have changed anything, but who knows?

If you see some of these signs, step up and show them that someone cares, and help them get in touch with a hotline or professional. If you can help a person through a rough patch, then why wouldn't you?

Afterward

Thank you for joining us on this journey through some rough spots and crazy situations. It's been a blast!

Did you like the book? That's great. Could you do us a favor? Go to Amazon.ca or Amazon.com, find our book, and leave us a review. It would help us out big time! Without reviews, books just mold away at the bottom of the pile.

We need your help to get the book noticed. Please, write us a review.

Come visit us at our website:

https://toolboxtalk.substack.com/

If you have a story, video, or picture you would like us to share, please, send it! **Email us at unreliablenarrator2019@gmail.com** or visit us at https://toolboxtalk.substack.com/ and drop us a line.

We are grateful for those who gave us the nightmare fuel for these stories. If it weren't for your ridiculous lives, we never would have had enough to fill a book.

Thanks again to all of you hardworking tradies. Without welders, pipefitters, electricians, plumbers, laborers, and all the other tradespeople, the world would grind to a halt. We appreciate you. Now, get back to work!

Manufactured by Amazon.ca
Acheson, AB